HIDE AWAY

Books by BV Lawson

Beverly Laborde & Adam Dutton Series

Steal Away
Hide Away
Burn Away

Scott Drayco Series

Played to Death
Requiem for Innocence
Dies Irae
Elegy in Scarlet
The Suicide Sonata
Deadly Dance (2020)

Hide Away

An Adam Dutton & Beverly Laborde Mystery

BV Lawson

Crimetime Press

Published in the United States of America.

For information, contact:

Crimetime Press
6312 Seven Corners Center, Box 257
Falls Church, VA 22044

Trade Paperback ISBN 978-1-951752-01-9
Hardcover ISBN 978-1-951752-02-6
eBook ISBN 978-1-951752-00-2

1

Monday, December 3

Adam Dutton stared at the snowman staring back at him from a yard across the street. Thirty years ago, Adam made a similar snowman with his godfather, Harlan Wilford—the same day Adam fell on a patch of ice with a spike sticking up through it that jammed into Adam's leg.

The river of blood that turned the ice red could have caused Adam to bleed out if quick-thinking Harlan hadn't fashioned a tourniquet and likely saved Adam's life. He owed Harlan, not just for that day, but for all the other things the man had done for Adam since his father's death. Even encouraging Adam to go into law enforcement. That's what made it all the harder for Adam to have to arrest him.

Adam squinted at the yellow and black sign that read "Tossed Treasures Antique Store," glinting in the early morning wintry blue sky like gold nuggets in a creek bed. He opened the door, ignoring the feeling of relief when Harlan's assistant, Prospero Rigas, was the one to greet him instead of Harlan.

Adam's face must have registered his mood because Prospero asked, "Everything okay, Mister Adam?"

"I need to see Harlan. He in this morning?"

Prospero nodded toward an office. "Back there."

"Thanks." Adam imagined how Prospero would react when he carted Harlan out of the building in handcuffs. That was one reason he'd come alone instead of bringing Jinks with him. Having two detectives on the scene somehow felt more official, more of a betrayal.

Harlan smiled up at Adam when he entered, but his smile faded when Adam quietly closed the door behind him. "Well now, Adam, you're not usually this dramatic." He managed a small laugh. "If you're here to discuss the Christmas party, I don't think it'll be a surprise for Prospero."

Adam eased into a chair opposite Harlan. He pointed at an ugly clock on Harlan's desk. "That's new. And hideous."

"That's a painted Syroco Clown Lux clock. Part of an estate lot that came to me recently."

"That wouldn't be the estate of Reuben Ryall, by any chance, would it?"

"As a matter of fact, it would. Why do you ask?"

"Did that lot contain a sword, a Medieval kind of thing, about yay big?" Adam held his arms apart about three feet.

"A reconstruction, ayah. Quite a beauty, that one. A Tritonia, based on a sword at the Museum of Medieval Stockholm in Sweden. The blades are hand-ground with a satin finish. Didja know those swords may date back to the thirteenth century?"

If it were any other time, any other day, Adam would have smiled at Harlan's enthusiasm over the piece. The man was an antiques acolyte to the Nth degree. "And did that sword have Reuben Ryall's name engraved on the handle?"

"Yes, yes it did. Why all this interest in a sword, Adam?"

"Have you sold that sword yet?"

"Why no, I haven't—"

"Can you show me the sword?"

Harlan scratched the top of his head. "Well, if you're that obsessed with the thing, why not?" He hopped up from his desk and opened the door, waiting for Adam to follow. They headed to a display case of swords of all types—short, long, plain-handled, some handles with elaborate carvings and gemstones.

Adam asked, "Which one is it?"

Harlan peered into the case. "Why, I don't see it. It was right there," and he pointed to an indentation in the fabric on the bottom of the case. Then he hollered over to Prospero, "Did you sell that Ryall sword when I wasn't here?"

Prospero yelled back, "Nope. No swords lately at all. Sold that green piano stool you've been trying to get rid of."

Adam put a hand on Harlan's shoulder to guide him toward the office, where he again shut the door. Neither man sat down this time, and Harlan asked, "Adam, what the hell is going on? Did someone steal that sword? Is that why you're here?"

"A sword matching that description, complete with 'Reuben Ryall' engraved on the handle, was found sticking out of a body tied to a tree. Are you sure you don't remember selling the piece?"

Beads of sweat popped out on Harlan's brow. "The man was murdered with that sword? Oh, dear God."

He opened his desk drawer and pulled out a ledger. "Prospero's working hard to get our computer database up and running. Until then, every sale goes into this book, you see." He flipped through several pages. "No swords. Not nary a one."

Harlan muttered to himself. "Prospero's been after me to get a security system. But I've put it off. Vermonters are too honest, I told him. They'd be insulted, don't you know."

Adam hated himself right then, but he had a job to do, one that had become part of his DNA. He couldn't let any relationship get in the way of that, even if it made him a traitor.

"Why did you never tell me you had a criminal record, Harlan?"

Harlan sank onto the edge of his desk. "You didn't know me before I started going to AA, Adam. You were too young. And I'm glad you didn't. After a few beers, I turned into one of those mean drunks. Kinda like the Incredible Hulk. Most of the time, I kept it under control. But there was this one time I let the demons get the best of me. Beat up a guy, got arrested for it. Since I was a first-timer, I got a month."

"The guy you pummeled, George Norwick. The arrest record said he'd sold you some antiques and then found out you'd undervalued them. By a lot. He confronted you, you hit him. That sound like what happened?"

"Ayah, near as I recall. I'm not proud of that. But I didn't cheat him. He was wrong about that part."

"I can't interview him, myself, because Norwick is deceased. Two years ago, heart attack." Adam rubbed his eyes. "Wallace Ryall accused you recently of the same thing about his father's estate, of cheating him. We have some witnesses who heard the two of you arguing, and that you poked him in the chest and said, 'You don't want to mess with me.'"

The shrewd, savvy Harlan who Adam knew, loved, and admired broke through the surface as the hard truth dawned on his face. "The man found murdered. It was Wallace Ryall, Reuben's son, is that right?"

Adam nodded. "The only fingerprints on that sword were yours, which we ID'd through the Vermont Crime Information Center records. We also found a bloody handkerchief at the scene of the crime, one of yours, and the blood matches Ryall's."

Harlan shook his head. "You can't think I killed Wallace, Adam, you've known me all your life. How could you possibly believe something like that?"

"It's not what I think or don't think, Harlan. It's what the evidence says, and if wasn't me standing here, then it would be Jinks or some other cop."

The other man blinked hard. "You'd rather it was you than someone else."

"If I'm not the one to arrest you, people will talk, and the integrity of the force and this investigation will be tainted. After the Forsythe debacle, the mayor is watching our department's every move. We have to do this by the book. And if 'by the book' it means having you arrested while still looking for the real killer, then that's what I have to do."

"The real killer?" Harlan managed a small smile.

"You know I shouldn't be talking about any of this without your attorney present."

"I don't need an attorney. I trust you."

Right then, Adam wanted to grab Harlan, streak across the border into Canada, and find sanctuary in some tiny coastal town where folks didn't ask any questions. Instead, he said, "You'll need to come with me to the station."

Harlan studied Adam's pockets. "Do I get to wear handcuffs?"

"It's too cold a day for handcuffs." Adam spied a pair of thick buckskin chopper mitts on a table and picked them up. "These'll do."

On their way out of the store, with Adam letting Harlan take the lead, Harlan yelled out to Prospero again, "Might be gone a while, Prospero. Hold down the fort, will ya?"

Prospero waved at the other two men, and Adam knew what Judas Iscariot must have felt like. Like being dropped on a planet where the gravity was so dense and heavy, it crushed you into a mangled ball of flesh. What he needed was something to lighten the load, some angel of mercy to help prove Harlan's innocence.

An image of a tall raven-haired woman flashed across his mind, and he pushed it aside. Beverly Laborde was certainly no angel. And he didn't need that distraction, especially if she found out about Harlan's arrest. Maybe it was a good thing he hadn't heard anything from her in two months. Harlan's arrest was proof positive Adam might be better off without the entanglement of relationships. No friends, no lovers, no regrets.

2

Beverly Laborde ran her hand along the cracked beadboard walls, barely avoiding a splinter. When she'd arrived in front of the building, the dirty white façade stained with streaks of mold told her this was no candidate for *Architectural Digest*. The sign spelled out, "ANT. . .S," the "I," "Q," "U," and "E" missing. And the interior wasn't doing anything to dispel her first impressions of the place.

Her companion, Agnes Flamm, picked up the broken remnants of a wooden captain's chair and carried them over to a trash pile. She smiled at Beverly. "I've got a local handyman coming 'round later today to patch up that beadboard and paint it all yellow. This place will look much cheerier after."

Beverly had spied a few rats outside the building and hoped they weren't going to be her friend's new shopmates. "Still not sure why you decided to turn this into a wine and gift store instead of antiques like you had before."

Agnes grabbed a broom and started sweeping the whitewashed, pickled wide-plank flooring, which looked to be in good shape. "As they like to say today, been there, done that. Too many memories, I suppose. And I thought it could be fun to try something new."

"Like a wine shop?"

"Seems less fusty than a tea shop, don't you think, dear?"

"You never did like doilies."

"Hate them with a passion. A tea shop would only bring in wrinkled prunes like me, while a wine shop, well. Lots of younger customers, laughing, smiling, full of life. Besides, aged wines are sort of antiques, aren't they?"

Beverly smiled at that. "True. I'll bet Gregory isn't too thrilled with your idea."

"My son wants me to move to Florida to keep an eye on me. I hate sand almost as much as doilies."

"I doubt he bought into that argument."

"Oh, he means well enough. But he has too much of his father in him. The controlling, manipulative part." When Beverly shot her a surprised look, Agnes added, "I know, I know. Shouldn't speak ill of the fruit of your own loins, but there it is."

"What's the real reason, then? Why a wine shop, why now? You've lived above your empty antiques store for, what, ten years?"

"Eleven. And it's all your fault."

"My fault? Whatever do you mean?"

"When you came to visit me in October, I started thinking about the days when your grandmother and I each had a thriving antiques business. And how much we loved finding that perfect bowl or statuette we just had to have. How much we enjoyed the customers, even balancing the books. So empowering for two old, single broads. Then there's the history of it all."

Beverly side-stepped a board with a nail sticking out and made a note to find a hammer. "You mean wine history? Or something else?"

"I'm tired to death of people casting away their heritage, their local history. We're one big throwaway society. If it's not bowls and paintings, it's kids, families, land, culture, pride."

Screw the hammer. Beverly picked up a rock and banged the nail into place. "Like those two young toughs I ran into last time, in this very room?"

The older woman nodded. "Who knows what their home life's like? Divorce, death, drugs, detention. You said they were after copper they could sell for cash. Cash to buy alcohol or drugs. Kinda makes you feel sorry for 'em, in a way."

"Didn't feel sorry for them at the time. As I recall, they threatened to rob me. Have you seen them hanging around since?"

Agnes laughed. "They're too afraid of you, the crazy lady with the gun."

"Maybe I should buy you a gun, too. In case they return."

Agnes leaned on her broom. "I've been meaning to ask you. Was one of those boys fourteenish? With shoulder-length floppy hair?"

"You know him?"

"Seen him around. Think it's Denny Morland's son, Blaine. Blaine's mother was killed when a tree fell on her while she was riding her bicycle in a storm. A freak thing, you know? Denny spends most of the time when he's not at work in the sawmill or Cold Creek Tavern. The boy pretty much fends for himself. Kinda like you do."

"You mean that I'm an independent, self-sustaining modern woman who doesn't need anyone to take care of her? Then, I take that as a compliment."

Agnes set the broom aside and put her hands on her hips. "You needed help when you went after Reggie Forsythe, didn't you?"

"That was different, I had to get other people involved to take that scumbag down."

"Other people like that handsome detective, Adam Dutton, you mean. You told him you're back in town yet?"

No, she hadn't, and Beverly wasn't sure why she hadn't. After she'd sent him that note in the form of a telegram offering to be his "partner" going after more of the corrupt members of the Northern Antiquities League, she hadn't written or called since. She'd started to—several times—but never followed through.

Agnes looked in her direction. "You look like a cornered animal ready to take flight."

Beverly chewed on her lip. "Guess I have a hard time settling down in any one place. Even for a few days."

"You know, you left town so fast last time, I never got a chance to tell you I'm sorry, Beverly."

That took Beverly by surprise. "You, sorry? For what?"

"For what it must be like to get involved with the Forsythes. To see your own kin murdered and turn into murderers. Estranged kin though they were."

"To be honest, I'm still not sure how I feel. One day, I'll stay still long enough to dissect it—the case, the murders, my feelings—all of it. Just not today."

Agnes appeared to take Beverly's hint to change the subject and walked over to a wall next to an archway. She patted the wall. "This is where I'm going to put one rack of wines, next to a display of chocolates. I've got the racks being delivered tomorrow, and the chocolates and wines the day after that. I'm keeping it as local as possible. The wines, meads, and ciders are primarily from Vermont and New Hampshire. And the candies are things like Vermont maple almond brittle and artisan truffles."

Beverly pointed toward the room beyond the archway. "What's going in there?"

"That is going to be a little cafe, with more wine racks, some tables and chairs, a small stage area, and a counter that'll sell coffee, soup, sandwiches, and pastries. Simple fare, but all homemade."

"You can't do this all by yourself. You'll need help."

Agnes peered at her over her eyeglasses. "Are you offering?"

"I'll be happy to help you get set up. I mean, there's bound to be a lot of cleaning and arranging and planning and staging, and then there's all the merchandise to load in, and there will be flyers and a notice in the paper because you'll have to do some advertising—"

"Beverly, dear, you're babbling."

Beverly chuckled, trying to cover up her embarrassment. "Like a brook?"

"Like someone who always has one foot out the door. Look, dear, there's no pressure from me to do anything. Come or go as you please. Besides, I admire an independent, self-sustaining modern woman."

She winked at Beverly, who felt her shoulders relax a fraction. That lasted for all of ten seconds when Beverly's cellphone rang, and she heard the familiar deep-tenor tones of her friend, the ever-mysterious "Mr. X."

His words put her mood into a plunge. "I hate to be the bearer of bad tidings, Beverly. Your friend Harlan Wilford was arrested for murder."

"Murder? That's insane. Harlan wouldn't hurt a cockroach. In fact, I once saw him putting out a dish of sugar for a cockroach. Whoever arrested him made a mistake."

"I'm afraid the whoever would be Adam Dutton."

Beverly gritted her teeth and counted. Thousand-one, thousand-two, thousand-three. . .

Mr. X's voice tolled in her ear, "Beverly? Are you still there?"

"I'm here all right. But you bet I'm going to have a word or two with Detective Dutton."

"If you don't end up killing the man and winding up in jail, yourself, you might stop by later and say hello to Yin and Yang."

"How did you know I was in the area again?"

When he didn't reply right away, she smiled. "Right. Mr. X knows all and sees all. Or should I say, 'don't ask, don't tell?'"

She could hear his grin over the phone as he said, "Dutton isn't all bad. Do kill him gently, won't you?"

3

Harlan was doing his best to put on a brave face, but he looked like he'd lost his best friend. Maybe he had, although Adam didn't want to think about that. Adam made sure Harlan was as comfortable as possible in the jail cell. He assigned him to a unit at the far end of the row of cells, away from the two other prisoners currently "guests" of the Ironwood Junction PD.

After processing the paperwork, Adam had Harlan brought to the interview room. Harlan continued to waive his right to an attorney, steadfastly proclaiming his innocence and his faith in Adam.

Adam was both touched and upset about Harlan's "faith." It made him more determined to get to the bottom of the case, but he had to do it without digging the hole deeper for Harlan.

Adam placed a cup of coffee on the table for his friend. "Okay, let's start at the beginning. Tell me how Wallace Ryall came to sell you his father's estate."

"Oh, he didn't *sell* me his father's estate. Reuben Ryall bequeathed me his collection. Sorry if I gave you the wrong impression."

Adam jotted down details in his notebook. "Why did he choose you for this honor?"

"Reuben and I knew each other for years. Mostly because he liked to scour the antiques stores looking for gems to add to his collection. He especially liked swords, knives, and military memorabilia. But he also had a fondness for books and kitschy items.”

“Like that clown clock?”

“And worse. Take this butt-ugly face jug piece he had. Looks like a child made it, with broken plates for teeth, but it’s nineteenth-century porcelain folk art. Some folks pay five thousand dollars for that type of thing. I kinda like that little clown clock, though I’d only get a couple hundred for it. Think I was the only in the world who liked clowns.”

“Why did Ryall leave his collection to you instead of his two sons?”

“Guess it’s okay to repeat what he said, now he’s dead and all. Every time he came in, he’d have something bad to say about those boys. The oldest, Ramsay, started out kinda shaky in his business endeavors but eventually did okay. I think he and his father were on the outs, though, something about his wife, I think.”

“And the youngest son?”

“The youngest,” Harlan paused to lick his lips. “That’s the one who was killed, Wallace. He was estranged from his brother. Hardly saw each other. Wally made all the right moves about doting on his father, or at least the appearance of doting. Reuben called him a major suck-up.”

“What caused the estrangement between the brothers?”

“A joint business venture that went south. Don’t know the details, you see.”

“This argument witnesses saw between you and the victim. What was that all about?”

“Wallace wanted to buy back his father’s collection. But he offered me a ridiculously low price for it all. And he didn’t want to buy it piecemeal, either. He was adamant he wanted every single last item. When I told him his offer was insulting, he threatened to sue me and put me out of business any way he could."

"The witnesses say you pushed him, told him not to mess with you."

"I poked him in the chest. Once. Like an exclamation mark, you see. I do it all the time. Even to you."

Adam knew that to be a fact, being on the receiving end of many an "exclamation mark" from Harlan. "And the part about not messing with you?"

"Now, there you've got me. I haven't a clue what those people *thought* they heard. I think I said something along the lines of 'I guess you'll just have to meet my price or walk away.' But that was it. Nothing threatening."

Adam wrote that down. After all the conflicting witness statements Adam had collected in his time, Harlan could well be telling the truth. "How much are we talking about, the value of Ryall senior's collection?"

"All told, about a hundred grand. Depends upon the market, you see. Collectible prices are worse than riding a roller coaster. Go up and down a lot faster."

"You had no idea the sword from that collection was missing?"

"None. It was there when I checked that case a couple days ago."

"Do you have any idea how a handkerchief with your monogram and the victim's blood ended up at the scene?"

"I keep a few of those handkerchiefs in my office desk drawer at the shop. I guess if the killer stole the sword, he could have stolen the hankie then, too."

Adam wrote down more notes, then paused to look up at Harlan. "And now for the sixty-four-thousand-dollar question. Where were you yesterday between one and five?"

"It's Sunday, Adam, my day off. And it's December. You know what that means."

Adam groaned. "Please don't tell me you went ice fishing."

"Of course, I did. Though technically, it wasn't ice fishing since there's not enough ice yet. But it sure felt icy due to the low temps, so that sorta counts."

"Alone?"

"Well, a certain detective doesn't want to go with me anymore, so yeah, alone."

Adam forgot for a moment the whole alibi issue. "It's dangerous to go ice fishing alone, Harlan."

"I've gone ice fishing on my own since before you were born."

"You're no longer in your twenties. Or thirties. Or forties."

"Bah. Don't matter. Besides, it'd be hard for me to drown with all the pollution. Could grab onto an old tire. Or all the chemicals and phosphorus from runoff would create mutant algae big enough I could use 'em as stepping stones."

Adam sighed and started writing in the notepad again. "Are you familiar with the remote forested area off Happy Valley Road? It's north of White River, abutting Pierce Wigley's farming property. But on the far side, where he doesn't go that often. The only reason Wigley found Ryall's body was that he was checking on some of his sapling sugar maple trees to see if they survived the last snowstorm."

"I know where old man Wigley's farm is, ayah. But I've never driven along that particular road, near as I recall. You'd need an off-roader for that, wouldn't ya?"

Adam was well aware that Harlan was notoriously opposed to giant vehicles that passed for "cars." Humvees, trucks with boat-sized wheels, monster SUVs. He didn't like to drive at all, though he tolerated his little Subaru.

That was another point in Harlan's favor since he was right—Happy Valley Road was tough even by Vermont standards and wasn't plowed recently. Being early in the winter season, some of the snow had melted, making the road passable, if just. Adam didn't tell Harlan the tire treads they'd seen on that road didn't match his Subaru, but then Harlan or anyone else could have used a borrowed or stolen car.

Adam flipped over a page in the notebook. "If we're looking for alternative suspects for Wallace Ryall's death, seems like his brother would be high on that list. Maybe his sister-in-law, too, from what you said. Anyone else who had a beef with the guy?"

"I wish I could help you there, Adam, but I really didn't know him that well. Only through what his father told me. And he never said boo about enemies."

Adam finished writing up his notes and closed the ledger. "Harlan, I hope you realize how truly sorry I am about all of this. Hopefully, the judge will take your limited flight risk into consideration tomorrow at the arraignment."

"If he does, what then?"

"Then, we can get you out on bail."

"And if he doesn't?"

Adam leaned back in his chair and swallowed the acid rising up in his throat. "We won't worry about that yet. One thing at a time."

He ushered Harlan to his cell and made sure the older man was settled in as comfortably as possible, then headed toward his own office. As he rounded a corner, he bumped into someone wearing his "standard" police uniform accessory, a perpetual scowl.

Sergeant Moody's frown grew deeper when he saw who had bumped into him. "Detective Dutton, either you're in a hurry, or you need glasses."

"Sorry, Mike. Distracted, actually."

"Yes, well, your distraction quite nearly broke my wrist."

Adam stole a quick peek at Moody's wrist, which looked

pretty normal to him. The baby.

Moody said, "Just be more careful, Dutton," and hurried off.

Shaking his head at the odd encounter, Adam arrived at his office and grabbed his address book. He flipped through it until he landed on Gilbert Deniere and dialed the number. "Gil, it's Adam Dutton. Got a favor to ask. You're a banker, so you must have known your late banker associate, Reuben Ryall."

"Ryall? Sure, we crossed paths many times. What's this about?"

Adam explained the situation and asked if Deniere knew about Ryall's antiques collection and hobby and if he was aware of Harlan doing business with the man. Deniere verified everything Harland said, which was a relief. But one thing he added made Adam's heart sink. Ryall, senior, was friends with Adam's nemesis, Mayor Titus Lehmann—enough to make a contribution to the mayor's re-election campaign.

Though that didn't bode well, Ryall apparently didn't have connections to Reggie Forsythe, Adam's other adversary. Only *that* one was currently lying in a coma and hopefully not able to try to attack Adam through Harlan and this whole murder case fiasco.

If Reggie Forsythe *weren't* in a coma, he'd have been Adam's number one suspect—a healthy Forsythe would be willing to do anything to get back at Adam, including hurting the people Adam cared about the most.

Adam thanked Deniere for his time and reached into his desk drawer for some antacids. This was one of those days he wished he'd become an accountant like his grandfather. And it wasn't noon yet.

He popped the antacids and picked up the phone again. Harlan was still in jail, and Adam would do everything he could to make sure the man didn't spend the rest of his life there.

He'd work non-stop, on his days off, on his nights off, even unpaid overtime. Whatever it took.

4

Beverly paced the floor of the Ironwood PD reception area, not caring if she carved out a groove in the black-and-beige checkerboard tiles. The receptionist, sporting the nametag Arline Newton, told her half an hour ago Adam Dutton was unavailable, but she'd let him know he had a visitor.

Beverly hadn't given the receptionist her real name, afraid Adam might duck out a side door if he knew who his visitor really was. So, she used the same name she'd used to con a robber baron out of a yellow jade Bianhu Qing Dynasty vase—after he obtained it by foreclosing on an elderly woman who fell behind on a four-hundred-dollar sewer bill.

The soulless monster bought the house and furnishings in a tax sale for seven hundred dollars and evicted the woman from the home she'd lived in for more than fifty years. Not wanting a traceback to the woman, Beverly sold the vase for forty grand and deposited the money in the woman's bank account anonymously.

Looking at her watch and noting that forty-five minutes had passed, Beverly was about ready to charge down the hallway to Adam's office, when the man himself walked through the reception door. He didn't see her at first until Ms. Newton pointed her out. Beverly was extremely satisfied to see the look of shock on his face—and a touch of guilt. *Good.*

Adam walked up to her slowly. "*You're* 'Lynnette Furmanski?'"

She made him stew for a moment, then said, "Either we go someplace and talk privately, or I create a huge scene right here. Which will it be?"

Adam rubbed the back of his neck, then silently held out his hand to indicate she should follow him. They ended up in an office that had his nameplate on the desk, although she didn't take the time to catalog the other details of the space like plaques on the wall and books. She was too steamed to care.

She sat in the chair farthest from him and folded her arms across her chest. "Are you going to tell me now why you arrested Harlan Wilford, one of the nicest, kindest, most law-abiding folks in the universe?" To drive the nail further in, she added, "The man who also happens to be a surrogate father to you?"

When he didn't answer right away, she said, "Why didn't you tell me?"

He retorted, "Why didn't you tell *me* you were in town?"

They glared at each other for a moment, then he said, with a touch of anger in his voice, "Hell, I almost arrested you a couple months ago. It's part of the job. I don't willy-nilly pick and choose who I arrest and who I don't. Especially when there's murder involved."

"Murder?" Beverly's voice rose an octave. "You're telling me you arrested Harlan for murder? That's preposterous."

Adam leaned his forearms on the desk and sighed. "I know."

"You know? What do you mean, you know? And if you know, why is he in jail?"

"He had an argument with the victim shortly before his murder, the murder weapon belonged to Harlan with only his fingerprints on it, and one of Harlan's monogrammed handkerchiefs with the victim's blood on it was found at the scene. And Harlan doesn't have an alibi."

Beverly settled down to think about that for a minute. "Obviously, he was framed."

"Obviously to you and to me. But not to anyone else. Yet."

"You think this is Mayor Lehmann's doing? To get back at you for humiliating him? Not to mention the fact his wife Zelda wants to have an affair with you. Even if she is your ex."

Adam got up briefly to close the door to his office. "No one else knows about that, and I'd like to keep it that way. But yes, I'd thought about that very thing."

He had the audacity to look surprised she'd thought of it. Damn the man. She thought they'd learned to respect each other's viewpoints more than that.

"Okay, then, we're on the same page." The iron weights of stress on Beverly's shoulders started to ease off, if just a little bit. "What about Reggie Forsythe? I know he's comatose after his suicide attempt, but what about some of his associates? They might try to get back at you through Harlan."

"Yeah, it's more likely than the Mayor Lehmann scenario. Lehmann's still gunning for the governorship. Wants to keep his image squeaky clean, especially after the way the Forsythe case turned out. The man's got more balls than I thought."

"That's not what Zelda thinks, is it?" Beverly smirked at him.

The ghost of a smile played around Adam's lips, but it disappeared almost as soon as it came. He stared at her for a few moments, as if examining her under a microscope. "It's good to see you again, Beverly. I was beginning to think I wouldn't."

"You got that telegram I sent?"

He nodded. "I believe you said something about settling down in Ironwood Junction."

She twisted a strand of hair around her fingers. "Settling has so many definitions. As in to place in order, or to pay a bill, or calm your stomach or stop from annoying someone, or it can also mean to make a liquid clear or cause something to sink down."

"Were you aware you babble when you're uncomfortable?"

She stopped twisting her hair and clasped her hands in her lap. "I've been told that, yes."

Then a small twinkle formed in his eyes. "You could at least have dinner with me. To discuss Harlan's case."

Beverly hesitated. Should she? It was just dinner. But an image of Harlan sitting alone in a small cell popped into mind, and she replied, "I have other plans tonight. I'm eating dinner with a friend."

The twinkle was replaced by a glint of something like hurt, though it disappeared as quickly as it had come. "That would be Mr. X, no doubt?"

"He invited me to stop by."

"I'm not surprised. I suspected he was the source of your information about Harlan's arrest. Wish we had him helping us since he seems to know about everything that happens around here."

"He likes you. Told me to kill you gently."

Adam uttered a humorless laugh. "Yeah. Gently." The raw look on his face almost made her change her mind, but he hurriedly added, "I know you asked me to help investigate Forsythe's cronies. To make the rest of them pay for what they did to your grandmother and others like her. But Harlan's case takes priority."

Beverly surprised herself by chiming in, "Of course it does!" Two months ago, she wouldn't have said anything of the kind. What had changed? For one thing, two of the NAL ringleaders, the Forsythe father-and-son duo, were out of the game. And for another, well. . .she'd got quite attached to Harlan.

Beverly frowned. "So, where do we go from here? What's Harlan's next step in the system?"

"He's got an arraignment scheduled for tomorrow at ten in the morning."

"You mean for bail?"

"That's right."

"What are the chances a murder suspect will get out on bail?"

"In Vermont, judges set bail based only on the risk the defendant will flee or otherwise fail to appear. If Judge Ponte is half the man I think he is, he'll agree to bail. But the amount could be pretty stiff."

"How much?"

"High enough a bail bondsman wouldn't touch it. I could deed over my property to the court to secure the release of Harlan on bail. But I don't think that would look right. And could be fodder for a prosecutor's claim I'm too close to the suspect, and any evidence I offer up is tainted."

Beverly blurted out, "Agnes could do it."

"Agnes? You mean your grandmother's friend, Agnes Flamm?"

"I'm helping her fix up her old antiques store. She's going to open up a wine shop and cafe."

"She doesn't know Harlan. Why would she do that?"

"She knows how I feel about him. And he's a fellow antiques lover." It was beyond presumptuous for Beverly to think of it, let alone mention it to Adam. So why had she?

Adam just stared at her again. She felt anew the way those lovely mocha-brown eyes of his made her toes curl and a warm tingling sensation wiggle its way up her spine. Why hadn't she let him know she was in town? And Mr. X hadn't exactly asked her over for dinner, so why didn't she accept Adam's invitation?

No, no relationship distractions, not in October and not now. Harlan's freedom depended upon it. With renewed resolve in her heart and that tingly spine firming up into steel, she hopped up from her chair. "Guess I'll see you at the arraignment."

He called after her, "Wait a minute. Are you staying with Agnes Flamm or at the Apple Valley Resort again?"

As she opened the door, she replied, "At the resort. Same room."

She said the last words louder, not caring what Adam's colleagues thought. If she were honest, she'd have to admit she was being a little wicked.

Still angry about the thought of Harlan warming a jail bench, she got into her car and drove around town with no real destination in mind. Then she remembered Harlan's assistant, Prospero. Surely he must know something?

She turned the car around so fast, she nearly hit a van headed in the opposite direction. Ignoring the finger he gave her, she raced to Harlan's Tossed Treasures store, parked, and tried the front door. Locked. Knowing there was a rear entrance, she hurried toward it and was pleased to see it unlocked.

After she slipped in, she headed to the front and spied Prospero at the counter. But right as she got ready to pepper him with questions, she noticed another man inside the store. He was on his hands and knees in front of a display case using something that looked like a cross between a radar gun and a camera. And he was wearing a blue police jacket with the name Brimm on the pocket.

She strode up to him. "Detective Brimm?"

He took off the goggles he was wearing and looked up at her. "Not a detective. Yet. A forensic technician. I'm not sure how you got in here, Miss. . ."

"Laborde. Beverly Laborde."

"Ah, yes. I've heard all about you. But it would be better if you came back another time."

Beverly glanced at Prospero, who was behind the counter and looking miserable. "Prospero, how did all this happen?"

Harlan's assistant wrung his hands together. "It's all my fault. I wanted to put in a security system. But Harlan was against it. People are friendly, he said, and it would drive them away. I should have insisted."

"It's not your fault, Prospero. Or Harlan's." She moved closer to Brimm, who put out his hand. "Please. Evidence. You really should go."

"Well, I'm here now. And I won't touch anything." Studying the device in his hand, she asked, "What's that?"

"ALS. Alternate light source. Contains ultra-violet, visible, and infrared components of light. Filters the light into individual wavelengths that enhance the visualization of evidence. Fluorescence, absorption, oblique lighting."

"For fingerprints? I thought you used powder."

"Sometimes. Despite what the TV shows say, fingerprint powders can contaminate evidence. This baby can also find body fluids, hair and fibers, gunshot residues, drug traces, and a lot more."

Had she blundered in the worst possible way? Contaminating the crime scene and hurting Harlan's chances of being proven innocent? But her curiosity couldn't help it. She asked, "Have you found signs of a break-in?"

"Not at the doors. Nothing like using a crowbar or a screwdriver or a bump key. Could have used a lock pick kit if they knew what they were doing. But I'll take some high-res photos and examine them in the lab to be sure."

Beverly nodded and then apologized. "Sorry for barging in. I didn't know you were here."

"Did you touch the back doorknob?"

"Yes, I did."

"Fortunately, I've examined that one. But just in case, I may have to get your prints to rule them out."

Her eyes widened at that. She'd always avoided getting fingerprinted out of fear her prints would be found at the site of one of her cons and get her arrested. She'd not only blundered on Harlan's behalf, but she'd thrown herself into the tar pit along with him. She apologized profusely to Prospero and Brimm, who stood up to unlock the front door with his gloved hands and let her out.

What should she do now? Adam would be furious with her. Well, more furious than he already was. She slid into the SUV and banged her head on the steering wheel. There was nothing she could do about it. With any luck, her stunt wouldn't set Harlan's case back too much. And her prints wouldn't have to wind up in a database.

But was she going to sit around and do nothing? Absolute not. Not proactive Beverly, no sir. Only one left thing to do— she needed a "dinner date," after all.

5

Adam put his head in his hands after Beverly huffed out of his office. He wasn't sure how long he'd stayed like that when a soprano voice chirped in his ear, "Morning, sunshine," followed by the sound of a cup being placed on his desk. "Coffee can cure anything. From Alzheimer's to the blues. Or so I've heard."

Adam glanced up at his partner. "Is that what Felicia tells you?" Jinks's live-in girlfriend, Felicia, was a self-appointed alternative medicine guru who was always trying to get Adam to eat tofu this or quinoa that.

"She doesn't know what I add to my coffee here at the station, though."

"I'd say six sugars and three creamers doesn't count as health food."

Jinks pointed at the cup on his desk. "I stopped by Dean's Coffee Bean and got you a quad espresso. Figured you needed it."

"What I need is for this nightmare to disappear."

"If you mean Harlan, yeah. But I think I also saw Beverly Laborde running out the building on my way in."

"She's back, all right. And as righteous as ever."

"About Harlan?"

"Let's just say I don't think I'm on her Christmas card list anymore."

Jinks plopped into a chair and opened the lid of her coffee to lick up the cream, leaving a white mustache on her light brown skin. "She probably knows it, like you and I know it, that this whole thing is bunk. Harlan was framed. So now we just have to find out who's responsible."

"Yeah. Easy."

"Sure, easy enough. After long days and nights and lots of interviews and phone calls."

"Didn't see you when I brought Harlan in earlier."

"I was already working on those phone calls. Our victim, Wallace Ryall, wasn't a very popular guy."

"I knew he and his brother were on the outs. And his father considered him enough of a suck-up to leave him out of his will."

"That's not all. He was Mr. Litigious. Sued people all the time. Over-compensation, you know? An average looking guy with an average intelligence and an average income. He probably even had an average haircut, and his favorite color was beige."

Adam pulled a photo of the victim out a folder and passed it over. Jinks took one look at Wally Ryall wearing a khaki-colored suit and gave Adam an "I told you so," look.

"Harlan told me he was in business with his brother, Ramsay, which failed, hence the estrangement."

Jinks slurped up more of the cream. "A snowmobile business. But when Wallace Ryall kept suing customers and suppliers, it eventually bankrupted the company. I can understand why his brother might be a tad miffed."

"He seemed to bounce back with his new business."

"I talked to one guy who said Ryall was a pretty talented wood craftsman. He made custom skis. But I don't think that ended his litigation obsession."

"So, we have a bunch of pissed-off litigants to add to our suspect list."

Jinks uttered a very unladylike belch. "Strange thing about the location of the murder. Be a lot easier to shoot the guy at his house. Why way out in the boonies? And why a sword, for God's sake?"

"I got an expedited court order for the phone records from Wally Ryall. I haven't chased down all the callers and callees on the day before and the day of his murder, but the few I've checked so far look benign."

"Maybe a phone call that lured him there was arranged to look legitimate? Or the murderer set up a meeting with Ryall in person? Or kidnapped him. Since no cars were found at the scene, the killer either drove Ryall there or he had an accomplice who drove Ryall's car back to his house."

"I've got the tech guys matching car tire treads and looking at Ryall's car right now."

"You got that list of phone records, lover boy?"

Adam handed it over, and Jinks scanned it. "I'll follow up with these. And we'll need a warrant to search Ryall's home."

Adam pulled out another piece of paper and flashed it at Jinks. "Right," she said, adding, "You've been a busy bee this morning."

He returned the copy of the warrant to the folder. "This came through yesterday. You were out on that McWilliams case at the time. How's that going, by the way?"

Jinks grimaced. "Sexual assault cases aren't my faves. But I'll have time to help with Harlan's case." She added, "We'll also need a warrant to search Harlan's home. Have to cover all bases. Appearances and all."

She didn't add, "In case Harlan really is guilty," but she didn't have to. If he were honest with himself, he'd admit point-blank he'd briefly entertained the notion Harlan could have killed Ryall. Very briefly.

"Warrants are us." Adam patted the folder.

"We'll get right on it then," and she put her feet up on his desk.

Adam smiled at her. "Miss Laborde and I independently came up with the idea Mayor Lehmann or one of Reginald Forsythe's cronies might be behind the frame-up."

"She's got brains in addition to the beauty. Just don't let Felicia know I said that."

"So what do you think? About Lehmann or the Forsythe angle?"

"Lehmann is a dickhead, and I'd love to be able to pin a murder on him. But I think he's too much of a coward to kill anybody. At least, physically."

Adam snorted, and she continued, "The idea that it could be a revenge move on the part of a Forsythe partner-in-crime— that's got some legs."

He replied, "Other than the Forsythe-Lehmann revenge angle, there could be other motives to frame Harlan. Hatred, convenience, an opportunistic killing, or something related to Harlan's business. A disgruntled customer, a competitor. Someone who might benefit the most if Harlan went out of business."

"That sure smells like a Forsythe plan."

Jinks inhaled a chocolate-chip muffin in two bites, crumpled up the wrapper, and did a perfect three-pointer into the trash. "The mayor's going to be on our asses over this. If he gets a whiff that we're going easy on Harlan due to our friendship. . ."

"And then there's Reuben Ryall."

"What about him?"

"That research I was telling you about. The Ryall patriarch, being of the rich, white persuasion, was a good bud of Lehmann's."

Jinks groaned. "How good?"

"Good enough to make a contribution to the mayor's re-election campaign, apparently."

"Here we go again."

"Me, I love carousel rides. Round and round and round." Adam gulped down some of his now-cooler espresso and wrinkled his nose. "Whoa. That's extra-black."

"Put some hair on your chest. Hetero women still like hair on a man's chest, right?"

"Depends upon the woman. And the hair, I guess." Adam tapped a pencil on the folder. "I checked into Reuben Ryall's death. To see if there were any signs he'd been murdered, too."

"And?"

"The medical examiner's autopsy listed natural causes. Brain aneurysm."

"Ouch. My cousin Shijo had one of those. He's still on crutches and slurs his speech two years later."

"Shijo. Let me guess which side of the family he's from."

"It's funny, but my African-American kin get along better with the Japanese clan than vice versa."

"Prejudice comes from every side. I'll bet cardinals turn up their beaks at sparrows."

"And all the dogs at the Westminster show love to hate on the poodles. Silly furry topiaries."

He grinned, knowing Felicia owned a large standard poodle with reddish-brown, curly hair. Minus the topiary. "In all those phone calls you made, you find any charges of prejudice, sexual assault, threats against Wally Ryall?"

"Not so much as a 'he looked at me cross-eyed.' Though pretty much everyone called him a self-absorbed, narcissistic jerk."

"Plenty of motive potential there."

"Where do you want to start?"

"Prospero. He said he didn't know the sword was stolen, and I found out he has an air-tight alibi for the entire day of the murder. He drove up to Boston with two friends to attend a matinee of *The Nutcracker* at the Boston Opera House. Ate at Fajitas & 'Ritas after."

"But he's a good place to start."

"Yep. And a search of the antiques store."

Jinks dropped her feet to the floor, guzzled the last of her coffee that was more cream than java, then stood up and bopped Adam on the arm. "Come on, man. Times a'wasting. We've got a potentially innocent man to save."

"Potentially?"

"As far as Mayor Lehmann is concerned, that's what we're going to call him. Officially."

"I'm sure the chief would appreciate it. He had me in his office yesterday with a friendly warning on that very subject."

Jinks looked at him out of the corner of her eye. "What about Beverly Laborde?"

"What about her?"

"She attracts trouble like mold to cheese."

"I don't think she'll get in our way. She's helping Agnes Flamm open a new wine shop. She'll probably be too busy for anything else."

Jinks gave him a full-on slow burn, and he chose to ignore her. Beverly had turned down his invitation to go to dinner, what, three times now? If that wasn't a clear sign she wasn't interested in him, he didn't know what was. His ex-wife was clamoring for an affair—thus cheating on the mayor no less—but Beverly couldn't seem to run away from Adam fast enough.

Romantic relationships all ended up in divorce or death or heartache. He'd take a down-and-dirty criminal case over that any goddamned day of the year.

6

Although the roads Beverly navigated were barely on a map, she could make her way to her target blindfolded. The thirty-minute trip gave her plenty of time to obsess about Harlan and his arrest. So much so, that when she screeched into the parking area, she paid little heed to the two yaks next to the fence nor to the creek circling the mini-castle as she stormed across the bridge.

The door automatically opened for her as she approached. Striding into the castle, she made a beeline for the study, where she flounced onto a sofa without the usual amenities toward her host. For his part, Mr. X seemed totally unconcerned and handed her a mug of a steaming-hot concoction. She took a few sips, but her mood was hotter than the drink, making it feel cool by comparison.

Mr. X relaxed in a chair and tented his fingers together. "I must be slipping. Or Yin and Yang are slipping. Is their yak milk hot chocolate not to your taste? I added a touch of mint."

She looked up at him for the first time. "What? Oh, yes, it's quite good, as always. I'm sorry. Here you invited me to drop by, and I'm being a horrible guest."

"'Horrible' and 'guest' aren't two words I'd put together when thinking of you, Beverly."

"At least someone is glad I'm back. Here I am, taking a chance to return to the Junction, and this is what greets me? Betrayal by Adam?"

"Oh, that word, betrayal. But remind me again why you came back?"

She sighed. "The whole NAL thing and the antiquities crime syndicate."

"You don't feel you've avenged your grandmother yet? Bringing Reggie Forsythe down was a pretty big coup."

"As long as there's one of those scumbags still out there, I can't give up. And Adam said he'd help."

Mr. X sprawled back in his chair and smiled at her. "So tell me, love. Did you kill our poor handsome detective? Or is he alive to sleuth another day?"

"He's very much alive. Although I'm not sure I like him very much right now."

"I suppose it wouldn't help to say he's only doing his job. And that's he's quite good at it?"

Beverly wrapped her hands around the mug. She was suddenly cold, and the warm drink was welcome. "If he's that wonderful, then I can only hope he finds out who's really responsible for killing that man."

"Wallace Ryall, you mean."

"Is that the name of the victim? I didn't stop to ask."

"Have you ever heard of him?"

She shook her head. She's the one who must be slipping— she hadn't thought to ask Adam about any details of the crime.

"Not terribly surprising. He's hardly memorable, a little rat of a man, although that may be too unkind to rats."

"A criminal?"

"Not in the traditional sense. He seemed to make his living from suing other people. Many of those lawsuits were baseless. But the hard fact is, businesses often settle claims out of court to make the bad publicity go away. Even if they're not in the wrong."

"Makes what I do for a living seem very respectable by comparison."

"But you're a female Robin Hood. I guess female is redundant since 'Robin' is an androgynous name. But you are a heroine in your own way."

"I'm not sure Adam and his kind would think so."

"His kind, love? Makes him sound like a caveman throwback."

She took another sip of the chocolate. The mint did add a nice touch. After sipping in silence for a moment, she spoke up, "I asked Adam if he thinks the person framing Harlan could be connected to the Forsythes. Or the Northeast Antiquities League crooks."

"It's not impossible. Although I'm not sure any Reggie Forsythe 'associates' liked him well enough to consider avenging his defeat."

"One of those associates did try to kill Adam two months ago. And then me, too."

Mr. X pointed out, "But that man is currently awaiting trial. And as Adam found out, that lowlife is not a criminal genius."

"What about others? Someone who might have it in for Adam and is getting back at him through Harlan?"

"Forsythe himself would have gladly done something like that for spite. And he's quite capable of murder, killing his own father as he did. But he's lying in a nursing home bed with tubes in every orifice."

"It's a pity his cowardly suicide attempt that put him there didn't work."

Mr. X put his feet up on an ottoman, and Beverly was glad to see his foot had healed since their last encounter when it was in a cast. He must have noticed her gaze and said, "Good as new. And no new murderous tree roots have reached up to grab me since."

She managed a small smile as his attempt at cheering her up. "Ah, that word. Murderous."

"I can help with those NAL crooks you mentioned. And it's good news, thanks to you."

"Thanks to me?"

"Indeed. Your ingenious methods at reverse cons, plus taking Forsythe out of the picture, and the murder of a state Representative, were too much for the spineless 'kingpins.' Most of the other NAL bad eggs have left the antiques industry altogether. I think we're down to two now. One is eighty-one and in poor health, so that pretty much leaves only a man named Ivon Kozak."

"I'm not sure I can take credit for all that. But I guess Grammie was avenged in the end."

Beverly got up, mug in hand, to walk to a rosewood marble-top étagère. "You've added a new piece." She ran a finger along the glass bottle. "It's 1920s René Lalique, isn't it? A 'blackberry' perfume bottle."

"So it is. Your grandmother taught you well."

She smiled at the thought of Grammie taking a little eight-year-old girl into an antique glass shop, to the horror of the owner. It wasn't until the young Beverly started teaching him a thing or two about a Loetz Titania Glass Vase that the owner relaxed. Even told her to come back and work for him when she turned sixteen.

Beverly picked up another piece on the étagère, a bronze statue. "Who is this?"

"Daniel Chester's bust of Ralph Waldo Emerson. The very same man who said, 'There is no den in the wide world to hide a rogue. Commit a crime, and the earth is made of glass. Commit a crime, and it seems as if a coat of snow fell on the ground, such as reveals in the woods the track of every partridge, and fox, and squirrel.'"

"Are you an Emerson disciple? I doubt many people could quote him at will."

Mr. X wagged a finger at her. "You look rather shocked, Beverly. Not all shady characters, even reformed ones, believe the only reading worthwhile is gun catalogs and porn magazines."

A blush of guilt crept along her cheeks until she saw the laughter in his eyes. He added, "Emerson has always fascinated me. A man who questioned everything and continued his quest for the truth despite losing most of his family and friends to illness. His words influenced almost every great writer and thinker since."

"If you're trying to make me feel better, it's not working very well."

"Then how about this Emerson quote, 'Trust your instinct to the end, though you can render no reason.' You have amazing instincts, Beverly. Trust them."

She returned to the sofa, but instead of sitting down, perched on the armrest. "I guess the shock of my uncle killing my grandfather and trying to kill Adam and me is clouding those instincts. I wanted the man who framed Harlan to be part of that case, too."

"Why?"

"I don't know. To make it easier to combine my two quests into one. Nail the killer, nail more of the NAL scoundrels at the same time."

"But your instincts aren't cooperating?"

Beverly drained the last drops of the cocoa and put the glass on an end table. "This is too in-your-face." She slid back down onto the sofa.

Mr. X agreed, in his usual soothing tones. "The Forsythes were more comfortable with manipulation and secret machinations. Not really their style."

"But who else would want to frame dear, sweet, dotty Harlan?"

"A competitor. An opportunist. A psychopath. Take your pick."

"In other words, this isn't going to be easy."

"Murders rarely are. But I take it this means you'll be poking your nose into Adam Dutton's business?"

"I'm not a patient person."

"He has to be thorough. Judges and jurors like that sort of thing. But as I mentioned before, poking your nose into a hornet's nest can—"

"Get you stung."

"Get you killed. You were lucky last time."

Beverly stared into her empty mug. "What do I do now?"

Mr. X arose to grab a pad of paper and a pen. "The victim belonged to this group. Not my style, but it seems like an appropriate place to start."

Beverly took the paper from him. "The Society for Creative Anachronism. They use swords and other Medieval weapons, don't they?"

He blinked at her. "Very realistic swords."

She reached up to give him a hug and said, "I knew I could count on you. And Adam Dutton better watch out because Beverly Laborde is on the trail."

"On the killer's trail or Dutton's?"

Beverly didn't dignify his quip with a reply, but she had to admit the thought of working with Adam again gave her an adrenaline rush. She wasn't about to stop and analyze why.

7

Tuesday, December 4

Adam made himself a breakfast of coffee and blueberry waffles from scratch. The berries made them a health food, right? Wonder what Jinks's Felicia would say about that? Besides, you couldn't be a true Vermont patriot sans something with maple in it or on it to start off your day.

Ordinarily, he'd make an asparagus frittata or some scallion goat cheese muffins. Zelda once loved his cooking, happy to try out his latest creations. But apparently, that love wasn't enough to keep her from leaving him for the town's mayor-turned-wannabe-governor. A man who could afford his own cook. And butler and gardener.

But today, Adam didn't feel like cooking, not when he knew Harlan was getting some lukewarm java and stale toast. Harlan liked to have the same thing every morning—one egg over easy, one strip of maple bacon, one English muffin toasted soft but not crisp, with orange marmalade.

That image of a forlorn Harlan sitting on the hard cot in his cell was enough to make Adam lose his appetite altogether. He hurriedly got dressed and flew down to the station, where Jinks was waiting for him in his office. She dangled a key in her hand. "Ready to make good use of all those search warrants?"

Adam pointed at the key. "Whose is that?"

"The victim's. He rented half of a duplex on Mayhew. Not too far from the train station. Used to be where the owner of Rory's Five and Dime lived, but his heirs chopped the place into two units."

When Adam and Jinks arrived in front of that duplex ten minutes later, Jinks added, "Looks like the heirs needed the money. Don't think they've spent any time fixing up this dump."

Adam got out of the car to peer into a window on the unit next to Ryall's. "Empty."

They used Jinks's key to get in and soon realized it wouldn't take long to investigate the place. He pulled out a pair of nitrile gloves and handed one to her. "Jim Riley said the tech guys would already be here, but I guess we can get started. Don't think it'll take the team over a half-hour to print the place."

Jinks surveyed the room, which was basically a long rectangular box with a small kitchen at the end and a narrow staircase to the second floor. She nodded at the staircase. "Start at the top, work our way down?"

They did, and though they were accustomed to home conditions of all kinds, this one was pretty pathetic. Not due to the usual piles of junk or trash lying around—in fact, the room was surprisingly pristine. But all it contained was one twin metal-frame bed with a faded maroon paisley comforter, a micro-chest-of-drawers, and one chair.

The only decoration in the room was a photo on the chest that Adam picked up. The face of an attractive, smiling blonde woman peered back at him. He turned it around to show Jinks. "Girlfriend, perhaps?"

Jinks snorted. "With a room like this? Maybe he cut it out of a magazine and framed it. Virtual girlfriend."

The downstairs didn't prove much more interesting, although they did focus on the shed in the rear of the house where Wally made some of his custom skis. A pair of half-finished skis lay on a worktable waiting for their crafter—who was never coming back.

Adam picked up a ski and examined it. "Your source was right. Ryall really was a pretty talented wood craftsman, if this is any indication. Too bad he didn't focus on these instead of lawsuits for a living."

They made one last sweep through the downstairs and were heading out when Joe Brimm and the forensics guys arrived with their gear. Leaving them to their work, they headed over to Harlan's home. This was much harder for Adam, and he had to take a deep breath before he headed inside.

Jinks shot him a sympathetic look. "I could do this one alone. Then Mayor Lehmann wouldn't have more 'conflict of interest' bullshit to sling around."

Adam shook his head and used his copy of Harlan's house key to let them inside. Knowing this place as well as his own, Adam would be able to make quick work of it, too, but he made sure they were slow and thorough.

Jinks stopped at one point and huffed. "What did you expect, Adam? Swords? Weapons? Bloody clothing? Harlan's face should be on a bottle of house cleaner, this place is so neat."

"That's Harlan for you." To Adam's immense relief, only did they not find dirt, they didn't find anything that could tie Harlan to Ryall.

Jinks did find another interesting unframed photo, which she showed Adam. "Beverly Laborde."

He studied it. "Wonder when this was taken? Somehow I don't think a con woman would want her picture out there."

"Don't you mean *former* con woman?" Jinks grinned at him. "Because if she's still in the biz, you might find yourself having to arrest her, too. Again."

Adam didn't grin back. He knew why Beverly had done what she'd done. Trying to help victims of the NAL misdeeds and right what she felt were wrongs. Even if it was technically illegal.

In reply to Jinks's ribbing, he merely said, "She knows better now."

Jinks said, "Um hmm," and replaced the photo.

§ § §

So it wouldn't be a total waste of a morning, they decided to head to the Tossed Treasures shop and chat with Prospero, who was holding down the fort, as Harlan had asked. This time, he wasn't waving or smiling, although he seemed determined to be polite.

The young man's mother had named him "Prospero" from a beat-up copy of Shakespeare's *The Tempest* she had as a girl, reading it over and over. She emigrated to Vermont from Puerto Rico at age sixteen with baby Prospero in tow—after an uncle moved here to work in the mining industry, saying Vermont had low unemployment.

They quickly settled in the Rutland and Barre area, the centers of marble and granite quarrying and carving in the States. Young Prospero had hated mining and hated the snow, but he stayed, anyway. He'd once told Adam he thought Harlan was about as good an employer as you're going to get.

Adam asked to see all the items Reuben Ryall bequeathed to Harlan in his will. Prospero dutifully showed them an array of swords, spears, blunt weapons, and some pieces of armor, as he said, "That policeman with the fingerprinting gear yesterday was quite thorough."

"Good." Adam looked around the shop. Couldn't tell Joe Brimm had been there, which was his trademark. Thorough but discreet.

Prospero added, "Although I think he was a bit upset when Miss Laborde arrived. Was afraid she'd tainted evidence."

Adam whipped his head around to stare at Prospero. "Beverly Laborde was here? Wasn't the shop locked?"

"We thought it was. But she came in through the back door."

Adam's blood pressure rocketed up through his body and launched into the stratosphere. The nerve of that woman. Giving him a hard time about arresting Harlan when Adam was just doing his job, and here she was, waltzing in and potentially screwing up everything.

He could feel Jinks's scrutiny as she butted in to ask, "So, Prospero. Adam said the murder weapon was a Tritonia sword? What's that? A sword looks like a sword to me."

"Oh my, no. There are hundreds, if not thousands of different kinds of swords. Asian, Egyptian, European. Your basic sword has a long, edged piece of forged metal, but it can have single or double-bladed edges. And the blade itself can be straight or curved."

Prospero started warming up to the subject with a string of information that made Jinks, who was writing everything down, grit her teeth, but Adam welcomed the tedious details. It helped him focus.

Harlan's assistant lectured on, "There's the arming sword, sometimes called a knight's sword, a single-handed cruciform weapon." He picked up another piece, "And then you have your falchion, kinda like a scimitar, with a curved blade. Or this long sword over here, often used with both hands, which is great for hewing, stabbing and slicing."

Jinks asked, "And the Tritonia?"

"Well, I can't show you that one." He chewed on his lip and hastened to add, "But I guess you've seen it, haven't you? Evidence and all. The Tritonia weighs about three and a half pounds, but it handles easily. Intended to deliver large cleaving strikes from horseback."

"Were there any other Tritonias in the Ryall lot?"

"No, only the one."

Adam spoke up. "You've checked all the estate items against your original catalog, and nothing else was missing?"

Prospero nodded. "There's something else, and I don't know if this will help. But a friend of mine thinks the victim was a member of the Society for Creative Anachronism."

Jinks said, "Those guys who dress up in armor and chain mail and pretend that indoor plumbing wasn't a good idea?"

A slow smile spread across Prospero's face. Adam almost had a smile to match at his partner's snarky sense of humor, a Jinks secret weapon that came in handy in interviews.

He asked, "Prospero, can you tell us anything more about the Society and Wallace Ryall's association with it?"

"No, 'fraid not. Detective. The Society is part-owner of a lodge and conference center next to the Nature Preserve. They can practice all that Medieval swashbuckle stuff in winterized comfort. And plenty of indoor plumbing."

At Adam's request, Prospero led them to Harlan's office, even though Adam could have simply barged in there. He wanted everything to appear by the book. After their search, which didn't turn up anything incriminating to no one's surprise, Adam and Jinks left.

Adam felt more like smiling when they were outside. "Well, now, our victim was a member of a sword-playing group and was murdered with a sword. Maybe things are looking up for

Harlan."

"I hope so."

The unhappy look on her face made him ask, "Anything I should know about?"

"I didn't want to tell you right off the bat, but Mayor Lehmann's stirring the waters into a tempest over this. He called the chief this morning. Wants to make sure Chief Quinn keeps you in line. So far, Quinn is trying to play both sides."

"Parrying, Jinks?"

"When in Rome. Or should I say, Hastings or Amesbury?"

They found the address for the lodge, and Adam called Chief Quinn to keep him up to date. Yep, by the book, i's dotted and t's crossed. Harlan's future depended on it.

8

Beverly picked up the menu to order a room-service breakfast but decided to hit the Apple Valley Resort's tea room instead. It gave her a chance to catch up with Gloria, the waitress who was still grateful for Adam Dutton putting her scoundrel husband behind bars.

Gloria couldn't sing Adam's praises high enough. Did she have her eye on Adam? But then Gloria told her how getting rid of her abusive ex—and realizing there were decent men out there like Adam—had encouraged her to date a better class of men.

After some of the tea room's espresso and locally famous hazelnut cream chocolate-chip scones, Beverly headed to her rental car. She plugged the address on the piece of paper Mr. X gave her yesterday into the car's GPS.

The pewter-colored skies threatened precipitation, but the above-average temps meant anything that fell would be a rain-snow mix. Most of the snow left over from a week ago had melted away. But, as she pulled into the parking lot of the lodge, she had to navigate around an obstacle course of plowed piles. They should be called "snowbiles," with soot and pollution turning them black.

The Salt Rock Lodge and Conference Center lodge itself was of a stereotypical New England faux-alpine style. The A-frame looked large enough to accommodate a few hundred people. Certainly large enough for a bunch of Medieval re-enactors to practice sword fights.

She opened the front door and easily found the office, where she introduced herself to the lone occupant as a "police consultant." The man's name was Braddon Hopper, who she learned served as secretary for the local Society of Creative Anachronism. He looked to be around thirtyish and athletic, with shoulder-length dark blond hair. How very anachronistic of him.

Right as she started to ask him questions about Wallace Ryall, in walked Adam Dutton and Eliot Jinks. When Adam caught sight of her, he scowled, but Jinks had an amused look on her face.

Adam quickly took charge, which made the confused Braddon turn to Beverly and ask, "Who did you say you worked with?"

"Them," and she pointed at the two detectives.

Jinks cleared her throat loudly, and Adam turned to scowl at her, too. He finally said to Braddon, "I understand Wallace Ryall was a member of your group."

"He's our Rapier Marshal. *Was* our Rapier Marshal."

"What's that?"

"The Rapier Marshal's responsible for safety on the battlefield. Oversees the Combat Marshal, looks for violations like non-combatants entering the field. And makes policy decisions. Has to know tournament protocol inside and out."

"Like a combination of referee and administrator."

"Kind of, I guess." Braddon frowned. "But it's more important than you make it sound."

"Sorry. Just trying to understand what Ryall did. You use swords in your tournaments, correct?"

"In Armored Combat events. But they're made of rattan. And the axes and maces are padded."

"You wouldn't use a replica sword made of steel like a Claymore, Falchion, or Katana? Or a Tritonia?" Prospero's lecture on swords didn't make Adam an expert, though it did give him a better understanding of Medieval weapons. But he was more interested in Braddon's reaction to the mention of the Tritonia.

Braddon didn't bat an eyelash as he replied, "No steel swords, antiques, or replicas. It's against the rules."

"You never use them?"

"Some of the guys use them for fun. But not for competition."

"Was there anyone in the Society who didn't get along with Wallace Ryall? Even threatened him?"

This time, Braddon hesitated. "No one I know about. You can come back some evening when there are practices and ask around."

"We'll do that. What is your role here?"

"I'm, ah, a secretary. But I hope to work my way up. This isn't my main job, though. I run my father's lighting business. And I teach fencing. Freelance."

"Fencing?"

"The Society uses a modified form of fencing for tournaments, but I won the American Nationals sabre fencing championship. Went to the Olympics."

Braddon seemed unusually defensive to Beverly. Did Adam see that, too? Braddon reminded Beverly of a former boyfriend, stuck in adolescent dreams instead of adult reality. Or maybe he'd realized he peaked in his early twenties, and it was all downhill from here. That happened to many athletes, one reason she'd stayed far away from sports. That, and all the pesky exercise involved.

She piped up, "Did Wallace have a girlfriend, Braddon? Someone in the Society, perhaps?" She ignored Adam's glare aimed in her direction.

"He used to date Fern Gery. She wasn't a member, so I don't know much about her. If it's the girl I saw him bring to a tournament once, she's a looker. Tall, blond, blue eyes. The model type. You know, like Candice Swanepoel or Gisele Bündchen."

Adam did a pretty job of masking his confusion, but Beverly could tell the names didn't register. She cast a sideways glance at Jinks, who had a smirk on her face.

Beverly asked, "They aren't dating now? What happened?"

"He didn't say, I didn't ask." Braddon waved his arm in the air, but in so doing, he knocked over his cup of coffee and grabbed some paper towels. "Great. There goes my mud coffee."

That was a new one to Beverly, so she asked, "Mud?"

"What I call it. Espresso, the more bitter, the better. With extra shots."

"I see. So Wallace didn't have any new girlfriends?"

"Don't know of any. But he's not the kind of guy to attract 'em, you know?"

Beverly wanted to press him on this, but Adam butted in again. "Did Wallace talk about his father much?"

"Plenty. One of those love-hate things. Or he loved his father's money more. Did everything he could to get in the old man's good graces. But look how that turned out."

"The will?"

"Hell, yeah. Wallace was livid when the estate went to that antiques store guy. Said he'd do everything necessary to get it back."

"Did he say how he planned on doing that?"

"Wallace was like a balloon, all gas and hot air. Pile the least little bit of weight on him and down he goes."

"I see. Thanks for your time, Mr. Hopper. We'll be in touch if we have any further questions. And if you think of anything to add," Adam handed over his card, "Call."

Beverly walked out of the lodge with Jinks and Adam, who wasn't saying a word. She waited for the tirade to come, but she got a reprieve when Jinks literally ran into a stranger outside the lodge.

Jinks apologized, then asked the man, "Do you work here?"

This man was slightly older and taller than Braddon. He had even longer hair with a full beard and mustache and definitely looked the part of a Medieval knight. Beverly had the notion she should look around for his white horse.

He said, "I'm a park ranger. Name's Joss Warder."

Jinks followed up, "But you belong to the Society for Creative Anachronism?"

"I am a Territorial Baron. You may address me as 'Your Excellency, Richard Symonnet.' That's my Society rank and pseudonym."

Jinks turned to Beverly and rolled her eyes. "Mr. Warder, I'm Detective Jinks. And this is Detective Adam Dutton, and Beverly Laborde, a—"

Beverly piped in, "Consultant."

"We're looking into the death of Wallace Ryall. Did you know him well?"

"Only through the Society. Our Canton of Vaodien is part of the Kingdom of the East. I knew Ryall as Dulcitius Vriend, our local Rapier Marshal."

Adam asked, "What about Braddon Hopper?"

"Braddon? You mean, Manfred Urdangarin. If you're looking for SCA members who might harbor Dulcitius—I mean Wallace—ill will, he'd be a good start."

"And why is that?"

"Braddon's been gunning for the Rapier Marshal position for years. Kept egging on Wallace to retire. They argued about it all the time. Poor Braddon. Had a bright future, going to the Olympics and all. Alas, when he returned, his father had a stroke."

Jinks whipped out her notebook to write down the details as Warder continued, "With no health insurance, Braddon had to take over his father's lighting business to pay for medical bills. That's why he hasn't moved somewhere he could teach fencing on a more competitive level, say a university or nationals."

Adam asked, "He went to the Olympics?"

"Placed eighth. That's a big deal in the fencing world, even if it isn't to Americans who only care if you bring home the gold."

Adam thanked "The Baron," who headed on inside. Beverly steeled herself for the lecture, but once again she was saved, this time by the ringing of Jinks's cellphone. From Jinks's end of the conversation, Beverly guessed it had something to do with her kids.

Jinks verified this when she hung up and told Adam, "Jacob's sick. The school wants me to come and pick him up."

He said, "Then you should go. You can drop me off at the station first."

Beverly gave him a sweet smile, "That will waste precious time. You shouldn't make a sick child wait. Jinks can take your car, you can ride with me, and *I'll* drop you at the station."

Jinks punched Adam on the arm. "Thanks, partner. I'll call you later."

Adam opened his mouth to protest, but Jinks was already half-way to the car. As they watched her drive away, Beverly said, "Where do we go next?"

"We? Next?" Adam shook his head at her, but Beverly added, "The clock's ticking for Harlan, Adam. Taking you straight back to the station will take a half-hour."

Adam growled. "I shouldn't be talking to you. Not after that stunt you pulled yesterday at Harlan's shop. We chatted with Prospero this morning."

Beverly felt a warm flush in her cheeks. "I'm sorry, Adam. Truly. I had no idea your officer was there. I only wanted to talk to Prospero. And when I found the back door open—"

"It really was unlocked?"

"Of course. Did you think I picked the lock?"

"I know you can pick a lock if you want to."

She sighed. "This is getting us nowhere. We both want the same thing, to exonerate Harlan. Let me help. I'm not just going to sit on my hands. So, I ask again. . .where do we go next?"

Adam matched her sigh with a bigger one. "There is one place I want to stop by, and due to your connection, maybe it would be a good idea to drag you along."

"Where?"

"Dartmouth-Hitchcock hospital. Where your uncle is in ICU."

She grimaced. "Make sure he really is still comatose?"

"Something like that."

"Okay, then." She wasn't looking forward to seeing The Monster again in person, even comatose. But she'd do anything for Harlan. And having Adam as company wasn't all that bad, was it? Her stomach did its impression of an Olympics somersault at the thought, and she could only hope Mr. X and

Ralph Waldo Emerson were right about that "trusting your instincts" bit.

§ § §

Beverly pointed the car along US-4 toward I-89, not daring to look at Adam. After a couple of minutes of silence, he said, "Do you not trust me?"

She was so surprised by his question, she almost veered off the road. "Absolutely, I trust you. You're an A-plus detective." And she really did mean it.

"Then why this go-behind-my-back stunt? After our last 'outing,' I thought we had an understanding. About that whole trust thing."

"Trust is something that comes hard for me."

"Apparently."

She bit her lip. "After my parents died in that car crash when I was four, I hated them for a long time. Told myself they'd deliberately died so they could leave me behind."

"Beverly—"

"It's okay. I'm over that now. Grammie was my anchor, but when Forsythe's political shenanigans stole her livelihood, she left me, too—going downhill fast, dying in that horrid nursing home."

"It isn't the same as committing suicide. She wasn't intentionally leaving you behind."

"Close enough. Losing everything she'd worked so hard for was rough for her, I get that. But I hoped having me in her life would give her something to hold on to."

"It wasn't you, Beverly. Stress can affect your immune system, your heart, lungs. If you're older and have a bad ticker, it can be deadly. From what you've told me, she would never abandon you. She took you in when your parents died, right? She didn't have to do that."

"I know. And if she hadn't, it would have been the foster care system for me. Adam, I'm sorry if it looked like I was trying to undermine you. It's just that, along with Agnes, Harlan feels like the closest thing to a family member I've got left."

"Me, too." He rubbed his hand along the dashboard. "But this has to be done right. The mayor's on my case, which means the chief is under pressure. And the prosecutor won't care squat about how we feel toward Harlan. Unless he determines our behavior constitutes an unfair bias."

"My offer to be your unofficial partner was genuine. And with Jinks's son ailing, seems like you could use the help."

He uttered a noncommittal "Hmm."

Beverly gave him a quick sideways glance. He had an expression she hadn't seen on him before—pain, but not the physical kind. Was Harlan the cause? Or was she? She couldn't think of anything to help, so she changed the conversation. "Why did she name him Jacob Jinks? I can only imagine the teasing he gets."

"She thought it was easy to remember. For when he's a rich doctor or lawyer someday. Or runs for office."

"Heaven forbid."

Adam grunted out, "Amen to that. Between Lehmann and the Forsythes, I've had enough of politicians and corruption."

"I do feel sorry for poor Representative Strudwick, though. Got caught in the middle."

"He was blackmailed by the Forsythes to push through their political agenda. When he became a liability, he was killed."

"After he talked to me."

"Beverly, that's not why he was killed."

She gritted her teeth so hard her jaw hurt. "It's true, and you know it. Sometimes I think I should have left everything alone. Maybe none of the deaths would have happened if I hadn't taken it upon myself to play avenging angel. Perhaps Zelda was right."

"Zelda?"

Beverly shook her head. She was not going to go there. Not then, maybe not ever. The subject of Adam's ex-wife was too testy for both of them.

Adam went quiet again, although she didn't feel as much tension radiating from his body. His very appealing body. Damn the man for knowing how to wear a suit, and that white shirt with the light silver tie was casually alluring. *Very unprofessional thoughts, Beverly.* What was there about this man that threw her composure totally out of whack?

"If it helps, Adam, Mr. X said he didn't think whoever framed Harlan is related to the Forsythe mess."

"Since Xenakis was an inside man in the Forsythe organization himself, once, I guess that counts for something."

"And the Society for Creative Anachronism lead seems hopeful."

"They all do, at first. We sometimes go through dozens of suspects in a case. It can take months to navigate all the lies and alibis."

The GPS voice cheerily chimed in, reminding Beverly to veer off onto I-89. She said, "I hate that voice."

Adam turned toward her. "Oh, really? She sounds a little like you."

"Horrors, no."

Adam laughed. "Actually, you have a much nicer voice."

"Thanks."

One more turnoff and they were soon pulling up beside the hospital. Beverly found a place to park but didn't turn off the engine right away. "So this is where they took my uncle after he shot himself."

"Yep. By helicopter."

The images from that night were etched as if lasered into her brain. Forsythe's gun pointed at Adam, getting ready to pull the trigger. Then the arrival of Jinks and the cavalry. Forsythe turning the gun on his own head, toppling like a bloody totem pole.

She said, "When I saw him lying there on the ground after he shot himself, I thought he was dead. And I felt anger."

"Not relief?"

"That came later. I was angry at the evil person he'd been, angry at what he'd done. To Grammie, to you. He tried to kill you—three times!" Her voice didn't sound all that "nice" to *her* ears. Shrill, scared, uncertain.

Adam looked at her intently. "Are you sure you're up to this? If you want to stay out here, I can—"

"No. Let's go in." She turned off the engine and climbed out of the car.

Once inside, Adam showed his credentials to the staff, and they were led to the new high-tech critical care wing. They passed a central nursing station, and their guide pointed to one of the patient rooms in the corner.

After the guide left, Beverly and Adam approached the room, only to find they weren't alone with the patient. A man as tall as Adam, but built more like a linebacker, stood inside Forsythe's room. He didn't look like staff, with his jeans and an auburn parka that matched his neatly trimmed red beard. The man took one look at Adam and ran from the room.

Adam said to Beverly, "Stay here," and gave chase.

What should she do? Adam was faster than she was, and her presence might distract him enough to let the stranger get away. Forsythe's room was the better option.

She tiptoed toward the bed then had to laugh at herself for it. What was a man in a coma going to do, make a charge at her? She'd hated this man for so long, now that she saw him like this, she wasn't sure how to feel.

She had thoughts of her grandfather whisking this man away from Grammie as a child and the family estrangement. Then Reggie growing up to be far darker and more sinister than his father. Unpleasant memories, all. Yet, she still didn't feel anything.

Maybe it was the fact this pale, shell-of-a-man in the bed—attached to a ventilator, feeding tubes, IV fluids, and monitors—hardly resembled The Monster she knew. Not someone capable of killing Wallace Ryall and framing Harlan. But he had a wide reach, with many tentacles of his octopus-like criminal enterprise still growing and thriving in a dark, dangerous sea.

Was it one of those "tentacles" who was in the room when they arrived? Whoever it was recognized Adam and didn't want to be seen here. But why run? If he'd stayed, he could have pretended to be a visiting friend

She didn't have to wait long all by herself when Adam soon strolled into the room with an exasperated look. "Couldn't catch him, and he had a driver waiting. They were off before I had a chance to get the plate."

"Did you recognize him?"

"No, but I can input his description into our database. Maybe he doesn't like cops." Adam unbuttoned his jacket and wiped some sweat off his forehead.

Beverly drew closer to the bed. "They say people in comas can hear you."

"Here's your chance. What do you want to say to him?"

"Other than call him a rat-ass heartless bastard, you mean?"

Adam smiled, and she added. "I guess I have one word to ask. And that's 'why?'"

"That, Beverly, is the question hounding us detectives each and every single day."

"He had everything. Money to buy anything, any woman he wanted. Why risk losing it all by scamming defenseless people out of their life savings?"

As she realized what she'd said, she reached for Adam's hand. "I'm sorry. I'd forgotten about the Ponzi scheme that broke your father."

He briefly squeezed her hand. "The origins of psychopathy are pretty murky."

Beverly shivered, prompting Adam to say, "We've seen what we came to see. I'm not sure I'd call it closure, but it's enough. Let's get back on the Harlan trail."

"You want me to come along?"

"Sure, why not? I want to see that ex-girlfriend of Ryall's. Having another woman around might break the ice."

Beverly nodded, enjoying the thawing in the frostiness between her and Adam as they made their way back to the car and drove away. As if to mirror her thoughts, a ray of sunlight cracked through the clouds above and illuminated the road in front of them. An omen? A promise? No, that was too clichéd. Mere coincidence.

She gripped the wheel tighter and stared straight ahead at the shadows in the road ahead. Determined not to cave in to ridiculous fantasies or superstitions, she forced all thoughts of her comatose uncle out of her head.

9

Adam opened the door for Beverly as they headed into The Gift Guru, where they'd learned Ryall's ex-girlfriend, Fern Gery, worked. Fern had heard about the murder on the news, so she wasn't surprised at Adam's request to chat with her.

Beverly liked the look of the shop immediately and started making mental notes of suggestions for Agnes's new wine cafe. The irony of the ex-girlfriend's name, Fern, wasn't lost on Beverly, and the woman herself pointed it out immediately after they introduced themselves. "Must have been ordained for me to work as a florist, right? It's something Wallace found amusing, too."

She looked over at a co-worker and said, "Sheila, can you cover for a minute?"

Fern motioned them toward a room in the back filled with flowers of all colors, shapes, and sizes in refrigerated cases. Shelves stuffed with plastic containers, floral foam, preservatives, wire, green tape, and ribbons lay against one wall.

Beverly stopped to admire vases of white roses, red carnations, blue hydrangea, purple alstroemeria, and orange gerbera daisies. It smelled like the inside of a perfume factory.

Adam sneezed, and Fern raised an eyebrow. "Allergies? We can go somewhere else."

"I'm fine," he replied. "How long were you and Wallace Ryall an item?"

"About six months. Our relationship burned bright and fast, even making it to the engagement stage."

"Who called it off?"

"I did, about five months ago. He was loving and supportive, a kind man. Misunderstood by others. Mostly bark with little bite, but that's because he lost his mother when he was a boy in a car accident."

Beverly stiffened at that remark. Something she had in common with the victim.

Adam asked, "Why end it, then?"

"He was also controlling and manipulative. And he had OCD, the kind where he thinks bugs are everywhere. Lived like a monk with few possessions." She shook her head. "I felt sorry for him in the end. Hated the thought of hurting him. But I didn't want to wear surgical gowns and masks the rest of my life."

"Can you account for your whereabouts this past Sunday afternoon?"

"An alibi, you mean? You can ask my new boyfriend, Bruno Giacometti. I call him my Italian Stallion." She wrote down his name and number on a piece of paper. "He and I were at the TD Garden in Boston. The Bruins versus the Maple Leafs."

Adam stuffed the paper in his pocket. "They're fifteen, three and two this year. Leading the Atlantic Division. Are you a fan?"

Adam perked up when Fern mentioned hockey, and Beverly noted the way he kept looking at the other woman. And why not? Braddon's comments about Fern resembling a supermodel weren't far off. But the way Fern was smiling *back* at Adam made Beverly wonder how stable her relationship with Bruno Giacometti really was.

Fern answered him, "Maybe not as big a fan of hockey as my boyfriend, but my father got me interested when I was a girl. He taught me how to ice skate, and I used to play around on the ice with him for fun."

"My father and I did the same thing." Adam had a wide smile now.

Beverly gritted her teeth at the flirtation and butted in to ask, "How did you meet Wallace? We talked to Braddon Hopper, who said you weren't part of the SCA."

Fern rolled her eyes. "Everyone has some sort of fantasy world they live in. Those folks are nice people, don't get me wrong. But dressing up in a chemise and a long, heavy gown and playing serving wench or basket weaver isn't my cup of tea. Or stein of mead."

She paused to rescue a plush bear that was in danger of falling off a tabletop. "As to where Wallace and I met? In the very unromantic cereal aisle at the grocery store. He asked my opinion on finding something that wasn't too toxic, and I offered it. We struck up a conversation, and there you go."

Adam asked, "Was he upset about the breakup?"

"At first, yeah. He called and called for weeks, but when he saw me and Bruno together, the calls stopped. It sounds horrible, but the breakup was a blessing in disguise. I wouldn't have found Bruno otherwise."

"Breakups can do that." Adam looked at Beverly this time as he spoke, and her heart did a little flip.

She picked up the stuffed bear, which had "I love you" printed on its T-shirt. "Wallace didn't date after your split?"

"He was a loner. Not a lot of friends. I think it would be hard for him to pick up girls easily."

Beverly stroked the bear's fur. So soft, it felt real. "Suing everyone around him likely didn't help. It's an odd hobby."

"I called it his Righteous Indignation Badge. Like a Boy Scout. Only instead of archery, Wallace tried to collect as many 'screw you' badges as possible. He had ego issues."

Adam piped up, "Did any of those 'screw you' people threaten him in retaliation?"

Fern paused to think. "There was one fellow. He fought Wallace's lawsuit tooth and nail. Said it had cost him his job, his wife, and his kids. But he died sometime in October, I think. I remember reading about it in the obits."

"And the man's family?"

"Seems like the obit said they lived in Maine now."

"Do you remember the family name?"

"Think it was like a dog's name." She thought about it a moment. "Rotheimer."

Adam took out a notepad to write that down. "You say you and Wallace Ryall broke up about five months ago. That was before Wallace's father died."

"I heard about that, too. Croaked without leaving either of his sons one red cent. But you're a detective, so you were wondering if I left Wallace after I found out he wasn't going to inherit any money?" Fern laughed up at him. "I never did think he'd get that inheritance. Wouldn't have mattered either way."

"Why not?"

"A handsome, honest, hard-working guy like you—now that's the kind of man to make a father proud. Wallace and Ramsay, well, they had a few too many deficiencies."

"We haven't talked to Ramsay yet. He's out of town and won't be back until tomorrow."

"There was bad blood between the two. Wallace would never tell me why."

"Was it bad enough to lead to murder?"

Fern leaned against the table. "No. Maybe. Wallace certainly seemed upset with him. I never met Ramsay the entire time Wallace and I dated."

"Wallace was never violent toward you?"

"Like I said, he was nice. Even had a tender side. One mixed-up, lost soul who couldn't find his way. Guess he never found his turtle totem."

Adam stared at her. "Turtle totem?"

"The turtle totem is a Native American symbol for being anchored to your path and walking it in peace."

Beverly didn't cotton much to folk wisdom. The universe was too complex, too mystifying to try to explain away in pithy sound bites. Adam didn't seem as disturbed. But he also didn't seem to think they were getting anywhere when he said, "That's all for now. If we have any further questions, we'll check back."

"Oh, I do hope you will, Detective Dutton." Fern batted her eyelashes, making Beverly fight the urge to frown at both of them.

Once outside, Beverly made a beeline for the SUV. Standing beside the car, she asked, "Waste of time?"

"Hardly anything in the investigation business is a complete waste of time."

She slid into the driver's seat and waited for him to join her in the car. "This is where a man might say how would an average loser guy like Wallace Ryall attract a beautiful babe like Fern Gery?"

"Some times average guys get lucky."

She imitated Fern's eyelash-batting, but in an exaggerated fashion with a smile she hoped was sickeningly sweet. "And how would you know that, since you're most decidedly not average?"

He smirked at her. "If you're trying to get me to buy you a fudge mocha latte at Uncommon Grounds. . ."

Beverly checked the clock on the dashboard. "I know you should get back. But I think I need the fortification of extra espresso shots."

"That makes two of us."

Too bad those Native American legends of Fern's hadn't pegged chocolate as an omen that an innocent man was going to get bailed out. But since chocolate cured everything else, why not? Maybe she'd get a chocolate-chip mocha latte. To be safe.

§ § §

Beverly couldn't deny the mocha latte, which was an Uncommon Grounds specialty, was pretty killer. Being seated across from Adam at the wrought-iron table was both awkward and agreeable. Not exactly the dinner he'd been angling for, but hopefully it would pacify him a bit.

They sat in silence for several minutes, and Beverly was half-dreading another scolding. But when he finally decided to talk, it wasn't what she expected.

"Seeing your uncle—evil though he is—in that condition must have been painful. I shouldn't have taken you along."

"I'm glad you did."

"You are?"

She sipped some more coffee. "I've had some nightmares. About Forsythe. And the kidnapping and near-drowning and, well, you can imagine."

He nodded but didn't interrupt. She set her cup down and continued, "Sometimes, to get rid of the nightmares, you have to exorcise the ghosts."

"And seeing him was that exorcism?"

"In a way."

Adam turned those lovely brown eyes of his directly on her face, which made it hard for her to concentrate. She quickly gulped some more of the coffee.

He said, "I never did get a chance to thank you for the fudge. And for the donation to the Indian College Fund. Unexpected, but nice."

"Very least I could do."

"Have to admit, I wondered when I hadn't heard from you in two months."

"Was it two whole months?" She was pretty sure he would see through her deflection. His frown confirmed it.

"Look, Beverly, you don't owe me anything."

"Adam, I—"

"You remind me of a wild cheetah. They're notoriously skittish. Loners. And fast runners."

"But they can also be pretty fearless, or so the nature documentaries tell me."

He smiled at that. "I wouldn't want to be your prey."

"You wouldn't?" She gave him a slow, come-hither smile and was rewarded by his rapid blinking and squirming in his seat.

Adam did a little deflection of his own by asking, "What did you do for those two months? Besides sending me fudge and donating to the Indian College Fund—and selling a certain solid silver statue, perhaps?"

"Oh, this and that."

"By 'this,' you wouldn't be referring to any more con jobs, would you?"

She glared at him. "And would it matter? Or did you expect me to dust off my résumé and get a job as a secretary in some cubicle fending off passes from my horny boss?"

He ducked his head and bit back a smile which only made her angrier. She added, "Oh, come on, Adam. I don't even know how to type."

"I don't see you as a secretary, no. But I'm worried for your safety."

She gaped at him. "My safety?"

"I want you to promise me something, Beverly."

"Promises aren't my strong suit."

"Promise me you'll try to avoid the con life. It's dangerous. And I don't want you to get into any more legal trouble. Mr. X and I may not be there to help."

Before she could retort, he headed her off. "You're not the damsel-in-distress type, I get that. Still, promise you'll *try* to go straight. Give it a chance. You might like it."

What could she say to that? She'd never tried it before, so how would she know if she'd be able to go cold turkey? She replied slowly, "I promise you I'll give it serious thought. And try not to get into any more legal trouble. Deal?"

"Deal." He didn't look entirely convinced, but she reached out her hand, and he shook it.

She'd never trusted anyone enough to get close to giving up the only lifestyle she'd ever known. But he was right about one thing with that cheetah crack. Every time she considered settling down, she had to fight the urge to run away. To hide away.

She picked up the coffee cup again to give her mouth something else to do besides talk. No talk meant no more promises and no lies.

10

Adam waved at Beverly after she dropped him off at the station. He hoped some of his words had gotten through to her. That she'd think twice about returning to her not-quite-legal ways. But he was a cop, and he'd seen it all. Habits, learned behaviors, personal codes—once they drove those ruts into your soul, it was hard to turn around.

After checking in with Jinks, he stopped by the lab and was pleased to see Joe Brimm hunched over his work desk. "Joe, my man, tell me you found something helpful at Harlan's antiques shop the other day."

Before he had a chance to reply, Adam added, "Are those new specs I see? What happened to the contacts?"

"Infection. The doc had these half-price, though."

"Sporty. Got a hexagonal thing going on."

Brimm took off the glasses to rub his eyes. "Finished the inspection of the knob from Harlan's shop." He waved Adam over so he could see the computer screen. "See that deep gouge and those small scratches below it? That's where a tension tool was used. Whoever did it was pretty skilled. Only used a light torque."

"You're saying someone did pick the lock?"

"Seems so."

"Well, well. That helps our case, though it's not enough by itself." He patted Brimm on the shoulder. "Good work. Keep me posted on anything else you find."

Adam grabbed the morning's *Junction Jive* from the reception desk and headed to his office. Looked like Sam Cowie was busy working on the Wallace Ryall murder case from his end. Adam scanned Sam's update in the paper but nothing new, at least to him.

He and Sam went way back. The man was an honest journalist and wouldn't let their friendship get in the way of covering the story no matter where it led. Maybe that's why they got along so well, a professional code of ethics.

Adam sat down at his desk for a moment glaring at the phone, then got up again and paced around. No way around it, he had to make a call he'd dreaded. Grabbing the receiver, he sat on top of his desk and dialed his not-so-favorite prosecutor, Philip Arment.

The clipped tones that greeted him on the other end were a sure sign Arment was as "overjoyed" to hear from him. "Yeah, Dutton, what can I do for you?"

Adam kept his voice neutral. He was proud of himself for that—should be made an honorary Swiss resident. "I'm calling about the Wallace Ryall case, Phil."

"And Harlan Wilford's arrest, you mean?"

"The arraignment."

"Quite frankly, Dutton, I'm surprised your Chief Quinn would let you handle this case. Conflict of interest and all."

"He trusts me. So should you."

"I don't have much choice right this moment. But rest assured, I'll be watching everything you do. One misstep, and—"

"You'll take me off your dance card for the Valentine's Dance. I get it. Thought you should know that Joe Brimm found definite signs of a break-in and someone picking the lock."

There was a pause on the other end and the sound of the phone being put down. When Arment picked it up again, he said, "If that's all you've got, Adam—"

"This case is hardly two days old, Phil."

"Why don't you hold a séance or something, Dutton? Look, the evidence against Wilford is still pretty tight. I'm going to ask for no bail."

Adam sucked some air through his teeth. "You do what you have to."

"I nailed Wilford last time, Dutton. I'm not worried. See you tomorrow?"

Adam hung up, still seething. When he'd found Harlan had the prior arrest for assault, he'd also learned that the newly minted prosecuting attorney on his case was none other than. . .Philip Arment. That's what made Adam even angrier. The nerve of Arment wondering why the chief had let Adam work the case—the same Arment who'd refused to recuse himself from Harlan's murder case.

But maybe he had a point. Adam was ordinarily expected to work with the State's Attorney, but this particular time, he was trying to help defend the accused. Or trying to help pursue the truth, which he hoped would exonerate the accused.

Adam checked the time. Six o'clock. He wasn't going to do Harlan or the case or justice any good if he was this keyed up tomorrow. He grabbed his coat and headed for the one place he knew he could take out his frustrations without getting himself arrested.

§ § §

When he arrived at Jim's Gym, half a dozen other cars peppered the lot. He might have a good sparring partner instead of the bag for a change. Adam grabbed his boxing gloves from his car and ducked inside.

He didn't have to inhale deeply to notice the familiar aroma of rubber, plastic mats, pine cleaner, and sweat. A testosterone gym, for sure—not too many feminine customers darkened its doors, and the owner was fine with that. Though they did install a woman's bathroom, in case.

Wonder what Beverly Laborde would say to that? Somehow, Adam thought she might be able to hold her own in the ring and put up a pretty good fight.

Adam was in luck. His occasional sparring partner, Frank Ethridge, was there and greeted him with a thump on the back. "Wondered what happened to you, Adam. Thought you were swallowed up by a blue hole."

"Blue hole?"

"Black hole wouldn't fit a cop, now would it?"

Adam laughed. "Guess not. Got your gloves ready?"

"I had 'em bronzed and mounted on my wall when I hadn't seen you in a couple months." The man guffawed at his own joke. "Nah, I kid. They're over there. I see you brought yours."

"I need this, Frank. And don't think I'll be taking it easy on you this time."

"Like you ever do." Ethridge tilted his head and squinted at Adam. "I know why you're here, though. Read about Harlan in the paper. Damn shame."

Adam took one of his gloves and popped it on the other man's head. "Less talk, more violence."

The two men headed to the small boxing ring in the corner and immediately settled into a friendly but jabbing exchange of punches and counterpunches. They happily added their own collection of sweat to the gym's catalog of aromas.

They'd been at it for only fifteen minutes when Frank's cellphone rang from the edge of the ring. He tore off his gloves and hopped over to check it, then apologized to Adam. "Gotta take this. It's my kid. She tried out for the school band today. Bassoon. Tried to get her to go for the flute. More jobs."

After Frank had stepped out of the ring and headed out the front door, chatting the entire way, Adam became aware of a presence behind him. He whipped around and saw the mocking mug of Sergeant Mike Moody.

Moody leaned across the ropes. "You up for a round or two, Dutton?"

Adam was tempted to take him up on his offer and wipe that smug smile right off his face. But he didn't think the chief would be too happy if one of his detectives beat one of his sergeants to a bloody pulp. "Would love to, Mike, but I'll have to take a raincheck. I've got an appointment in an hour."

"Appointment? You mean date, right? With that sexy Beverly Laborde? You must be doing it with her, right?"

Moody was baiting Adam, angling for a fight. But the image of a bloodied and battered Moody would have to do for now. "It's a case I'm working on. A reason I made detective so fast—a lot of overtime, paid and unpaid."

Adam said those words through a clenched smile, playing it cool. He knew how his words would affect Moody, who'd made no secret of his career-climbing ambitions. And it did wipe the smile off the other man's face, even it not nearly as satisfying as a left hook.

Adam left the ring, waved at Moody, and headed outside the building. Frank was finishing up the conversation with his daughter and must have seen the dark clouds forming on Adam's face. "What got into you, sport?"

"Sergeant Mike Moody. A man who thinks he's God's gift to, well, everything. He's not my biggest fan."

"I can't leave you alone for a moment without you getting into trouble. You should hire me as your official bodyguard."

"I'll run it by the chief, Frank. I'm sure he'll be happy to put you on the roll. For free, of course." Adam pointed at the phone still in the other man's hand. "Daughter make the band?"

"She made it through the first round. Says there's another girl gunning for the same seat. Kinda like her own Mike Moody."

"She has my sympathies. Give her my best. And tell her she's got good genes on her side. How could she possibly lose?"

Ethridge grinned at him. "You are so full of it, cop-man. But I'll tell her. Better than my prepared pep talk of 'always drink upstream from the herd.'"

Frank had a way of cheering Adam up, and Adam parted ways feeling less nervous about Harlan's arraignment tomorrow. And with any luck, Moody wouldn't find out that Adam's "appointment" was with the TV and a beer while flipping through case notes about Wallace Ryall's murder.

11

The drizzly gray morning should have served as an omen—the minute they entered the lobby of the Superior Courthouse, Adam spied trouble. Mayor Titus Lehmann was talking to a man Adam recognized as a prosecutor's assistant, his arms waving in the air a sign of his agitation.

Adam turned to Beverly and said in a low voice, "Lehmann's already suspicious of me and my role in this case. Seeing you might set him off."

Beverly frowned at him, but after a glance over at the mayor, she said, "You don't think I should sit in on the arraignment."

"I can explain to Harlan later. He'll understand."

Adam hated asking that of her and half-expected her to throw her own tirade back at him, but instead, she looked around the lobby. "Where should I go?"

"There aren't any lounges for visitors. And you do have the SUV."

She seemed to take the hint, although he detected the bitterness in her voice as she replied, "Shopping. Just the thing a woman needs to take her mind off the fact she's a liability to her friends."

"To Lehmann. Not to your friends."

He was relieved when she turned her bitterness toward the mayor, with a dark scowl in the man's direction. "Maybe I'll buy some rat poison since I have a problem with them."

"I'll call you when I have word, Beverly. Besides, you're my ride to the station, remember?" He wasn't happy about that arrangement, but when his car wouldn't start this morning, he'd reluctantly had to ask for her help.

She relented, and he watched her go with a mixture of relief and disappointment. He didn't even have Jinks by his side today. Guess it was him against the mob. Although one judge and one prosecuting attorney didn't count as a mob. And he wasn't entirely alone since he'd finally persuaded Harlan to hire the best defense attorney around, Duane Sher.

It was a delicate dance when a cop was friends with a suspect. Adam had immediately offered to recuse himself from the case when Harlan was pinpointed as the main suspect, but Ironwood Junction wasn't a major metropolitan area. Almost everyone knew everyone else a little. And the chief had given Adam his support, especially when Adam insisted he should be the one to arrest Harlan.

Duane Sher was already in place in the courtroom, wearing his customary navy suit, and didn't acknowledge Adam as he entered. He and Sher were often on opposite sides of the legal fence, but they respected one another. Do your job well and honorably to the best of your abilities, rinse, repeat. Adam and Sher actually had several shared interests, but defense attorneys and police detectives were rarely best buds.

State's Attorney, Philip Arment, was also there, shooting not-so-friendly glares Adam's way. Most of the time, they were not only on the same side of the legal fence, but they were practically in bed together. Adam tried not to look at the folder

Arment was currently scanning, knowing it contained details on the very evidence Adam obtained against Harlan.

Adam swallowed the acid in his throat when the bailiff ushered Harlan into court. Fortunately, Harlan wasn't handcuffed or shackled, and he wore his street clothes. When he was led to the defense side next to his attorney, he turned his head toward the area where Adam sat.

The only other person in the defense box was a petite elderly woman dressed in a blue paisley dress with a purple felt cloche hat. Harlan didn't have any sisters. Who was she?

One other person caught Adam's attention. But it was hard to miss the yellowish glint of light off the shiny bald head of Mayor Lehmann, who hunkered down in his chair with a scowl that made him look like a Halloween skull mask.

The State's Attorney presented his case matter-of-factly and argued for a charge of first-degree murder with no bail. The mayor nodded his head at the conclusion of Arment's statement. Might as well have given the attorney a thumb's up sign. It was no great secret to Adam that State's Attorneys were often on the fast track to political office or appointments. Just as it was no secret Lehmann was gunning for the governorship. Birds of a feather.

But Lehmann's presence was hardly needed. In fact, it was the first time Adam had ever seen him attend an arraignment. Overcompensating? After all, he'd been caught doing business with the same Forsythe henchman who'd tried to kill Adam. Or was he wanting to see his plan of revenge against Adam and Harlan come to fruition?

Duane Sher spent his turn at bat working forward from Harlan's "not guilty" plea with a recitation of the low flight risk Harlan presented. As a long-time member of the community and business owner, Sher argued, Harlan should be granted bail in light of the "paper-thin" circumstantial evidence.

Adam should have winced at that. But in truth, the evidence *was* quite circumstantial. Sher concluded with the motion that Harlan's case be dismissed due to the lack of hard proof and the evidence of a break-in at the antiques shop.

Harlan had drawn one lucky break with the judge on duty, the Honorable Lena Mollin. She was known as the "Julep Judge," for her mixture of smoky toughness and sweetness, depending upon the case, but was generally considered to be fair.

The questions she put to Sher were enough to give Adam hope until she announced her decision about dismissing the case. "I find there is enough evidence to proceed with this case, but not clear and convincing evidence of guilt to be held without bail. Given that Harlan Wilford does not present a threat to the community or a substantial flight risk, I am willing to set bail at two hundred fifty thousand dollars."

Adam's heart sank at the amount. Even if they could get a bail bondsman interested, they'd be out the ten percent at the end. And twenty-five grand wasn't chump change for Adam or Harlan. Adam had half-hoped for an unsecured appearance bond, but that possibility disappeared in a puff of unhappy smoke.

Then Sher did something unexpected. He turned to the elderly woman beside him, who handed over a piece of paper. Sher transferred the paper to Judge Mollin, who read it carefully. "This appears to be a property lien."

Sher replied, "It is, your Honor. A copy was filed with the town clerk's office and the courthouse. Miss Agnes Flamm here is a friend of the defendant's and wishes to offer this property as a surety bond. You will see that it's worth more than two hundred fifty thousand."

Adam scratched his chin. Beverly had told him her friend Agnes would put up the building she was turning into a wine shop to bond out Harlan, but Adam hadn't believed she'd really be willing to do it. Either she was a saint, or Beverly's charm vortex had pulled her into down into its alluring waters, too.

Miss Flamm smiled up at the judge who turned to the State's Attorney. "This appears to be legitimate, Counselor."

Arment's face turned boiled-lobster red. Although he didn't argue, he did give a quick glance in Mayor Lehmann's direction.

Judge Mollin added, "In light of this lien, I hereby agree to release Harlan Wilford on bail until trial. He will surrender his passport, be limited to his home, business, and any medical appointments, and must agree to electronic monitoring."

Mollin looked directly at Adam. "Mr. Wilford will also be required to check in with the Ironwood Junction police, as designated by Chief Caldwell Quinn. Does the defense agree to these conditions?"

"We do, your Honor."

"Then I release him to your custody, counselor. And I expect you and Miss Flamm will also make certain Mr. Wilford returns for his next court appearance?"

Sher answered in the affirmative, while Agnes Flamm was as calm and unflappable as a deep river on a windless day. The attorney whisked Harlan out a side door, meaning Adam didn't have a chance to chat with him. Not that he would have, thanks to Lehmann glaring at Adam with a face that was a more apoplectic shade of crimson than Arment's.

As Lehmann leaned over to whisper to a flunky, Adam took the opportunity to slip out of the courtroom. He hurried to a quiet spot near a small vending machine area and called Beverly on her cell to give her the news.

"Agnes offered the wine shop as bail?" Beverly sounded incredulous.

"You didn't put her up to it?"

"I mentioned to her what you'd said about putting your own house up, and how it would look suspicious. And though I mentioned off-handedly to you the possibility of her using the shop, I didn't ask her to do this and never dreamed she would."

"And she's never met Harlan?"

"Not as far as I know."

"Well, you can come pick me up now. That is, if you've finished shopping for shoes and rat poison." He didn't add that he planned on investigating Miss Flamm's background to be safe. He didn't want there to be any blindsiding of Harlan's case by unexpected skeletons in the closet.

"Where's Harlan now?"

"His attorney is taking him home. I can't exactly visit him there. Not unless it's an official visit."

"But I can."

"First things first. Drop me off at the station so I can update the chief."

"I'll be right there." She paused and then added, "What was the mayor's reaction?"

"Let's just say he's not going to sleep well tonight."

"I almost pity Zelda. Almost."

Adam had half-expected Zelda to make an appearance since they'd shared many happy times together with Harlan during their marriage. Maybe the mayor had decreed that she stay home. Maybe she didn't care anymore.

He was so deep in thought, he ran into someone, and when he looked up, the flash of short, red hair made his pulse race a little. Speak of the devil. Not seeming to care if the mayor or anyone else saw, Zelda wrapped Adam in a bear hug, holding on longer than was necessary for a standard greeting.

She smiled up at him, "Harlan didn't do it."

"You know this for a fact?"

"And so do you."

"Your husband would disagree."

She ran a hand through her hair. "Oh, he's only desperate to appear tough on crime. And the murdered man's father was his golfing buddy. It's always all about Titus."

"Titus makes no bones about his dislike for me. And by default, Harlan."

Zelda Lehmann wrinkled her brow. "I admit Titus can be obsessive at times. But to frame Harlan? That's what you're suggesting, isn't it?"

"Have to check all angles."

"He knows how I feel about Harlan. If Titus loves me, he would never think about such a thing."

Adam didn't believe Titus was capable of loving anyone other than himself. Would he even care if he knew Zelda had asked Adam point-blank to have an affair and keep it quiet? Okay, maybe he'd care because of the appearances.

Zelda had a knack for reading his mood, and she asked, "Have you reconsidered what we talked about last time you came to my house?"

Adam looked toward the ceiling. Perhaps some God somewhere would take pity on him and cause an earthquake. She didn't wait for his reply as she continued, "Titus is going out of town in two weeks. And he'll be gone for eight days. I'll be all by my lonesome."

She stepped in closer, pressing her body against his. Then she reached into her coat, pulled out a key, and slipped it into his pants pocket. "I'll be waiting," she whispered.

With a quick kiss on his lips, she disappeared around the corner, leaving him still plastered against the vending machine. Good thing those Snickers bars and Cheez-its couldn't talk.

Was his ex-wife really still interested in him? Or was this all an elaborate trap on the part of her mayor-husband to ensnare Adam and finally get him fired?

He turned around to look at the machines, hoping for one that dispensed coffee, although bourbon would be better. With a shake of his head, he headed toward the front of the courthouse to wait for Beverly. That cheered him a little. Definitely nice to have something better to think about than attorneys, arraignments. . .and affairs.

12

Beverly's heart sank as she drove up to the courthouse and saw the canyon-sized frown on Adam's face. When he climbed in, she asked, "I thought Harlan being released on bail was good news?"

"That part's good, you're right. But poor Harlan has to wear an ankle monitor. And be almost a prisoner, stuck at home and work only. It'll make him feel horrible. And how's that going to work with his customers? Seeing him wear that thing?"

Beverly didn't like the image, either, but replied, "His customers know him, Adam. Know he wouldn't do what he's accused of. And Prospero can hold down the fort if necessary."

"Hope so." Adam rubbed his temples. "And thanks for dropping me at the office. I'll arrange for a mechanic to stop by the house and fix my car since the station can't give me a loaner. Jinx can take me home later."

They drove in silence the rest of the way to the station. Adam was probably as lost in his thoughts as Beverly was in hers. She felt so sorry for Adam being put in this position in the first place. Not being able to check on Harlan must be eating away at him.

When they arrived at the PD, Beverly said, "I'll give Harlan a chance to settle in at home and check in on him later. I can let you know how he's doing, right? I mean, surely that doesn't break any ethics laws."

"None that I know of. Tell him. . .no, you'd better not relay any messages from me. And thanks, Beverly. For being chauffeur and for being Harlan's friend."

She hated to leave Adam in his downcast state and gave him the most encouraging smile she could as she waved goodbye and drove off. She figured she'd give Harlan a couple of hours before she stopped by. Which meant she had a couple hours to burn.

Merely spending it at the Apple Valley Resort sitting around doing nothing wasn't her style. Better to be proactive. She headed for the Salt Rock Lodge and Conference Center to chat with Braddon Hopper again.

But right as she arrived, Braddon climbed into his car and started to head out of the parking lot. "Alright then, Beverly, what now?" she said aloud to herself. Follow him, that's what. Her initial excitement at what she might find turned to disappointment when he stopped at a dry cleaner, carrying what looked like costumes.

She parked down the street and waited until she saw him exiting the shop. She took a quick photo of him on her cellphone and then hurried toward him. When she called his name, he turned toward her. "Miss Laborde, isn't it? The one working with the police?"

"Yes, but I'm just heading in to pick up some dry cleaning. Thrilled I don't have to launder all that clothing, myself."

"Tell me about it. Try getting black currant mead stains out of tunics and tabards."

She smiled. "You don't use mutton fat or wood ash soap?"

He snorted. "Hey, I have a cellphone and a TV. What goes on at the SCA stays at the SCA."

"And modern society thanks you for using deodorant, too." She fished around in her purse as if looking for her claim ticket. "I'm surprised Wallace Ryall would be interested in the SCA since he was a germaphobe, according to his ex-girlfriend, Fern Gery."

"He hid it pretty well. Washed his hands all the time."

"You said the other day that you thought it was hard for Wallace to find another girlfriend after Fern. Why is that?"

"Well, the whole germ thing, but that's not all. He could be a bit violent and had impulse control issues. Kinda wondered if he'd assaulted Fern, quite frankly."

That was news to Beverly since Fern had said Wallace was a sweet guy. "You never saw him hit her?"

"No, they seemed okay together. But even my ex-girlfriend Jane worried about the assault thing. It's not just me."

"It's a shame Wallace was so troubled."

"Guess he came by it honest. Dysfunctional family and all." Braddon unlocked his car. "Been nice chatting with you, but I've got to get some flowers for my current girlfriend. It's her birthday."

"Happy Birthday to her, then."

Before he slid into the car, he asked, "You think red roses or pink? We've only been dating two weeks."

"Go talk to Fern Gery at her shop, The Gift Guru. I'm sure she'll help you choose something nice."

He headed off, and Beverly had the brief idea to keep tailing him, but that might be too obvious. Although she *could* say she was getting flowers for Harlan. Definitely too obvious. Making up her mind, she headed to Tossed Treasures, and this time, the front door was unlocked.

Prospero looked up when Beverly headed in, a small smile on his face. Beverly marched up to him. "I must apologize to you, Prospero. I didn't know about the police technician the other day when I blundered in here. Hope I didn't get you in any trouble."

He put down a clock he was fiddling with. "I think that policeman, Joe Brimm, was secretly amused. Though he didn't admit it. And I don't think you kept him from doing his job."

"You're a very perceptive young man. Must take after Shakespeare's Prospero. Wise and magical."

He grinned. "Then I think Harlan doesn't pay me enough."

The mention of Harlan's name dimmed Prospero's smile. Beverly asked, "Did anyone call you about the arraignment this morning?"

"Harlan did. He tried to sound like his usual self, but I think he was down in the dumps. But it's good, right? No more jail cell?"

"And he can continue to come to work, too."

"Just in time. We got in a delivery of old advertising signs. Professor Flint's Horse and Cattle Powders, Big Ben's Sodas, Oilzum Motor Oil. And I have no idea how to catalog them. Or where to put them."

Beverly smiled. "Harlan will set you straight. I know he appreciates your invaluable help. Sure hope the police don't suspect you had anything to do with this." She'd entertained the idea herself until Adam told her Prospero had an alibi for the time of Wallace Ryall's murder.

"I told Mr. Adam I'd willingly take a hundred lie detector tests and swear on a stack of Bibles—King James, American Standard, English Standard, you name it."

"He'd take you up on it if it would help."

She headed to the cabinet with the swords and peered inside. Mostly full. Except for a section where an indentation on the fabric in the bottom of the case showed one sword was missing. "Who would have known the missing sword was here?"

Prospero joined her beside the case. "The sons of Reuben Ryall? Or Reuben told some of his friends, maybe."

"Did he even have any close friends? I'm getting the impression his murdered son wasn't very well-liked. Like father, like son?"

"His father was less prickly. And I believe he was friends with the mayor."

If Adam knew that, and he surely did by now, he'd probably hit the roof when he found out that tidbit. She noted the dark circles under Prospero's eyes. The man had likely gotten less sleep than she did. "Have long have you known Harlan, Prospero?"

"Since I came to work here. About nine years ago. He hired me on with no experience. I needed the job, and I guess he saw that. I owe him a lot."

"Harlan has the knack for rescuing lost souls."

The young man smiled and absently fingered a Replogle art deco ocean globe on a nearby stand that looked newly dusted. In fact, everything in the shop looked dusted and tidy. Harlan had a good eye for people as well as antiques.

She asked, "Did Harlan ever mention being threatened by anyone? Or did you ever see anyone argue with him?"

"He never said any such thing. But now you mention it, Mayor Lehmann came by to see him once. They went back to Harlan's office and closed the door. Couldn't hear what they were talking about, but I did hear raised voices. After, the mayor stormed out. And Harlan had black clouds over him all day."

That was both surprising and not surprising. Surprising because Adam had never mentioned it. Which meant that Harlan may have never told him. And not surprising because of how Lehmann had it in for Adam—and Harlan, by proxy.

"I don't suppose you ever saw a man in here, thirtyish, athletic, shoulder-length dark blond hair? Name of Braddon Hopper?" She showed him the cellphone photo she'd taken earlier.

Prospero bent over the phone to peer at the photo. "No, can't say as I have." Then he snapped his fingers. "Wait, I think there was this one time. I was working in the back while Harlan was at the counter. This fellow there, I think he came in, but his hair was up in one of those man buns. He wore a yellow scarf, too, the color of his hair. But I'm sure of it now. It was the same guy."

"I wonder what he wanted?"

Prospero closed his eyes and concentrated for a moment. "I'm not sure. But I think. . ." He opened his eyes suddenly. "The swords. I think he was looking at the swords."

"He belongs to the Society for Creative Anachronism. That wouldn't be a big stretch for him to be interested in weapons like that."

"Could be. But you don't think—"

"I don't know. Adam and I talked to Braddon the other day. He didn't mention coming here."

Prospero bounced on the balls of his feet. "Oh, maybe this is, what do they call it, a break? In the case?"

"I'll tell Adam and let him take it from there."

Beverly looked around the store and didn't see any customers. "Since you're here all by your lonesome, you can't take time off as often. Why don't you head on out for a bite of lunch? I learned all about antiques from my grandmother's shop. Happy to help out."

He hesitated. "I brought my lunch. Didn't think I'd be able to leave."

"Well, then, you can go to the back or Harlan's office, have your lunch, get some coffee."

With a broad smile on his face, he thanked her and headed to the break room. Beverly wandered through the store, admiring some of Harlan's latest acquisitions. A cast-iron "hornet's nest" bird house. Victorian D&K brass conical incense diffusers. An Asian-themed porcelain dish, Imari, if she wasn't mistaken. She picked it up and looked at the tag. Eighteenth-century Edo Japanese, Arita Kakiemon style.

The bell over the door to the shop rang, and a woman walked in. But she didn't browse, she came right up to Beverly and asked, "I need something for a man who's hard to shop for."

Without missing a beat, Beverly replied, "Does he have any hobbies?"

"Not many, no. But he does love gardening and nature."

"Does he, by any chance, enjoy bird watching?"

"Why, yes he does. Not right now, naturally. But when spring arrives again."

Beverly picked up the bird house. "This dates from around 1910. It's an unusual bird house made from cast iron. You see a little bit of wear, where the three layers of paint show through, the bottom cream, the middle red, and the top green coat."

The woman frowned. "Cast iron? Wouldn't that be too heavy?"

"These used to be quite popular. They're usually on stands, and when hung, often in the form of a Victorian-style house. This one here is very unusual. Only one of its kind I've ever seen." She pointed to the screw on the top. "And you attach it to the eaves of your house or to a tree."

The woman picked it up and turned it around in her hands. Then she beamed at Beverly. "He'll never guess what this is. Oh, yes, it's perfect."

Beverly went behind the counter and saw that the register was one she was familiar with, fortunately. She rang up the purchase, saw a box and tissue under the counter that she used to wrap it up, and watched as the satisfied customer left the store.

Right as she left, Prospero hurried into the front. "I thought I heard the bell." He looked around, disappointed.

"I sold the hornet's next bird house. The cast-iron one."

He stared at her. "You sold it?"

Beverly felt her cheeks grow warm. Perhaps that was an item set aside for someone else? Had she made another of her reckless blunders?

But then Prospero reached over and gave her a hug. "That bird house has sat there for two years. Couldn't give it away."

Beverly grinned. "I would ask for my sales commission, but I think Harlan needs all the good luck he can get."

13

It took every bit of self-control Adam had to keep from heading to Harlan's house to see how he was doing. He'd have to console himself with the fact Beverly would check on Harlan later. The only cure for his worries was work, and he had plenty of that.

First up was a check of local property records to look for a "Rotheimer," the name Fern Gery gave him for one of Wallace Ryall's lawsuit victims. The same victim whose efforts fighting the lawsuit had allegedly cost the man his job, his wife, and his kids. He did find a Payton Rotheimer who'd died a year or so ago. Adam made a note to dig further into his family and whether they'd be livid enough with Ryall to kill him over it.

When Adam's cell rang, he was surprised to hear Beverly's voice. Afraid it was bad news, he rushed to ask, "Is Harlan okay?"

"I haven't been over yet, but I will. I made a stop at Harlan's store to talk with Prospero."

"Beverly—"

"It was to apologize, okay? For barging in when your Joe Brimm was there fingerprinting."

"You're only calling to tell me that? I mean, I'm grateful for the heads-up, but you didn't have to."

"I asked Prospero if Braddon Hopper visited the store recently. And Prospero thinks he had. And get this, he wanted to look at swords."

"Swords? Very interesting. We'll check into it. Thanks for the tip, but don't make this solo act of yours a habit, 'kay?"

"A habit is what a nun wears. I have no intention of getting those any time soon. And you're welcome."

When she hung up, he felt a twinge at the way his comment had come out like he was ungrateful. But headstrong Beverly had a way of getting herself into trouble, and Adam didn't need that on his overflowing plate along with everything else.

He rubbed his temples and stared at the computer screensaver—of a llama dressed in a cop uniform Jinks had installed as a joke—that seemed to be mocking him. This day was getting better and better.

As he hunched over his computer, a hand moved in from his left and dangled something he didn't recognize in front of him. "What's that?" He caught a whiff of something exotic that smelled like cardamom.

Jinks replied, "I know you hate donuts in principle, but this isn't a donut. It's a kolompeh."

"Never heard of it."

"A gourmet chef like you? I'm shocked. Felicia works with a woman from Iran, and these are a big deal there. Cookies made from flour and a bunch of stuff like dates, walnuts, cardamom. And I think saffron. And sometimes sesame."

He studied it. "It's quite intricate. How do they make these? A press?"

"There's the chef I know and love coming back to me. Yep. Then decorated by hand."

She placed it on a napkin on his desk. "Think you've dropped a couple of pounds over the past few days. Time to fatten you up."

"They do say the best diet is stress."

"Amen to that. But don't leave me in suspense. How did Harlan's arraignment go?"

"Good and bad. He was released on bail with home monitoring."

"Okaaay. That's good. I think. So why the long face? I mean, other than the prosecuting attorney being the same guy who defended a man Harlan beat up years ago."

"Said prosecutor is also good friends with Mayor Lehmann, who was there today, so there's that. Plus, it's the whole thought of Harlan being treated like a pariah. Ankle monitor and all."

"He'll be fine. He's strong, and he's got the best detective on his case. Make that plural, if I'm helping." She grinned, and he relaxed a degree or two.

"Speaking of cases, Jinks, how's that sexual assault thing going? Mariel McWilliams, right?"

"The girl's still traumatized but putting up a brave front. I'd dearly love to nail the evil bastard. A date rape drug, following her out of a very crowded bar, attacking her when she's most vulnerable. Alas, no witnesses."

"Keep at it. I'll help when I can. More of that teamwork you mentioned."

"Batman and Robin."

Adam shook his head. "Not getting me to wear tights."

"Aw, you'd be adorable."

"Deplorable is more like it." Adam tapped his pen on the desk. "Think I'd like to head back to the crime scene for a fresh look. Care to come with?"

"I'd dearly love to slog through leftover snow and mud with you. But I have a new lead, myself. Meeting one of the bar regulars where Mariel was drugged."

"I could go along with you instead."

"I've got a feeling this is another dead end. Hardly worth wasting your time." Then she winked at him. "Maybe you should take Sergeant Moody."

He glared at her, and she laughed and gave him a quick wave, leaving him alone with his thoughts and the kolompeh cookie. He took a tentative bite. Damn. Flaky, delicate, not too sweet. He wolfed the rest down and made plans to find a recipe so he could try making some himself.

Jinks was right. He *had* dropped a few pounds recently without trying. He grabbed a sugary soda on the way out of the building—with a silent apology to his dentist—and headed to his car. He'd honed a pretty good sense of direction working cases in this neck of Vermont through the years. But he was still grateful for his GPS that helped him navigate right to the site of Wallace Ryall's murder.

It wasn't all that far from Harlan's favorite ice-fishing spot, one that Adam hoped his friend would be able to visit again in the not-too-distant future as a free man. The police tape was still there, cordoning off the area. He'd already got a call from Farmer Wigley fretting about when that tape would come down, with Adam having to placate him that it wouldn't be much longer.

Adam made sure to park down the road. Since the police and EMTs and their vehicles had slogged through the scene, he didn't expect to find any new tire tracks. Not that he was sure *what* he hoped to find. They were pretty thorough, but it wouldn't be the first time a police unit had overlooked something.

He ducked under the tape and made his way to the tree, still stained with blood and still sporting a sword tip-sized hole in the trunk. The snow had partially melted, leaving some of that mud Jinks "loved" so much. He took in the sights, sounds, and smells. Dirty snow had a different smell from fresh snow—or else it was all the exhaust fumes from cars and pollution it absorbed.

Winter was one of his favorite times of the year. Quieter, for one, just the sound of the wind and a few crows. Balsam fir trees perfumed the air with their woodsy scent, and every now and then, wood smoke from chimneys wafted his way.

He spied some animal tracks in what remained of the snow and studied them. Not a muskrat or a mink. Most likely a snowshoe hare. He followed the tracks for a few feet and then noticed a second pair of tracks—a fisher. Fishers were known to eat hares, but since he didn't see any signs of blood or a struggle, maybe this bunny got lucky.

Winter was the season of death, wasn't it? But why Wallace Ryall and why now? And why here? It was away from prying eyes, sure, but if someone were trying to frame Harlan for the murder, there were much easier and neater ways to do it, like Jinks said.

If not a frame-up, then nothing about it made any sense. The murderer could have killed Ryall in such a way to make it look like suicide. Why draw attention to it?

When he heard a noise not far from where he'd parked his car, he whipped around to see if he was no longer alone. But no new vehicles or even fisher cats. Probably nothing. As often as Beverly Laborde turned up at times like this, he half-expected *her* to pop out from behind the bushes any minute.

It was bad enough Adam's ex-wife was doing some kind of peculiar dance making him question that relationship, but Beverly. . .she was a more complicated conundrum. And she seemed determined to undermine him at times, accidentally, willfully, or subconsciously, hard to say.

He'd never known a con woman—make that a hopefully *former* con woman—before. Definitely none any smarter and more beautiful. He slapped the side of his head at that thought. Focus, bucko.

Adam closed his eyes to recall the GPS map of the area. Whoever drove the car creating the tire tracks that fateful day traveled down the one-way Happy Valley Road. He would have had to turn around a quarter of a mile down from the crime scene in the lone gravel cut-out. Did the murderer simply happen upon it by accident?

Adam had to laugh at the thought of their killer saying, "Well now, this looks like a nice little spot for murder."

A sudden squawking from above turned his attention to the trees. The source of the earlier sound, no doubt. About a dozen crows perched on the gray branches of a leafless maple like ornaments on a noir Christmas tree. One of the bunch swooped down by his head, making him jump back, starting a cacophony from the crow-ish "choir." The swooping-crow dropped to the ground and seemed to be interested in something shiny on the ground. Adam shooed the bird away and squatted down to get a better look.

It was a small silver metal circle with a hole in the center. A tiny bit of the circle was missing like the object had broken and fallen off something, but what? It didn't look antique, but it certainly wasn't dropped by a fisher or snowshoe hare. He carefully carried the piece to the car to place it in a baggy for safekeeping.

He returned to the site of the find and carefully sifted through the snow to see what else he might turn up. They must have missed this earlier. Wasn't dropped since then, half-hidden as it was under the old snow.

But after a methodical grid-pattern search, he came up empty. With his luck, the damned crow dropped this and was coming back to retrieve it. Crows were known to be attracted to shiny objects and even carry them off.

He looked over at the swooping-crow who'd hung around watching Adam, making clicking noises as if laughing at his failed efforts. Adam called out to it, "Thanks for nothing, bird."

Despite the crows and Farmer Wigley's nearby farm, this was a lonely place. Wallace Ryall's killer had gagged him before running him through with the sword, but it wouldn't have mattered. Any screams would get carried away on the wind and be indistinguishable from the ungodly screeching of a fisher cat.

It was difficult for Adam not to feel empathy for a victim's pain and suffering, but objectivity was critical. Still, the image of Ryall tied up and gagged, watching helplessly as the sword was pulled back before being plunged into his chest, was hard to take.

Adam gave one last glance around before heading to the car. He didn't know why, but he waved at his crow. The bird flew to the hood of the car and stared at Adam through the windshield. Then, with a flapping of his blue-black wingtip feathers spread out like fingers, it took off.

Too bad crows couldn't talk. The one thing Adam desperately needed right then was a good witness. With a sigh, he headed back toward the office. There would be many a phone call and investigative mile to go before he slept tonight.

14

Beverly stopped by Bistro de Bardot for some supper takeout and made her way to Harlan's. His home was the typical Vermont style cottage she loved—an early nineteenth-century Cape-style house, simple but sturdy with a steeply pitched roof and massive central chimney.

She wasn't sure if she'd get to see the inside if Harlan wasn't home, or worse, didn't want her company. But when she knocked on the door, he dragged her inside and wrapped her in a hug while she was still holding the bag of takeout.

She put the food down on the counter as she studied him. "You look pretty good for a dangerous criminal and newly flown jailbird."

He took a bow. "It's all that five-star prison cuisine." He sniffed the bag on the counter, and she pulled out several containers, starting with some Vermont cheddar and caramelized-onion focaccia rolls and maple cinnamon raisin bread.

"I wasn't sure which kind you liked, so I got both."

He grabbed a cheddar roll and started munching with a look of bliss on his face. Then he pointed to the styrofoam boxes. "What other delights do you have in store?"

"This one is lemon-garlic brook trout."

He wrinkled his nose, and she placed her hands on her hips. "Adam said you liked to fish. Don't tell me you don't eat fish?"

"Fishing is all about the experience. The air, the sunshine, the peace and quiet. It's not about eating the fish."

"Well," she opened up the other box. "Good thing I also got some applewood smoked ham."

"Ah," he smiled and nodded. "Now that's what we call a Vermont delicacy."

"Delicacy? Ham?"

"Comes from the same word as delicious, don't it?"

Beverly was a former art history major, not English, but she wasn't about to argue with his logic. She was just happy to see him looking so relaxed and untroubled by his recent ordeal.

They ate in silence for a few minutes. Beverly had purchased four coffees and got up to hand him a fresh cup. "You know Adam wanted to be here, don't you?"

He took a sip of the coffee. "Feel sorry for him. He's smack dab in the middle and doesn't know which way to turn."

"It's not your fault."

"Not directly. Though I still feel responsible somehow. If I'd got that security system Prospero's been bugging me about." He slurped more of the coffee, then added, "Sure wish I could thank Adam for arranging that attorney fellow. Got me out on bail. Don't know how he did it, though. Magic wand?"

"You have Agnes Flamm to thank for that."

"Isn't that the woman who was friends with your grandmother? The antiques store owner?"

"Former antiques store owner. She's opening up a wine shop now. And she put up her property as bail money. It's a lien, essentially."

"Now why in tarnation would she do something like that? She doesn't know me. I mean, we've run into each other a couple of times, both being in the biz. But that's it."

"She doesn't like injustice any more than I do. And she knows how much you mean to me. Guess that's all that mattered."

"Huh." Harlan pushed the remains of his dinner away, what little was left of it, and went over to sit in his favorite green recliner. "A wine shop, you say?"

Beverly sat across from him on the plaid sofa. "She wanted to try something new."

"It's a pain in the ass setting up a new store. Might take her a while to get stocked up. I could loan her some things on consignment to get her going. I've got a couple of great wine racks collecting dust."

"I have a feeling she'd appreciate that."

"I'll call up Prospero and have him send some things over this very day."

Beverly collected up the empty food containers and put them in the trash before curling up on the sofa next to Harlan. "Maybe Adam can't talk to you about the case, but I can."

"Wouldn't want you to get into any trouble."

"That's my middle name." She smiled at him. "Adam has one good lead, a man named Braddon Hopper, who belonged to the same Society for Creative Anachronism chapter the victim did. Was quite jealous of him, in fact. And an expert swordsman."

"Sounds too good to be true."

"Maybe, but it's a start. And Mr. X is helping work on the Forsythe angle."

"Mr. X?"

"His last name is really Xenakis, and—"

"Xenakis?" Harlan's eyes turned dark with suspicion. "There was a man by the name who was a Forsythe henchman. Very secretive and mostly stayed invisible. But I heard lots of rumors. Beverly, please tell me it's not the same guy."

"It is, but—"

"Oh, Beverly." Harlan shook his head. "Either you're betraying me or this fellow is taking you for a ride. I don't trust him."

Beverly winced at that. "Dear Harlan, I would never betray you, you mustn't think like that. Mr. X left the Forsythes' employ when he saw what they were like. He's retired from the business now, but he still has connections. He's a valuable resource. And he's on our side, please trust me on that. *I'd* trust him with my life." And she surprised herself to realize she truly meant it.

Harlan leaned back in his chair. "I do trust you, Beverly. So I'll trust him."

She smiled at him. "Thank you. Some day I'll let you meet him."

"Sure would be interesting, I'll hand you that." He looked around the room, then frowned as he pointed to some tackle boxes on a shelf. "I don't remember leaving those open. You think a burglar's been in here?"

Beverly cleared her throat. "More like a couple of detectives, I'm afraid."

"Oh." Harlan slid down further into the recliner. "Guess they had to do that. Kinda feels—"

"Like you've been violated?"

"Betrayed again. But that's not fair. And better them than a burglar, right?"

"Any day."

Harlan put his feet up on the recliner's footrest. "Well, now, you said suspects, plural. Are there more?"

"The estranged brother. There's also an ex-fiancée and her new boyfriend. And several pissed-off people the victim sued could also be on that list."

Harlan sighed. "Sounds like a cider-barrel of work for poor Adam."

"That's what he gets paid for. Although I think he'd take this case on pro bono if he had to."

"You don't think he's going to get fired, do you?"

"The mayor would love to arrange that. I'm pretty sure the chief's got his back."

"He damn well better."

Beverly tipped her cup at him. "There is one other strange thing that happened."

"Strange as in how?"

"Adam and I paid a visit to Forsythe in his hospital room. He's still very much comatose, but there was a man in his room who ran when he saw us. Big burly guy with a red beard. Know anyone fitting that description?"

"'Fraid not. Some criminal type afraid of the police?"

"Some Forsythe henchman who's afraid of the police. Or Adam in particular. Might even be the real killer of Wallace Ryall who arranged all of this to get back at Adam."

Harlan grumbled, "Well, none of this makes any sense, does it? I mean, there are simpler ways to get back at Adam than through me with this murder business. Too convoluted. Like using a jackhammer to crack open a nut."

"Maybe you've made some enemies yourself, Harlan. Or our red-bearded mystery man works for one of the NAL crooks and wants to put you out of business. Like he did my grandmother and other antique store owners."

"I don't think I'm important enough to have enemies. Too James Bond. Russian spies and all that."

"You have to admit the NAL angle makes sense."

"But I'm a lowly small-business owner. Not worth their while."

A faint thud outside caught Beverly's attention. She put up her hand, motioning for Harlan to be quiet, then listened harder. Another thud was followed by the sound of a scraping noise, like a key on a glass pane.

Beverly got up and whispered into Harlan's ear, "Keep talking. About the weather or fishing."

As her heart raced, she tiptoed toward the back part of the house and grabbed a flashlight from a counter in the kitchen. A solid Maglite, which she weighed in her hand. Good. Heavy enough to make a dent in someone's skull.

She crept through the kitchen, staying in the shadows as much as she could. The scraping noise started up again, and she stopped to listen some more. The sound was coming from the porch, so she hoisted the flashlight above her head and swung open the kitchen door.

She found herself face to face with the same red-bearded man she and Adam had seen in Forsythe's hospital room. Beverly didn't dare take her eyes off him for a second to look and see if he had a weapon. The gun in her purse in the living room was no help.

The intruder stared at her for a moment, then smiled when he saw her flashlight. He took a step closer toward her. But a sudden look of shock spread across his face, and he took off into the yard into the darkness of the night and vanished.

Beverly swirled around to see Harlan with a loaded rifle perched on his shoulder he was aiming at the intruder. "Come back here, you lily-livered coward!"

He made motions like he was going to give chase, but Beverly stopped him. "Better call the police, Harlan."

"But Adam can't come, can he?"

"Jinks or the beat cops can."

He relented and watched as she propped a chair under the porch door knob. She explained, "To make it harder to get in. He'll have to break the glass."

"That guy will think twice about returning for a second go-round, now." He patted the gun. "This ole girl here is going to sleep with me tonight."

"That ole girl can sleep with you, and this ole girl will take the couch." She smiled, and when he started to protest, she shook her head. "I've been told I'm more stubborn than a mule."

Harlan laid the rifle on the kitchen counter. "That maple cinnamon raisin bread will make a right tasty French toast in the morning. Since you bought it, guess you should get to enjoy it."

"That's the spirit." She grabbed her cellphone and dialed the Ironwood Junction PD, a number she knew by heart now. She half-hoped Adam and Jinks would show up, but knew it would look better if they didn't. What was Adam up to? She didn't dare think about such things. Not right now.

15

Adam yawned as he watched the sunrise with its pink fingers spreading apart the gray clouds. He hadn't got much sleep. Then again, his car didn't make the most comfortable bed, and trying to watch Harlan's house from down the road had kept him awake most the night. As he drove to the station to pick up Jinks, she was waiting for him outside and hopped in, wordlessly handing him a cup of steaming black coffee.

They sipped in silence for a moment until Jinks asked, "How's Harlan? That attempted break-in must have been a shock."

"Shaken up, but okay. We've got a BOLO out for our redheaded burglar."

"He turns up in two places—first Forsythe's hospital room where the man's in a coma, then at Harlan's. If it's the same guy."

"Beverly swears it's the same one. And how many 'ginger' crooks do you know?"

"Point taken. How much sleep did you get? An hour?"

"Or so. Enough." Wanting to change the subject to distract his heavy eyelids that kept threatening to close, he asked, "How's Jacob?"

"Looks like a chipmunk with its mouth full of acorns. You have had the mumps, right?"

"Think so."

"That's good. Can make adult males sterile."

"Felicia keeping an eye on him?"

"Her job owes her some sick days, but my mother's doing the honors today."

"Guess that means lots of ice cream."

"And cavities. And whining about how Nana does so-and-so better than I do. Gotta win the lottery so I can afford daycare."

Adam winced. Jinks and her mother had a prickly relationship even on good days. She'd never approved of her daughter's desire to become a police officer and definitely didn't approve of her relationship with Felicia. It was times like this he was glad he'd never had kids, mumps or no mumps. "If you need the time off—"

"Don't want to put Chief Quinn on the spot since I'm outta sick days. Not with Mayor Lehmann breathing down the chief's neck."

"It's me he hates. I don't like him giving you or the department any grief on my account."

Adam took some sips of the coffee. Pretty good, but he needed some mini-jacks along with it to keep his eyes propped open. "I thought about taking a job in New Hampshire."

Jinks frowned. "And let that conniving snake-of-a-mayor win? Don't you dare. Besides, I just got you broken in."

"So that's what all those newspapers are doing on the floor of my office."

"Here," Jinks handed over a bag with a cream-cheese muffin. "Puppy chow."

Adam took the muffin gratefully, surprised at how hungry he was. "Any leads on our red-bearded mystery man?"

"Not in the databases, no. By description or the fingerprints from Harlan's porch."

"First Forsythe's room, then Harlan's home. Not seeing the connection unless our theory about avenging Forsythe has legs."

"And I'm not liking that theory."

"Maybe the victim's brother, Ramsay Ryall, can enlighten us since he's back from his vacation or business trip or whatever it was. You got the address?"

Jinks pulled out her cellphone. "About ten miles down in the Brookhaven area. You drive, I'll navigate."

Adam was grateful for many aspects of living in Vermont. One was the lack of traffic on the roads, even during the so-called "rush hour." More so in the winter after the leaf-peepers and snowbirds were all back down in their hot, humid, winter havens.

Not that Adam couldn't use some of that Florida sunshine, but with the sunshine came the bugs. Lots of bugs. And malaria and dengue and bird flu and chikungunya and God knows what else.

A mere twelve minutes later—after a stop for Adam and Jinks to get more coffee—they reached their target. Ramsay Ryall's house was in stark contrast to his brother's OCD-constrained duplex. For one thing, it was a house he owned, not rented, and it showed he wasn't doing all that bad financially, unlike his brother. Not a palace, but a good three acres or so, with the house's stone facade looking as good as new. A blindingly white picket fence surrounded the yard.

Ryall led them into a den that hinted of a woman's touch, with blue-and-green curtains matching a braided rug and the aqua and periwinkle fabric on the furniture. He motioned for them to sit and grabbed a seat for himself near the fireplace. "I cut my trip short and got here as fast as I could after your department called me. I'm still in a state of shock."

Adam started the questioning with Jinks serving as scribe. "When was the last time you saw your brother Wallace, Mr. Ryall?"

"Guess the last time was Dad's funeral. In June."

"How would you describe the relationship between yourself and your brother?"

Ryall rubbed his temple. "You probably know all about that, so I'll tell you right out. It wasn't good."

"When did it turn sour?"

"It's always been touchy." He pointed to his cheek, where a scar stretched from his eye down to his mouth. "See this? Got it when we were kids. He dared me to jump off a tree into a snowbank, knowing full well there were boards underneath the snow. I was lucky I only broke my leg and got this scar."

"And more recently?"

"We had a snowmobile business together for a couple years. But Wally had one huge problem. He took exception to every least little slight and made it a habit of suing people. After a while, some of those resulted in countersuits. Long story short, he bankrupted our business."

"How did your father feel about all of that?"

"You'll have to arrange a séance and ask him. We weren't on speaking terms. Hadn't been for years."

"And why is that?"

"My wife, mostly. She was Vietnamese, a beautiful, loving, talented woman. But my father served in the Vietnam war. Perhaps he had a touch of PTSD, for all I know. He hated everything about Vietnam. Ranted and raved about me marrying a 'Commie.' Hinted that my wife might be the relative of someone who killed his buddies."

"Your wife is deceased?" Adam knew this already but wanted to see Ryall's reaction.

The man got tears in his eyes and turned his head to stare into the fireplace. "Breast cancer. And you know what the cold-hearted bastard father of mind said when she died? That he was glad she was dead. That now she could go and join her Commie ancestors in hell."

Adam cleared his throat. "I'm sorry to hear that, Mr. Ryall. I'm also guessing that's part of the reason he left you out of his will."

"Left Wally out, too. That surprised me. Wally made himself out to be this upstanding, righteous honorable guy. Put on a good act with Dad, trying to buy his favor. Guess it didn't take."

"Where do you work now, Mr. Ryall?"

"I'm a tour guide for the Apple Valley Resort."

Adam's ears perked up. The same place where Beverly was staying. "What kind of tours?"

"You name it. Sugar-mapling in the spring, horseback riding in the summer, fall colors, cross-country skiing in the winter. I enjoy the work. Much less stress than running your own business. And a steady paycheck, to boot."

"Although you and your brother weren't close, were you aware of anyone who had threatened him recently? Anyone who hated him enough to kill him?"

Ryall's hands curled into fists. "Braddon Hopper. He and Wally were in that Medieval group together. The ones that dress up and play with fake weapons."

"Jealousy?"

"Wouldn't know about that. I was referring to Hopper's former girlfriend, Jane Campen. She and my wife were friends. Jane confided to my wife that someone forced himself on her once. A bar in an alley, and it was dark. But the guy sounded like Wally and was the right size. And Wally was also in the bar that night."

"She didn't file charges?"

"Couldn't be sure it was him. She screamed, the guy ran off."

"You said ex-girlfriend. Where is she now?"

"California, I think. Couldn't take the Vermont winters."

Adam looked over at Jinks, who was faithfully writing everything down. "Any other enemies besides Braddon Hopper?"

"Folks Wally sued, I guess."

"Do you have anyone in mind?"

Randall hesitated. "I suppose his neighbor, Dr. Vernon Atkinson. He owns the house in back of the duplex Wally rented."

"Medical doctor?"

"College professor at Hardin Tech. Teaches Sustainable Design and Technology, whatever that is."

"When our department tracked you down to give you the news, you were in Bangor. Business or pleasure?"

"I met this woman. At the resort, a few months ago. She and I kinda hit it off. I'd been promising to go up and visit, and this was a slow period at work."

"Were you with her last Sunday afternoon?"

"Not exactly. I'd just got into town and was trying to find my way to my hotel."

"When did you check in?" Again, Adam knew this from his preliminary research, but this was a crucial alibi linchpin.

"That evening. Guess it was eight or so."

Adam didn't have to look at Jinks to know that even though it took four hours from Ironwood Junction to Bangor, Randall Ryall would have had plenty of time to kill his brother, then drive up to Maine and check into the hotel. "I'd like the name of the woman you were visiting if you don't mind."

Randall recited her name and address for Jinks to jot down.

Adam asked, "One more question. Did you know Harlan Wilford?"

"That's the antiques store guy, right? Don't know which shocked me more—that Dad would cut Wally out of his will or he'd leave everything to that Wilford guy. Still, after all my father said to me and my wife, I wouldn't have touched his cursed blood money. Wilford can have it and good riddance."

After they'd left Randall's house and were seated in the car, Jinks said, "That story about Wally forcing himself on Braddon Hopper's girlfriend in a back alley. Sounds awfully familiar."

"Your current sexual assault case? Mariel McWilliams?"

"Same type of M.O."

"But Hopper's girlfriend didn't get a good look at the guy. It's all hearsay."

"True. But if it was Wally, the perp is dead."

"Body's still with the medical examiner, though."

"I'll ask about getting DNA from Wally's body in the morgue to see if it matches evidence from my case."

Adam nodded. "We can get the paperwork started."

Jinks raised her voice as Adam cranked up the car's engine. "Our victim, Wally Ryall, is turning into more of a scuzzbucket every day. Makes me wish I was the one to skewer him. Shishke-Wally-bobs." Jinks stabbed her finger in the air.

"Ramsay Ryall has plenty of good reasons to kill his brother. He seemed sincere enough when he said he didn't want his father's money. But he could be a great actor."

"Maybe that money *is* cursed."

"Jinks, you're about as superstitious as an atheist at mass."

"Mass? You gotta be joking. I'd never be able to tell all those saints apart."

Adam laughed, and Jinks added, "Since we're on the subject of saints, how's Saint Beverly? Is she okay after the break-in last night?"

"She's fine. But really, *Saint* Beverly? She's as much a saint as, well—"

"As I am. You can call me Saint Jinks from here on. And since I've been canonized, I want a raise."

"Don't tell Beverly. God only knows what she'll want."

Jinks looked at him with a wicked smile. "Oh, I think I know what she wants."

Adam turned on the radio to VPR and was rewarded with Mozart, or as Jinks derisively called it, "bunny hop" music. That would shut her up for a while.

16

Beverly hadn't slept well at all, waking up at every bump or thump or creak at Harlan's house. The sense of relief from getting through the night without any additional intruders was shattered when she got the call from Agnes Flamm. Beverly fixed Harlan a quick breakfast, then dashed over to Agnes's wine shop and hurried inside.

Agnes had a broom in one hand, sweeping up some broken dishes. She stopped when she saw Beverly. "Guess it's a good thing the wines and food aren't scheduled for delivery until this afternoon."

Beverly looked around the room. Agnes had been hard at work since Monday when Beverly first stopped by, with shelves and chests and racks all filled with cookbooks, knick-knacks, and a few antiques. But it was equally evident someone had rifled through those shelves, with items askew or knocked on the floor in the burglar's haste.

"Oh, Agnes. When did this happen?"

"Some time overnight. I *would* have been upstairs in my apartment, but I'd gone over to Forestville to pick up some supplies. Got a hotel room since I'd be getting back too late. And when I arrived this morning, I found the place like this."

"Anything missing?"

"Not as far as I can tell. So far."

"We should call the police." And how would they react to that, seeing as how she'd called them just last night for another break-in at another location?

"I'm not so sure about that. I mean, nothing was taken. A few things are broken, not enough to add up to much. And that dear Detective Dutton and his colleagues are so busy with Harlan's case, I don't want to bother them."

"But—"

"Beverly, I don't think it's a good idea."

Agnes's firm tone of voice caught Beverly by surprise. Why would she not want anyone looking into this? "The fingerprints alone would probably catch the guy. You don't want him getting off scot-free, do you?"

Agnes didn't answer for a moment, so Beverly prompted her again. "Do you?"

"There's those young men, you know."

"The ones I encountered in October? The young toughs who were going to rob me here?"

"I'm familiar with the older two, Herman Villers and Fritz Gailey, and they're lost causes. But there's the younger boy who hangs out with them, Blaine Morland. The one whose mother was killed in that freak accident? I worry about that boy. He only seems to be going along with the other two. Not sure he's really into it, but what else does he have to do? He looks haunted. And underfed."

Beverly almost had to smile at that. As long as she'd known Agnes, the older woman had hated to see any creature go hungry. Whether it was a robin or squirrel or junkyard dog. Or one motherless boy. "Somehow I don't think feeding Blaine Morland is going to stop him going with the wrong crowd."

"I suppose not."

"Let me take some photos of the damage, anyway."

"Feel free, although I'm not going to report this to my insurance company. I just got insured and don't want my rates to go up. Might end up costing me more than replacing the items."

"As you wish, Agnes, but I'm only agreeing under strong protest."

Agnes handed her the broom. "If you don't mind finishing this up, I'll go get the dustpan."

They made short work of setting the place back to rights, but Beverly couldn't help adding, "Having second thoughts about moving down to Florida?"

"Not a chance. We native Vermonters are made of sturdier stuff than that."

"Aren't you afraid the thief or thieves will return?"

"Maybe. But that young man from Harlan Wilford's shop, Prospero, isn't that it? Such a lovely Shakespearean name. Anyway, he dropped some items off from Harlan's shop yesterday. Quite the thoughtful thing to do."

Beverly started to butt in, "But—"

"And he told me about a security system he was installing at Harlan's shop. Said he could do it for me, too. That should take care of it."

Beverly thought she'd noticed a few familiar items. Bless Harlan and bless Prospero. "All right, I give in. By the way, you haven't seen a red-bearded man around here, have you? A big, burly guy?"

"Can't say I have. Sounds like a lumberjack. I'd expect to see him wearing plaid flannel."

"I think it was more like jeans and a red parka. He's run from me twice now. Once at Reginald Forsythe's hospital room and again last night, at Harlan's home, where he tried to break in."

"You do lead an exciting life, Beverly. Not sure your grandmother would be thrilled to know you're playing cops-and-robbers."

"More fun than dolls and tea parties."

"I was more of a dancer, myself. Mitch Miller and Les Baxter. The jitterbug, the Chalypso, the bunny hop."

"Dancing sounds more fun than dolls and tea parties, too." Beverly straightened some cookbooks on a shelf, picking up one titled *Romantic Entertaining*, which she hurriedly put back. Not so hurriedly, it seemed, that Agnes didn't catch her looking at it.

"You can keep that one if you'd like. Someone you have in mind to entertain? A certain detective?"

"As you said, he's too busy with Harlan's case."

Agnes perched on the edge of a rattan chair. "You know why I decided to open this shop?"

"I figured you were bored with retired life."

"That. I was also tired of looking over my shoulder. Tired of glimpses of what I'd left behind. Fond memories. Good friends now gone. Missed opportunities. I figured as long as I had breath in me, I could find meaning and a little happiness."

Beverly blurted out, "But what if something happens to Harlan? You'll lose the shop since your fate is tied to his now."

"Then I'll find something else." Agnes got up to rescue the book on entertaining and handed it to Beverly. "From me to you. A gift."

"Oh, Agnes. I don't know—"

"I have a feeling you'll find some use for it."

Beverly hugged the book to her. "Guess I've never stayed in one place long enough to need something like this."

"Maybe it's time you did."

A gust of wind rattled the windows, and the last traces of the recent snow on the roof cascaded down the glass in a mini-blizzard. Despite Agnes's calm demeanor, Beverly couldn't shake a feeling of gloom. Two break-ins in two days. The Red-bearded Menace, as she'd decided to call him. Thieving young toughs. One violent murderer. And Harlan, who could be sent back to jail at any moment.

What *would* her grandmother think of her now? Would she be proud? Mystified? Angry? Disappointed? One thing was sure—Grammie always said she wouldn't raise a fool, and Beverly was nobody's fool. Not even a fool for love.

§ § §

Beverly didn't drive back to the resort right away. She couldn't stop thinking about the Red-bearded Menace. What was it that Agnes had said? That Beverly's description of him sounded like a lumberjack. Wouldn't hurt to do a drive-by of the local Formby's Timber Company, would it?

Grateful for her rental SUV's tinted windshield, she pulled her car over, down the road from Formby's, and scanned the place. Though an industrial company, the main building still had a cheery red roof and cabin feel to it, like so much of Vermont's architecture. In the back, covered barn-like structures filled with boards lay next to rows of wooden logs taller than she was. The smell of resin and wood dust made her sneeze.

She scanned the property for her red-haired target but didn't see much activity outside at all. Probably wasn't the right time of year for much in the way of logging or building. Might explain the lack of workers?

Sharp rapping on her car window made her jump. A man with graying hair peeking out from under a baseball cap and a green shirt that said "Formby's Timber" gestured at her. Maybe it would be smarter to peel off and get away from the guy, but instead, Beverly rolled down the window and gave the man a big smile.

He was *not* smiling as he said, "You lost, little lady?"

"As a matter of fact, I am. I don't know how to use this GPS thingie in my car, and I'm trying to find the Salt Rock Lodge and Conference Center."

He pulled off his cap to scratch his head. "You're way off track there. If you turn around here, you can pick up Hunter's Run and take it down to Karn's River Road. That dead-ends into Woodstock Boulevard. 'Bout five miles down, you'll see the signs for the center."

Beverly beamed at him. "Oh, you are such a gentleman, helping a lady in distress like this. When I saw your face, I was so afraid I'd got myself into some kind of trouble. My husband does tell me to take maps with me, but I always forget."

The expression on the man's face relaxed a bit. "Glad to be of help. And sorry if I seemed too threatening. Can't be too careful these days."

"Too careful? I don't understand? I didn't think this part of Vermont was dangerous."

"There's the occasional deer or moose you might hit. But I was thinking more about corporate espionage."

Beverly blinked at him for a moment. That wasn't at all what she'd expected. "Timber spies?"

"Competition everywhere is pretty fierce. You develop a new process or get a new patent, and all of a sudden, you're a target."

"I had no idea. I guess I *could* be accused of spying—at all those lovely wooden beams over there. My poor husband isn't going to be too happy when I tell him the idea I had of re-doing our rear deck."

That elicited the first smile from the staffer. "You get ready to build, call us. We got the best wood. We guarantee it."

"Thanks so much. You're an angel."

With a big wave and blowing the man a kiss, she dutifully turned around and headed back in the direction she'd come.

That was a bust. What had she expected? For the Red-bearded Menace to come bounding out and pose for her while she took a video? She envied Adam and his "official" authority. He could flash that badge, and doors opened fast.

Beverly wasn't "official," but she knew a thing or two about getting people to talk freely. She just had to get a bead on where to head next. She'd worry about the talking part later.

17

Adam drove around the corner next to Wally Ryall's duplex. The place was every bit as dark and deserted-looking as when he and Jinks were inside yesterday. The forensics team had come and gone, with not much interesting to add to the former occupant's murder case. No weapons, no blood, no secret threatening notes, and the only fingerprints were Ryall's and the ex-girlfriend's, Fern Gery.

But this time, Adam and Jinks were more interested in the house behind the duplex where Professor Vernon Atkinson lived, as neat and homey-looking as Wally's was unwelcoming. Despite the last traces of snow on top of dormant brown grass, the fastidiously trimmed bushes, plant stakes, and wire frames in back were signs of a gardener's obsessive touch.

The man who welcomed them inside was the quintessential college professor, complete with sweater and patches on the elbows and a pipe. Adam would have suspected the man was playing up the image for their benefit if Adam hadn't gone on the college's website and found photos of Atkinson with that same getup.

Their host introduced them to an olive-skinned woman he identified as his wife, Nyssa, who joined him on a Victorian-era loveseat. Adam asked the man, "You're a professor of Sustainable Design and Technology at Hardin Tech, is that correct?"

"You're going to ask what that is, so I'll beat you to the punch."

Adam had a pretty good idea of what it was from the website, but he'd play along.

"We take tree-hugging to the next level. But instead of hugging the trees, we find ways to keep from cutting them down. Or to do so in a way that eliminates negative environmental impacts. Sustainable design is about creating projects that don't require any non-renewable resources."

Adam thought he heard Jinks stifle a disgusted grunt trying to keep up with the man's words as she wrote it all down. Adam asked, "You must hold some patents, then."

"I do. Most are the college's patents."

"Was Wallace Ryall a student of yours?"

"I doubt that young man was college material. Although I could see him becoming an attorney. The ambulance-chasing kind."

"I understand you were one of the objects of his litigious pastime."

"Pastime makes it sound like knitting or playing basketball. This was more a pathology."

Adam looked around the room. Very. . .scholarly-looking. "What prompted his lawsuit against you?"

"I was a tad overzealous with my wildflower garden. I tried a new chemical touted as all-natural and only toxic to certain weeds. Some of it seeped onto the neighboring property. Not long afterward, an elm tree fell on top of his car. Smashed it in two."

"And he claimed the weed killer you used weakened the elm tree, causing it to fall?"

"Naturally, I protested my innocence since that tree was old and fell after a bad storm. But the jury didn't agree."

"They found in favor of Ryall?"

Atkinson rolled his eyes. "And that should have been the end of it, even though I disagreed with the outcome."

"What happened next?"

"The win in court emboldened Mr. Ryall. And the harassment started soon afterward."

"What type of harassment?"

"Several of my plants started dying for no apparent reason. I would have suspected the weed killer if my dog hadn't fallen sick about the same time."

Adam hadn't seen any pets. Maybe that explained it. "Poison?"

"That's what the vet said. She's a good vet, and Muttley survived, but we had some huge vet bills resulting from that. Not to mention chronic kidney problems."

"Did the veterinarian determine the type of poison?"

"She said it might be borax. But she couldn't tell from a blood test whether it was intentional or accidental."

"Anything else happen?"

Atkinson uttered a snort of disgust. "One morning when I left the house for work, I noticed someone keyed my car. That resulted in a big bill for a new paint job. Then, there were the windows that were egged. And red paint was splashed on the sidewalk in front of our home."

"Did you ever see Wallace Ryall doing any of these things?"

"He was very clever about timing. It all happened at night or when we were out of town. And we weren't about to let Muttley outside to act as guard dog after the poisoning incident."

Atkinson patted his wife on the hand. "It got so bad, my wife was afraid to go outside for fear she'd run into the man."

Adam looked at Nyssa Atkinson, quiet up to this point. She didn't appear frightened, more subdued and tense. Tense at the presence of police? They got that all the time, so it wouldn't be surprising. But he sensed that wasn't it. If her body language was any indication, she was ready to bolt from the room and out of the house. Adam caught Jinks's eye and used a little surreptitious sign language for "you, now."

Jinks took the hint and turned to Nyssa to ask, "I know this is all very upsetting to the both of you, Mrs. Atkinson. We have to ask the same questions to everyone, you understand. So forgive me when I ask you where you were Sunday afternoon?"

Her voice was soft, so soft it was hard to hear. "Visiting my sister. For the birth of my new niece, Joy Anne. Joy Anne Li. My sister is Melinda Li."

"At Dartmouth-Hitchcock hospital?"

Nyssa nodded. "A C-section."

Jinks waited for her to add more information, but the woman cleared her throat and looked down at her hands. Her husband jumped in and said, "And I was here all day, grading papers. Didn't even go out to get meals, thanks to Nyssa here, who prepared everything for me in advance. All I had to do was pop it in the oven."

Jinks smiled. "Then you're one lucky man, Mr. Atkinson. My kids are lucky if they get a can of Spaghetti-Os when I'm not home."

Atkinson chuckled. But Jinks's trademark humor didn't make one dent in Nyssa's gloominess as she continued staring at her fingers.

Adam posed his next question to Atkinson. "Did you ever report these acts of vandalism or the poisoning to the police?"

"We did. But without proof, what could they do? They asked Ryall a few questions, he denied everything."

Adam thought back to his survey of the small shed behind Ryall's duplex. He did recall seeing a can of red paint and some borax, a highly toxic weed killer in high doses. "Did you complain to the landlord who owns the duplex?"

"We did. But the family lives in Connecticut. The patriarch owned old Rory's Five and Dime, did you know that? The business hadn't done so well in later years. Guess that's why the family didn't want to make any waves about Ryall. He paid the rent on time, and that was all that mattered."

"I'm surprised he didn't sue them for the fallen elm tree instead of you."

"Guess he figured they had more money than a college professor to hire good lawyers. Even with their fortunes in decline, he was probably right."

"Mr. Atkinson, did either you or your wife see any unusual visitors at Ryall's place recently? Or witness any arguments?"

"That man had no visitors, far as I could tell. There was that nice young lady who he dated for a time. I remember her name because of the botanical connections. Fern, Fern Gery. But I never heard them argue. If anything, she was a saint for putting up with his eccentricities. I guess even saints get tired of wearing a halo."

Adam thanked the professor and his wife for their time, and he and Jinks retreated to the car. Jinks summed it up pretty well, saying, "One petty lawsuit, one poisoned dog, a few dead plants, a keyed car, eggs on the window, red paint on the sidewalk. Hardly seems enough motive to impale a man into a tree."

"I'm equally interested in Nyssa Atkinson's reactions. She was too quiet even for a woman who's had a brush with murder. Seemed afraid. Of her husband? Worried he's really a killer? Or even knows he's a killer?"

"Her story about the sister should be easy to check out. I'll add her to the list of characters I gotta research." Jinks shook her head. "Maybe it's that ugly baby-shit yellow paint on their living room walls that's giving her a bad mood."

Adam started the engine and put the heat on full blast. "Spaghetti-Os, Jinks?"

"Remember that casserole I made for the department picnic?"

"Oof. That one almost sent me to the emergency room. I'll have to remember that the next time we need to incapacitate a suspect. Better than pepper spray."

"Speaking of Spaghetti-Os and kids, I promised Jacob I'd check on him after lunch."

"No problem. You can do some of that character research you mentioned from home, right?"

"Chief Quinn didn't seem to mind when I brought it up the other day."

"All right then. Go forth and research."

"What about you, Dutton?"

He squinted up at the sky. "I was thinking of getting a drink. An Irish coffee."

Jinks gave him a knowing smile. "Say 'hi' to Cray for me, will ya?"

18

A quick call to Agnes verified some valuable information the older woman had given Beverly earlier, namely, the names and spellings of the two "young toughs" who'd tried to rob Beverly months ago—Herman Villers and Fritz Gailey. The same boys Agnes suspected were behind the break-in at her shop. And not only names, Agnes had heard where the duo worked—at the local lumber mill, which was open twenty-four hours.

Looked like this was going to be Beverly's "wood" day. Appropriate, since she'd been in town five days, and wood was the traditional gift for the fifth wedding anniversary. Not that she'd ever had to worry about that, never having made it to five before.

Before any showtime, one needed a costume. She headed for what had become a favorite store, the Cluttered Closet. The taxidermied eel in the window was no longer in sight, replaced by a stuffed gopher sporting a little top hat and sequin vest. But the mannequins guarding the entrance were still there, one dressed as a Viking, the other as a Goth.

The clerk and Beverly were on a first-name basis now, and the minute Beverly walked in the door, Cherry said, "We got in a new shipment of wigs. They're awesome. I thought of you when I saw them."

Cherry wasn't kidding. When Beverly headed to the back of the shop, her eyes lighted up at the array of hairpieces. She cooed over a real-hair blond wig with long, dark roots and long, wavy strands that fell to chest-height. That one went in her cart. Along with a black Cleopatra-style item with bangs and another that looked like what Dolly Parton would wear if she was a redhead.

Beverly also purchased a pair of red boots and two jackets, one red and the other green. After carting the items to her SUV, she opened the trunk and put them next to the costume kit she always kept in the trunk of whatever car she was driving. She had a brief pang of remorse as she studied the kit.

She wasn't entirely honest with Adam when he'd asked her to put aside her con-woman ways. For she couldn't bear to part with that kit—false eyelashes, glasses, face prosthetics, makeup, and all. And she hadn't *exactly* promised she'd give it all up, right? Only that she'd give it serious thought.

A quick trip to a restaurant bathroom was in order, and it was a one-seater, so she wouldn't be disturbed. Moments later, she headed out again as a redhead wearing a red jacket and red boots underneath her skirt. The fuller cheeks and green contact lenses were a nice touch if she did say so herself.

After one more stop at another store to pick up a leather portfolio, she headed for the lumber mill. As she found out when she arrived, the place was also a stone quarry. Guess if one business failed, they always had the other, right?

She soon saw a reason for the latter when she spied the layer cake of granite cuttings behind the main building. As for the wood part, it was hard to tell, since all the materials seemed to be hidden from sight in several outbuildings. But the sound of a loud whining, buzzing sound in the distance was a dead giveaway.

Time for some quick research on her phone to get the lingo and details just right. Or close enough. One deep breath and a quick look at her getup in the mirror reassured her, and she grabbed the portfolio and marched into the office. "Good afternoon, I'm here to speak with Mr. John Davidson."

The clerk tore his attention away from some paperback and squinted at her. "Do you have an appointment?"

"I did call ahead, yes. Ms. Joan Sutherland, sales rep from Frugaltech Wood Dryers."

"Oh? What's this about?"

"Counterflow continuous kilns. As you know, our kilns improve energy consumption, give higher throughput, and improve drying consistency and product quality."

The clerk rubbed his chin and frowned. "I don't remember the boss saying you were coming. He flipped through a ledger and shook his head. Guess he didn't make a note of it." The clerk picked up the phone, but after a minute of no reply, he hung up. "Sorry, ma'am. I'll have to go track him down."

"Thanks very much. Mister—"

"Franklin."

Right as the clerk headed off into the back, Beverly spied a clipboard on the wall with the heading, "Shift Schedule." Elated, she hurried over and ran her finger along the names, looking for Herman Villers and Fritz Gailey. When she got to the page for yesterday's shifts, the pair were listed as having been on night duty.

Beverly bit her lip so hard, she drew blood. Damn. Another dead end. If those boys were working last night, there wasn't any way they could have trashed Agnes's shop. Her disappointment wasn't enough to override her fear of getting caught, so she hurried back to her car.

Agnes was helpful in another way—she'd also passed along the name of Blaine Morland's aunt, whom he lived with.

Beverly wanted to believe like Agnes did that the young motherless boy was a decent kid sucked in by a couple of hooligans, but she was more cynical than Agnes. Life had taught her that being any other way was dangerous.

Her new quest meant another change of clothes, this time in a different bathroom and something more matronly. The green jacket with a black shirt and sensible flats was more the ticket. Plus, an entirely different makeup job, the Cleopatra wig, and brown contacts.

The woman who opened the door reminded Beverly of her Grammie, and she choked up for a brief moment. She almost backed out of the ruse with the woman but instead steeled her resolve. When Beverly introduced herself as a "Diana Shore," a social worker, Mrs. Trier welcomed her in and gave her some warm cider.

Beverly thanked her and apologized for the intrusion. "I'm checking up on Blaine to make sure everything is okay. A standard courtesy check for the schools."

"You're lucky you caught me as I got off work. I've got a 7-3 shift at Sweets for the Sweet."

Beverly knew the place well. A popular local tourist candy and fudge store. "I'm grateful for your time."

Mrs. Trier clutched her own mug of cider and fidgeted in her seat as if sitting on tacks. "I'm trying to do my best by poor Blaine. When my sister Tabitha died, it was hard on all of us. Blaine, especially. Has he been acting out in school?"

"No, nothing like that. Although he's hanging out with these two boys who aren't the best role models. I do hope Blaine has activities to keep him busy."

"There's homework. I make sure he does that. We watch TV most nights. Like last evening. I have him watch the eleven o'clock news with me because I want him to be educated in the real world. Not stuck in some virtual world like so many game-playing kids nowadays."

"And I see here," Beverly checked her non-existent notes, "that he went to school at the normal time this morning?"

"Gets up at five-thirty every morning. Since I have the early shift."

Beverly breathed a sigh of relief at that. Although Blaine could still be the culprit in the break-in, he'd only have from about midnight to five-thirty. Beverly was fairly certain his aunt would have heard him going out or coming in.

"Have you seen any unusual psychological stress in Blaine? Does he appear depressed or angry?"

"About the usual things, I reckon. Girls, grades, and games." At Beverly's raised eyebrow, the aunt added, "Oh, I know he plays those things. I try to keep it to a minimum."

"I don't know, they have video game tournaments now. And bachelor's degrees in game design. Programmers can earn up to five thousand a month."

Mrs. Trier's jaw dropped open. "You don't say? Guess I was a little too quick to stop him."

"I don't think so. There will still be plenty of time for that. You're only young once."

Blaine's aunt leaned back on her sofa and balanced her mug on an armrest. "You must have children, Miss Shore."

"Actually, I don't. But I was young once, too. And I know how much of that youth I squandered. The old 'if I could only go back and get a do-over' routine."

Mrs. Trier frowned. "I don't want that for Blaine. Aside from the loss of his mother. If God thought it was time for her to go, it was time. And nothing could stop that."

Beverly was feeling pretty guilty about bringing up painful topics with this woman, so she hurriedly said, "It sounds like you're doing a wonderful job with Blaine. I wish all of our cases were like that."

The other woman beamed at that, and Beverly hoped she'd set her mind at rest somewhat. She thanked the woman again for her time and returned to her car, thinking. She didn't agree with Tonya Trier on one thing—there was no way some deity up there was playing dice with people's lives.

While she was relieved to find it unlikely Blaine was involved in the break-in, it didn't clear him completely. But she was also beginning to understand why Agnes felt so sorry for the young man.

A call on her cellphone pushed away some of her gloominess. Fern Gery, Wally Ryall's ex-girlfriend, wanted to meet for dinner. Getting business and pleasure thrown in her lap without trying? Maybe it would turn out to be a good day, after all.

19

Adam stared up at the Ironwood Pub & Brewery sign. The building was newish in the Junction but designed to mimic the style of "traditional" Vermont, with post and beam architecture like something out of frontier days. Harlan once said to Adam that Vermonters make everything that's old look new and everything that's new look old.

Adam said aloud, "And leave it to the Junction for one of the biggest buildings in town to be a bar."

Not surprising, really, considering Vermont sported the highest number of brewers per capita in the U-S-of-A. Something to keep in mind, if Mayor Lehmann ever was successful in getting Adam fired. Built-in job security for bouncers since people were always going to drink.

One of the most determined drinkers Adam knew was waiting for him as he walked into the pub, waving Adam over to a booth in the back. Adam slid into the seat across from a human-bear. Six-five, shaggy black mane and beard and about the same size as a smallish grizzly. "Why, Creighton Querry, fancy meeting you here. Still bouncing?"

"Thanks to you and the little mention you worked into the papers after the Forsythe case, I'm back to being a full-time private eye. And I take it from your phone call earlier you might have some work for me?"

"What makes you think I don't just want to share a drink with my best bud?"

"Best and bud don't quite describe this," Cray gestured from Adam to himself.

"Cray, you wound me." Adam picked up the drink menu and rolled his eyes. "I can just see the marketing gurus who got paid big bucks to sit around and think of these beer names."

"Named after famous Vermonters. What's wrong with that?"

"Calvin Droolidge? Ethan Howlen? Rudyard Dripling? Maria von Trappist?"

"Okay, so they're on the kitschy side."

"Here's one I'm not familiar with. The Wilson Repently. Menu says it's named after Wilson Alwayn 'Snowflake' Bentley, the first photographer of snowflakes. Died of pneumonia after walking home six miles in a blizzard."

"Should have photographed seashells instead. Nice warm Bahamas seashells."

Adam handed the menu to the waitress when she arrived and ordered a coffee. Cray went with the Droolidge, but raised an eyebrow at Adam. "You're on duty?"

"Working a murder case. You may have heard about it."

"That Wallace Ryall fellow, I'll bet. Also heard Harlan Wilford was arrested for it. You do the honors or recuse yourself?"

"It was me."

"That's harsh, my friend. You do take that duty stuff serious."

"What else was I supposed to do? Take time off? Head off after some of those Bahamas seashells?"

"You don't think he did it?"

"Hell, no."

Cray took a sip of his beer when it arrived and gave Adam a thumbs up. "Harlan's always been straight with me. No pretentious shit, none of that smarmy salesman act. He sold me some desk gear. It was after my client list dried up, and I was running on empty. So he let me barter some work for him. Did some odd jobs to fix up the shop."

"Sounds like Harlan."

"I guess what I'm saying is, you want my help on clearing his name, I'm in."

Adam smiled over his glass of teetotaler Irish coffee. "He could use all the help he can get."

"Any primo suspects?"

"His estranged brother. A jealous fellow member of the Society for Creative Anachronism, Braddon Hopper. An ex-girlfriend, Fern Gery, although he had more reason to harm her than vice versa. And the victim's neighbor, a Professor Atkinson, a victim of Ryall's vendetta."

"Is that it?"

"Outliers include the neighbor's wife, Nyssa. Mayor Lehmann, who hates me enough to get to me through Harlan. Or a Reginald Forsythe crony. Like this one guy, burly but not quite as big as you. With a red beard."

"I can squeeze in some time for Harlan. Even with my current case."

"More marital infidelity?"

Cray sipped some of the beer, letting it trickle down his throat. "Something more interesting. A rare-earths shipment went missing."

"That's a new one. What's a rare earth?"

"Rare earths are just that—very rare. Minerals only found in small amounts that are hard to mine. Ironically, the windmill turbines those rare earths are used for are considered 'green' technology, but the mining process creates a bunch of toxic waste. One of the few mines in the U.S., outside the Mojave, was shut down because of that."

"All very interesting. But I'm more interested in Harlan's case." Adam handed over a couple of Ben Franklins. "That'll get you started, a mini-retainer. Anything you can find."

Cray looked at the bills. "Adam—"

"Go ahead, take them. The bail money's being put up by a friend of Beverly Laborde's. I got more to spare than I thought I might."

Cray pocketed the money and nodded toward the front of the bar. "You mean *that* Beverly Laborde?"

Adam peered around the tall seatback of the booth and caught sight of a familiar figure with long raven hair. Then he noticed she wasn't alone. She was talking animatedly to her companion, none other than Fern Gery. Adam slid farther into the booth, closer to the wall to avoid being seen.

Cray took another sip of his beer. "How's your love life, Dutton?"

Adam glared at him and started to retort when a woman slid into the booth next to him. "Cray, darling," she said. "It's been a long time. Too long."

Cray smiled at Zelda Lehmann. "Hell, the last time I saw you was right after you and Adam took that trip up to Nova Scotia. You couldn't stop talking about all the amethyst you found at Cape Blomidon."

"I've still got that amethyst. The big crystal is on my dresser, and the smaller ones I made into jewelry."

Adam was shocked she'd taken anything collected during their marriage to the mayor's home, even if it was gemstones. Zelda poked him in the ribs. "You remember that trip, don't you, Adam? We took that whale-watching cruise and saw the finbacks and minkes."

Okay, that made two surprises. She recalled all that? Cray didn't look as surprised as Adam felt, saying, "Feels like old times, doesn't it? The three of us sipping brewskis, watching the Patriots on TV."

Zelda laughed. "Now, you really are taking me back. That was when you were clean-shaven and had a crew cut."

"And as I recall, your hair was down to your waist, missy. And our favorite lawman here sported a mullet. Ah, the folly of youth."

She smiled at the two men. "I think you're right. You look much more intimidating with the beard, Cray. And Adam definitely looks sexier with his hair cut shorter." She ran her fingers through Adam's hair.

Adam tried not to notice how nice her fingers felt. And he tried even harder to ignore Cray's smirk. He made a surreptitious scan of the bar to see if he could spy Beverly and Fern, but they must have been ushered to another corner—or even another floor—of the cavernous joint. Not seeing any signs of her, he relaxed a little.

But then he had the sudden thought as to why he was trying to hide from Beverly. Or was it hiding Zelda from Beverly? All he needed was Mayor Lehmann to show up right then.

After several moments with no sign of Lehmann or Beverly, Adam allowed himself to enjoy the company. Just some friends getting together for old times' sake. All aboveboard and harmless.

Apparently, Zelda hadn't got the word about "just friends." A feminine hand squeezed his thigh under the table and moved too far north for comfort. But jumping up like a rabbit running from a fox would only bring attention to their table, and he desperately wanted to avoid that.

And damn that Cray—he winked at Adam. He knew, all right, and was enjoying every moment of Adam's embarrassment. *Goddamn* the man.

Zelda caught the waitress's attention to order a Maria von Trappist. While she waited, she grabbed Cray's beer and took a quick sip. "Adam, darling, you must tell me what happened with Harlan at the court the other day."

"Your other half didn't fill you in?"

Zelda made a big deal of rolling her eyes as if faux exasperated, but Adam could tell from the crinkles around her eyes she was truly pissed. "Titus doesn't tell me much of anything. Not that I don't eavesdrop, of course."

"Of course." Adam peered at her over his coffee. "What did you overhear?"

"Not sure who he was talking to. But he was pretty steamed."

"Harlan got released on bail."

"That's why he was steamed."

Adam was getting steamed, baked, and broiled himself. "Now why would he care if Harlan stayed in jail or got released to home confinement?"

"I think you know the answer to that."

"He hates Harlan because of his connections to me."

"I don't think he cares one way or the other about Harlan. Harlan is, well. . ."

"A weapon to cut me down?"

She grabbed her beer as it arrived to take a large gulp. "I tried to tell him what a lovely man Harlan is. And how Titus needs to spend more time on his career goals rather than personal vendettas."

"You said that?"

"Not in those exact words. But I hope he got the hint."

Adam didn't know what to say to that. He was grateful, sure, but he couldn't figure out Zelda's angle. The career part he got. That was why she'd married the guy in the first place. Up, up and away—all the way to the governor's mansion. But whose side was she on, really?

He must have had a seriously gloomy expression since Cray finally took pity on him. "Yo, Dutton, you tried the wings here? They got these killer spicy Moroccan Harissa wings. You'll need a refill on that coffee. Better make that an iced coffee. With lots of ice."

Adam gave Cray a grateful smile and waved at the waitress to place their food orders. He had the fleeting thought to go seek out Beverly and recommend she try the wings, too. Another time, perhaps.

20

Beverly studied Fern Gery as Fern studied the menu. She was quite striking, with her natural blond hair and pale blue eyes. Just like at the flower shop, she was also dressed sensibly. Jeans, albeit a designer brand, knee-high brown boots, and a yellow cable knit sweater—Ralph Lauren? Eileen Fisher?—which set off her hair nicely. What had this woman seen in Wallace Ryall? Well, they do say opposites attract.

Fern ordered some ale and seafood chowder. Beverly opted for a soda, since she was driving, and a vegetarian Reuben. She said, "This is my first time here. It's huge, but the crowd makes it look small."

Fern leaned over the table. "And loud. To be honest, this is my first visit, too. Wallace hated eating out, and my Italian Stallion prefers quiet romantic dinners. We tried the new French bistro in Windsor last weekend. I highly recommend it. Both for the food and for getting your man in the mood."

Beverly smiled. "I'll keep that in mind."

"That handsome detective you were with. Adam Dutton, wasn't it? Are you and he—"

"We're not." Beverly rushed to reply. "We're associates. And friends." She grabbed the soda as the waitress delivered it and took several gulps. Why had she said that? Why didn't she rush right in there and stake out her territory?

"I wondered. A hottie like that shouldn't go to waste. And I didn't spy a wedding ring."

"He's divorced. His ex married the mayor of Ironwood Junction."

Fern scrunched up her nose. "I've seen the mayor of Ironwood Junction. Definitely not a hottie. She must be a gold digger."

"I've never met her." Beverly didn't add, *And I hope I never do.*

"Her loss is the world's gain. Nice to know your detective is on the market in case my relationship with Bruno doesn't last."

"But Bruno is a big step up from Wallace, isn't he?" Beverly was glad for the segue into the real reason she'd asked Fern to join her at the pub, trying not to appear too eager to discuss the topic.

"Believe it or not, I still miss Wally. After my first marriage, which ended disastrously after my ex cheated on me, I'd hoped Wally was The One. Guess I'm unlucky in love. Maybe I'd do better as a gambler. Isn't it unlucky in love, lucky in cards?"

"I thought the saying was 'lucky at life, unlucky at love.'"

Fern laughed. "Or, in my case, both."

"I don't know, you've got a nice job you enjoy."

"That was another sticking point between Wally and me. With his OCD and fear of bugs and germs, he was always worried I'd track some dirt to his home."

"How did he justify being part of the SCA? Running around in a field, playing with swords and all."

"They wear armor. Not full-blown armor like ye olde days of yore, but I guess he thought it enough to ward off men and microbes. Well, that and all the scrubbing and long showers he took after SCA get-togethers."

"You said you weren't into all that SCA business, yourself."

"Not at all. I tolerated it for Wally's sake."

"What people do for love."

"You got that right." Fern swigged some more of the beer and uttered a satisfied burp.

"Did he talk about Braddon Hopper much? I understand they didn't get along one bit."

"Ranted and raved about him all the time. Braddon was after Wally's Rapier Marshal gig. But Wally thought he was too immature. I must admit, from what Wally said, I sometimes thought Wally was a teensy bit jealous."

Beverly's ears picked up at that. "Jealous?"

"Of Braddon's Olympics bid. And Braddon had more friends than Wally."

"Why didn't the ACA folk vote Wally out and Braddon in?"

"Doesn't quite work like that. They've got this incredibly complex hierarchy. More layers of bureaucracy and 'royal' appointments and decrees than the real thing."

Beverly wrinkled her nose. "More bureaucracy doesn't sound like fun to me."

"Wally liked the structure. And being Rapier Marshal made him feel important. He needed that."

"Were there any other reasons Braddon might have disliked Wally?"

Fern toyed with her spoon on the table. "Something about Braddon's girlfriend, Jane Campen. I guess I should say, ex-girlfriend. I heard them arguing once, but they shut up when I arrived. I heard some rumors."

"Rumors?"

"I discounted them. They were about Wally and Jane."

"An affair?"

Fern started to reply, but a woman's shrill laugh stole their attention. The sound wasn't exactly hard to miss, practically shaking the rafters. Fern stared at the source of the laugh, a young blonde woman. "You can tell a lot from a person's laugh.

And that woman is uncomfortable. Or fearful. Guys and bars, you know. Not always a good mix."

"Sounds like you speak from personal experience."

Fern took her time answering. "Have you ever been assaulted, Beverly?"

Beverly was startled by the suddenness of the question. And then she had a moment of panic as dark images she'd thought were suppressed punched through her subconscious. She clenched her fists by her sides, willing the images away again. "What woman hasn't experienced unwanted advances?"

"I mean truly assaulted, as in rape."

"If you count marital rape, perhaps."

Fern's eyes widened. "That would almost be worse."

"It's ancient history. Did Wally assault you?"

"No, not even close. Let's just say he wasn't a confident lover."

Beverly waited for the waitress to put down the newly arrived Reuben sandwich and took a tiny bite. Pretty good. She took a bigger bite and munched for a moment, then picked up her cream soda and enjoyed the sweet-tart taste. "I hope you won't take this the wrong way. But you and Wally seem like an odd match."

Fern sighed. "We got that all the time. When I was a girl, I was the kid in the neighborhood who picked up the strays. Cats, dogs, a couple of mice. I guess Wally struck me as another stray I needed to protect." She grabbed a wallet from her purse and slid out a photo which she handed over.

"That's you in the middle, with Wallace on one side. Who's the other man?"

"That's his brother, Ramsay. At our engagement party. One of the few times the two brothers were in the same room at the same time."

Beverly studied the photo. They may have been in the same room and same photo, but the way they stood unsmiling with tense body language, facing slightly away from each other, spoke volumes. "Was Wallace's father there?"

"He was invited, but he didn't show. I only met him once, and he was friendly to me. But I think he was going downhill fast. Neither of our fathers was there, his being ill, mine long gone."

"You said your father taught you how to ice skate?"

"You have a good memory. But that was from better days. He left me and my mother when I was only ten. Mom threw all his belongings out on the lawn and set fire to them. A huge bonfire of lies, she called it."

"Lies?"

Fern rubbed her finger around her glass. "I hated her for a long time, thinking it was all her fault. Later, I learned my father was seeing another woman. I felt sorrier for Mom after that. My father and I didn't stay in touch, and I found out later he'd died of a heart attack. Like Wally's father."

"That's awful. When you're young like that, it's hard to make sense of it all."

"I'm not sure I can make sense of it now."

Beverly hadn't had to deal with unfaithful fathers or spouses, like Fern. But learning your grandfather was a crook and your uncle a murdering son of a bitch wasn't *Father Knows Best* family territory, either. "Wallace's murder must have hit you pretty hard. Even though you're no longer together."

"The word 'shock' doesn't begin to explain it. And when I heard they arrested that antiques shop owner, I was floored. Why would he do that?"

"It's not clear he was the actual murderer. It's a very circumstantial case."

"But didn't Wallace's father leave his estate to that man? That's what Vernon Atkinson said."

"Who?"

"Dr. Vernon Atkinson. He's Wally's neighbor. He and Wally weren't on speaking terms lately, but when Wally and I first started dating, I chatted a few times with Atkinson and his wife. Nice people. I ran into him yesterday, and he told me about the will. I think it was in the newspapers, too."

Adam had warned her there would be a write-up in the *Herald-Post*, if not the *Boston Globe*. He'd talked to his reporter friend, Sam Cowie, about it, trying to be as professional and fair as he could. But something like that couldn't or shouldn't be kept out of the press.

She said, "I'm sorry to hear Wallace seems to have lost yet another friend. This neighbor of his. Dr. Atkinson, did you say?"

"He's a very distinguished-looking guy. Brown curly hair. Has these unusual half-frame eyeglasses. Wears tweed with patches on the elbows."

Beverly tried not to roll her eyes at the professorial cliché. "And yet, they didn't get along?"

"At first."

Fern didn't appear to want to discuss it further, so Beverly didn't press her about it. But it did make her wonder. What was so horrible it had caused the neighbors to stop speaking to each other? Beverly asked, "So if the antiques owner didn't end up killing Wallace, this neighbor could be a suspect?"

"It's not impossible. He seems too mild-mannered for it. They say it's always the quiet ones, though, right?"

"Can you think of anyone else who hated Wallace? Enough to kill him?"

Fern laughed. "You got all night? He pissed off a lot of people. People who hated him. But enough to murder him? Wow. That's so hard to wrap my head around."

Beverly prompted her, "Surely someone comes to mind."

"His brother. I think they started hating each other when they were still in diapers."

"Sibling rivalry?"

"Their mother died of an aneurysm, I think, when they were boys. Guess trying to compete for their father's affections was what did it. As you yourself said, when you're young like that, it's hard to make sense of it all."

Another woman's loud laugh caught their attention, and they looked toward the door where a woman with short red hair was batting her eyelashes at her male companion. The woman was clearly Zelda Lehmann, and the man was equally clearly Adam Dutton.

Beverly gritted her teeth and didn't say anything but did take note of another man who seemed to be with them, a large bear-of-a-man she didn't recognize. Maybe a business thing?

Fern noticed them, too. "Who's that with Detective Dutton?"

"His ex-wife."

"The new Mrs. Mayor?"

"She and Adam parted on good terms. Well, amicable enough."

"From his expression and hers, looks like his ex thinks they parted on much better terms than he does."

Suddenly, Beverly wasn't interested in the rest of her sandwich, and she pushed it away. Too bad she was driving. Fern's Maria von Trappist ale was sounding pretty good.

21

Friday, December 7

Adam stared at the spinach omelet he'd made, then poked at it with a fork. He'd slept pretty well and woke up thinking he was hungry. But then he'd remembered Zelda's antics last night at the bar, and his appetite faded.

Was that a metaphor for how he felt about her? It wasn't a red-haired woman he'd had dreams about last night. No, Beverly Laborde had played the lead role, and it was a doozy. A pinch of Shakespeare and *Lady Chatterley's Lover* but steamier. He felt a little guilty about it, like he should ask her permission before she appeared in his dreams.

He was never the shy, geeky kid in school, but he also was no Romeo. Beverly Laborde was the first woman to come into his life who made him wish he was good at all that hearts and flowers and poetry shtick. No, she deserved better than shtick. Hell, she deserved better than him.

Adam chucked the rest of the omelet in the trash and decided to grab some coffee for Jinks on the way to work. Miralee's Market and gas station had some of the best java in the county. Hot, always fresh, and fifty cents a cup.

As usual, he ignored the donuts and grabbed a couple of protein bars. Jinks referred to them as "bachelor kibble," but she was quick to take one when he offered it to her in his office a half-hour later.

She munched away absently, and he pointed at the bar. "Breakfast of champions."

"Enjoy it while you can, champ. I was supposed to tell you when you came in that the chief wants to see you."

"Harlan's case?"

"If you mean the mayor's on the chief's case about Harlan, yeah."

"That's not a secret."

"No, but I saw Lehmann chatting all friendly-like with Sergeant Mike Moody the other day, outside the post office."

"Moody?"

"Watch out for him, Dutton. He's trouble."

"Yeah, I know. I've had problems with him ever since he transferred here from Concord."

"And the mayor may have pulled a few strings with that. Considering Moody is the mayor's cousin."

Adam groaned and then took a big bite of the protein bar, tasting like a cross between sawdust and date paste. He wolfed the rest of it down and grabbed his cup of coffee, with a tip of the cup at Jinks. "See you at the funeral."

"Whose?"

"Mine."

It must be his imagination running away with him, but Chief Quinn's hair looked grayer than the last time Adam saw him. And that was two days ago. The man was slumped behind his desk, and his eyes were uncharacteristically bloodshot, which made Adam wonder if the man had been crying. Couldn't be, right?

The real reason came to light when Quinn grabbed some tissues and sneezed into them, then gulped down a pill with some water. "Zinc," he explained. "The wife says it'll cut a cold short by half."

"Sorry to hear you're not feeling well, sir."

"That's the least of my problems. And I think you have a good idea what my main problem is right now."

"A certain elected official?"

"Diplomatic of you. This 'elected official' hasn't let up about cutting our budget."

"He did that during the Forsythe case, too."

"And he's still doing it, although I think he's getting some of the councilmen to listen. Or at least reconsider their previous positions on the subject."

"Sounds awfully close to a threat, sir. Or blackmail."

"Considering the source, I'd say a bit of both. He reminded me that our meager budget only allows for two detectives. And hinted it would only take one small misstep from one of said detectives to pressure me to fire him."

"We've been through this before, sir."

Quinn looked at Adam through bleary eyes. "True. But Lehmann pushed a new hire through the application process. The man was the most qualified candidate at the time, so I gave final approval."

"Mike Moody?"

"I think you know where this is headed. I know now Moody is as much a schemer as his cousin, the mayor. He's gunning for your job, Dutton. If the mayor and town council put pressure on me to fire or demote you for any reason. . ."

"Perhaps it'll work in your favor. If Lehmann wins the governorship as he wants, and you play your cards right, you could get a nice gig out of it."

Quinn sputtered, and his face was red, but when he spoke, it became clear it wasn't due to the cold. "If you're implying I would sell you out for that lowlife scumbag, you're dead wrong.

Maybe it seems like I'm on his side at times, but things aren't always as they appear."

Quinn sneezed again, wadding up the tissues and catapulting them into a trashcan halfway across the room. "One day soon, we'll have to go out for a beer. Not in Ironwood Junction, but over in Hanover. And talk."

"Should I speak with Sergeant Moody, Chief? Set the record straight?"

"I can't stop you from talking to him, but if I were you, I'd steer clear of him. Only interact as little as you have to. I've already had one complaint about him."

Adam rubbed his nose. Colds don't spread that fast. Must be sympathetic nose itching. "Complaint, sir?"

"My secretary. She overheard Moody saying he thinks he'll be making detective real soon. But it won't be Jinks who leaves, because we'd be too 'scared of a discrimination lawsuit' to fire a half-black, half-Asian lesbian."

A flush crawled up Adam's cheeks, mirroring the chief's red face right then. "Jinks is a damn fine detective. She's worked hard, and she earned it."

Quinn held up his hand. "Preaching to the choir." Quinn stood up and paced behind his desk. "The mayor may yet see someone fired from this department due to a 'misstep.' Only it may not be the person he hopes."

Adam stood up, too. "Lehmann isn't going to keep me from doing my job. Speaking of which, I hope you've had a chance to read the reports I gave your secretary about Wallace Ryall's murder investigation."

"Got caught up this morning. The State's Attorney still thinks he's got a good case against Harlan Wilford, but I'm leaning in the other direction."

"I promise to follow the facts. Wherever they lead."

Quinn sneezed again, then gave Adam a watery smile. "That's all I ask, Dutton." He held up a bottle of pills. "And you might want to take some zinc. In case this thing is going around."

Adam headed back to his office, where Jinks was seated with her feet up on his desk. "Well?" she asked.

"Safe for now. Chief Quinn thinks the Ryall investigation is headed in the right direction. Keep at it, yada yada. As for Moody, well, that's a minefield."

"I've got something fer ya. You remember Dr. Atkinson saying the victim may have tried to sexually assault Braddon Hopper's former girlfriend, Jane Campen?"

"Yeah, why?"

"A friend of a friend of Felicia's said she knew Ramsay Ryall's Vietnamese wife. Before the wife died from cancer. This friend says Wallace Ryall tried the same thing on his brother's wife, too. Same M.O.—trying to pressure her in a dark alley after leaving a bar."

"Was the wife sure it was Wallace Ryall? Atkinson said Jane Campen wasn't entirely certain."

"Ramsay's wife swore it was him. But she didn't want to talk about it, so the details are kinda shaky."

"Gives the victim's brother more fodder for murder."

Jinks grabbed some wintergreen gum and started chewing. "Braddon Hopper, too."

"Yeah, could be they teamed up to kill him together. He was an accomplice who drove Wallace's car from the crime scene."

"Time for another interview of those bad boys."

Adam bounced on his feet but not from the protein bar. This was the kind of lead he'd hoped for, and it felt like their first big break in the case. "Well, Jinks. If this pans out, I owe

Felicia something nice. Does she love Norwegian lutefisk like you do?"

"She loathes it. Better try chocolate-covered strawberries instead."

22

Agnes had been up since before dawn when Beverly arrived at the wine shop, explaining she was burning the candle at both ends to get the place ready. The vandalism had set her back, but she remained her usual cheerful, optimistic self.

Beverly surveyed the older woman's handiwork, admiring how much progress she'd made in less than twenty-four hours. The wine racks, baskets, extra shelving—and a gumball machine from Harlan's shop—helped tremendously. And yesterday's delivery of some wines, cheese, crackers, and chocolates made it feel like a store ready for customers.

"Have you set an opening date?" Beverly asked.

"I was thinking next week. For the store part. The cafe may have to wait a little longer. The permits haven't come through yet. I was quite shocked at all the red tape you have to wade through to open a small cafe."

"And it's a matter of waiting for the red tape to clear?"

"The state paperwork was a breeze. A lot of it hasn't changed since I ran my antiques store. The local clerk's office is the main holdup. They keep saying it's a few more days."

Beverly didn't like the sound of that, not at all. Because Mayor Lehmann wasn't only angry with Adam, he had a bead on Beverly, too. If Lehmann knew Beverly and Agnes were friends, he might be spiteful enough to drag out Agnes's application. And if that *were* the case, there wasn't much Beverly or Agnes, or even Adam, could do.

Beverly didn't mention her suspicions to her friend and pasted on a happy smile, hoping it would fool Agnes. But Agnes wasn't looking at her. She was staring at the door with her mouth agape.

Beverly looked over and saw a tall, slender man in black slacks, a plain black shirt, and a black scarf around his neck that contrasted with his pale skin and platinum-colored hair. Like a yin-and-yang symbol. Fitting, since the man was none other than Mr. X in one of his rare public outings.

He carried a box in his arms he brought in and laid gently on the floor. He opened it without a word, and Beverly peered inside. "Where in the world did you get those?"

"You told me about Miss Flamm's unfortunate incident that resulted in the loss of several blue Wedgwood cheese plates and a cheese dome. I happened to have something similar lying around and voilà."

Beverly eyed him skeptically. "Lying around?"

"Lying around somewhere." He glanced over at Agnes. "I have no need of such items. But I hope you can find them useful."

Agnes looked from Beverly to Mr. X and back again. "I don't know what to say."

Beverly smiled. "Say yes and thank you. And if there's a way to sell yak milk hot chocolate in your cafe, we'll work that out, too."

"Yak milk?"

"I'll tell you about it later." Beverly added, "Can I drop by and see how you're doing in a few hours? I'd like to have a chat with Mr. Xenakis here."

"Of course, dear. That would be fine." Agnes couldn't stop staring at Mr. X. "Be careful."

As Beverly and Mr. X walked out the door, he asked, "Your SUV or mine?"

"I can't believe you're driving."

"The foot is much better, but driving can be challenging."

"Then, my SUV. I have someone I'd like to check out. It would be nice to have the company."

"With such a lovely chauffeuse, how can I refuse?"

"Chauffeuse? Is that a real French word?"

"Close enough. In Greek, it would be θηλυκό σοφέρ."

"Someday, you're going to have to fill me in on your sordid past. I'm dying to know about your family and where you're from."

"It's not as interesting as you think."

"Try me."

He raised an eyebrow at her, with one corner of his mouth turning up, as close to a smile as he ever got. "Who is this person you want to investigate?"

"It's the neighbor of Wallace Ryall, our murder victim. He's someone Wally sued successfully. Quite a bit of bad blood between them."

"Would he be at home this time of day?"

"He's a professor at Hardin Technical College. I looked him up, and he teaches a class there in forty-five minutes."

Mr. X settled back in his seat. That was one of many things she liked about him—he only asked questions as needed and eschewed small talk. It only took five minutes to reach the campus, and Mr. X served as navigator, directing her to the right building.

They had just pulled into a parking space when Beverly nudged her companion. "That's him. He was described to me as having brown, curly hair, unusual half-frame eyeglasses. And tweed with patches on the elbows."

"If that's your man, who is the young woman he's with?"

They watched at Atkinson flirted with a girl half his age who giggled and followed the professor into his car. As the pair drove off, Mr. X looked questioningly at Beverly, who said, "You bet your life we're going to follow them."

Atkinson and the young woman, whom Beverly assumed was a student, drove to a small house where they parked and headed inside. Beverly and Mr. X took up a position down the street and waited. After a half-hour had passed, Beverly started to say they should head back, when Atkinson popped out again, with a rumpled shirt and carrying his tweed jacket.

He drove off, minus the girl this time, with Beverly keeping a discreet distance, prompting Mr. X to say, "You're pretty good at tailing. I'm impressed."

Beverly pulled over as Atkinson did, finding an unobtrusive spot down the road. To her surprise, Atkinson stopped to pick up another passenger, this time, a man. Mr. X looked at Beverly as she sucked air through her teeth. "Someone you know?" he asked.

She'd seen this man recently in a photo Fern Gery showed her at the pub. "That's Ramsay Ryall, the murder victim's brother. And a chief suspect."

"Well, well. The plot thickens. I believe that's what they say on those TV cop shows?"

Atkinson dropped Ryall off at a hardware store. As Atkinson drove off, Beverly and Mr. X continued to follow until the professor returned to the college, got out of his car, and stalked inside the building.

Mr. X said, "Not what you expected to find, is it?"

"I was going to pretend to be a student wanting to major in Sustainable Design and Technology and ask him some questions. Guess that will have to wait for another time. But after what we saw, might not be necessary."

"That's too bad. I know you are itching to drag out some of your disguises."

She looked at him out of the corner of her eye. "I've gone straight, remember?"

"Officially. But a piece of the con woman will always remain."

"Like your own less-than-ethical past?"

"Naturally."

She turned on the radio, but when a newscaster started talking about Wallace Ryall's murder and Harlan Wilford, she flipped it off. "Poor Harlan. He must be going through hell."

"As one who has been there and back a few times, he'll survive."

Beverly started humming and didn't realize the tune until Mr. X asked," That's from the *King and I*."

"What?" She thought about that for a moment. "Whistle a happy tune, so no one will suspect I'm afraid?"

"Beverly, Harlan will be fine. Detective Adam Dutton is on the case."

Beverly felt a smile creep across her face. "Adam is pretty special."

"Hmm." Mr. X turned his gaze toward her, his heavy-lidded eyes as inscrutable as ever.

She hastened to add. "You're pretty amazing, yourself. For helping out Agnes like that."

"My pleasure. From one old antiquer to another. It's in the code."

"The code of the good guys, maybe."

But Beverly's efforts over the past few years battling crooked members of the Northeastern Antiques League had made her realize professional "codes" could mutate— depending upon the character-DNA of the user. She started humming again, only this time, "Bridge Over Troubled Water."

§ § §

Mr. X raised an eyebrow as Beverly rescued her kit and a few other items from her trunk. "That's an unusual way of 'going straight,' Beverly."

"I know I promised Adam, sort of. But desperate times call for desperate measures."

"How many wigs do you have in the trunk?"

"Enough."

He whistled as she slid into the driver's seat and opened her kit. "Impressive. In all that time running around avoiding being caught by the NAL or police, where did you store these?"

"Kept a few in my suitcase. Bought others new in each town and then donated them to a charity or tossed them in the dumpster as I left."

"That's quite practical. I approve."

"Did you ever use disguises during your days at the NAL?"

"It was far more effective when people saw me coming as I am."

Beverly had only seen Mr. X as a benign guardian angel. But he also carried an imposing air about him, and every now and then, she'd seen a flash in his eyes that gave her chills. "I guess it's the same as not asking an assassin about his job. And I have a feeling you were pretty good at doing whatever it was you had to do."

"I was never comfortable with the role, I happened into it. Something of a family business."

"What changed your mind?"

"Watching Forsythe and the others go off the deep end was the last straw. I do have a personal code."

She nodded and left it at that. Although she'd love to know someday where he'd "hidden the bodies."

As he watched her don the blond wig, eyeglasses, and a fake mole, he asked, "What did you have in mind for those disguises today?"

"I have a sudden interest in hardware."

He chuckled, and they drove back to the store where Atkinson had dropped off Ramsay Ryall. It must be their lucky day because the man in question was exiting the store when they pulled up.

Beverly hopped out and strode up to him, using a hint of vocal fry as she said, "Why Ramsay Ryall, as I live and breathe."

He stared at her with pinched brows. "I'm sorry, do I know you?"

"Sherry, a friend of mine, bought one of your snowmobiles way back when. It was a beauty."

"I'm not in that business anymore."

"That's too bad. Say, wasn't it your brother I saw in the papers? A murder or something?"

Ramsay winced. "That's right, my brother Wallace. I hope you don't mind, but I'd rather not discuss it."

"Oh, that's heavy, I get it. Such a close relative and all. Must be hard."

He hesitated, shifting the shopping bags in his hand. "Well, not that close, to be honest. We'd been estranged."

"Guess that's why my friend who bought the snowmobile said she got weird vibes from Wallace. Don't want to speak ill of the dead and all, but Sherry thought he might have been on something. Said he came on to her. And not in a nice way."

"I didn't know about that. And I'm sorry for your friend."

"Did Wallace do that often? You know, unwanted advances on girls?"

Ramsay frowned. "As I said, we weren't on good terms. It's not something I want to discuss. Especially not out here in the open."

"Sure, sure, I understand." Beverly smiled up at him. "So, why leave the snowmobile business? Seems like a natural for around here?"

"Wally ruined everything he touched."

"Really? I don't understand. I thought the biz was doing great."

Ramsay hesitated, and Beverly egged him on, "Must have been pretty bad, then."

"We'd snagged an International Snowmobile Congress award."

"You know, I think my friend Sherry might have mentioned something about that."

"It was right before our falling out. Could have meant more sales and an international market push."

"Oooh, that must have hurt. I'd have throttled him if it was me."

Ramsay's neck flushed a bright red, and his hands shook so hard, Beverly worried he'd drop the bags he was carrying. "Look, I've got to go," he said as he rushed off.

When she climbed back into the car, Mr. X gave her a brief smile. "You have a real knack for this disguise business. Did you make that all up on the spot?"

"Practice makes perfect. So they say."

He had a thoughtful look. "I'm not so sure Adam Dutton asking you not to practice your craft is the right way to go if it's part of who you are. Perhaps you'll have to take up acting at the local community theater."

"Theater?"

"An improv troupe, naturally."

She laughed so hard she almost had to pull over. Her performance with Ramsay Ryall hadn't won any awards—or discovered evidence except to verify Ramsay hated his brother and possibly knew more about his brother's misogyny than he let on. Despite his denials.

But she had to admit it was fun. *Was* it all part of who she was? Would she be able to give that way of life up for one man's approval?

Life imitates art imitates life. She wasn't sure what role she was playing or what role she wanted to play in life, but being an avenging angel for Harlan right now was good enough for her.

23

Adam and Jinks had just climbed into their car when Beverly called. Adam listened without saying anything during her account, finally adding a "Thanks for the report. We'll follow up later," which made Jinks give him the slow burn.

"That voice leaking through sounded like Beverly Laborde."

"It was."

"Follow up what?"

"She was out driving and 'happened' to drive by Hardin Technical College in time to see Professor Atkinson escort a young woman to a house off-campus. He then proceeded to pick up Ramsay Ryall from another location."

"Sounds like he's running a friendly transport service. Hardly a crime. Unless the woman wasn't exactly legal."

"Atkinson was at her place for thirty minutes."

"Maybe they were discussing an exam."

"He came out a bit disheveled, according to Beverly."

"So, it's a hands-on exam."

"Sounds like it."

"And Ramsay Ryall?"

"I think it's time we paid another visit to the not-so-grieving brother of our murder victim."

"Can we stop by Miralee's and get some Dr. Pepper and venison jerky? I'm starved."

"You should write a diet book titled *Always Eating, Always Thin.* I smell a runaway bestseller. You'll never have to detect again."

"And allow that smarmy bastard-cousin-of-the-mayor, Mike Moody, to take over my job? I like you too much for that, Dutton."

"Thanks, Jinks. I'm touched. Truly."

This being a Friday, they had to track Ryall down to the Apple Valley Resort, where he was between tour gigs. A staff receptionist pointed them toward the barns in the back of the resort—although "barns" was not the right word for the huge space filled with top-notch ski gear and gleaming snowmobiles. There was also an impressive array of ATVs, canoes, kayaks, and fishing tackle.

Adam surveyed the latter with a twinge in his gut. If the damned fool Harlan had listened to him and not gone out ice fishing by himself, he'd never be in this predicament.

Adam spied Ramsay Ryall in one corner, waxing a pair of skis. He strolled up to the man and pointed at the skis. "Your brother make those?"

Ryall shook his head and kept on working. "I know someone who bought skis from Wally. Said they were top-notch. But we don't have any here."

Jinks piped up, "Guess it's a good thing. Not to have any reminders around."

Ryall looked over at a nearby snowmobile. "That's a reminder. Of our former business."

Adam ran his hand over the closest one to him. "This one's a beauty."

"That one has one-seventy horsepower, with a turbocharged two-cylinder, four-stroke engine. Costs almost as much as I made last year."

Knowing the resort's rooms went for upwards of two-fifty a night with a long list of pricey add-ons, Adam wasn't surprised by the expensive gear to impress the high-end guests. But paying a staffer the same as it cost to buy a snowmobile seemed harsh. No doubt, Ramsay Ryall could have used the money from his father's estate—if said father hadn't willed the lot over to Harlan.

Adam said, "Were you friends with Wallace's neighbor, Dr. Vernon Atkinson?"

"We've gone out for drinks. Guess he bonded over our mutual dislike of Wally."

"When did this friendship start?"

"A year or so ago, I reckon. Vernon came to me to see if I could reason with Wally about vandalism he blamed on Wally. That was before he realized Wally and I weren't speaking to each other."

"I see." Adam nodded. "One other thing, Mr. Ryall. We have sources who say your brother forced himself on your late wife. And she may not have been the only victim."

Ryall stopped working on the ski and wiped his cheek with his hand, leaving a smudge that covered up his scar. But it didn't cover up the red flush spreading across his face. "Mai came home from a night out with her girlfriends. About a year before she died. I could tell she was shaken up. She didn't want to discuss it, at first. Then she told me Wally pressured her for sex. She didn't mention the word 'rape,' but in Vietnamese culture, rape is often seen as the fault of the woman. Since he didn't go through with it, thank god, guess she wanted to brush it off. Be the good little soldier."

"How do you know he didn't go through with it?"

Ryall sat down on the snowmobile. "There weren't any bruises, for one. And. . ."

"Yes?"

"I don't expect you to understand this. But all guys are one hair away from cavemen. Anyway, I took her into the bedroom right then and there. Made love to her. Some might say I wanted to mark my territory. I'd like to think I wanted to show her what sex between a man and a woman was supposed to be."

"How did this help you determine Wallace hadn't raped her?"

"She smelled the same. And felt the same. I would have known. If he'd. . .well, I would have known."

"Why didn't you tell us this before?"

"My wife died nearly two years to the day Wallace was killed. How do you think it would have looked if I'd told you?"

"About the same as it looks now."

"I didn't kill him. I swear. Although if you make me take an oath on a stack of Bibles, I won't say I'm sorry he's dead."

Jinks's cellphone beeped, and she pulled it out to look at the text message. She shook her head at Adam's questioning look, but he decided to wrap up the interview. "Did your wife mention any other women Wallace pressured into having sex?"

"Mai would never have discussed such things with me. That Asian reserve and all."

Adam tugged on Jinks's elbow to let her know they should leave. When they returned to the front of the resort, he counted to ten, waiting for her tirade. He wasn't disappointed.

"That Asian reserve? What the hell? He can come over to my house anytime. Or my parents' house. Reserve, my ass."

"Since his deceased wife isn't around for us to question, we don't have her side of the story. Maybe she was reserved, maybe not."

Jinks calmed down. "And maybe she fabricated that story to make her husband jealous. Or was another member of the Wallace Haters Club."

Adam looked over at the house, half-expecting Ramsay to be looking at them out of the window. "Did you run down that woman Ramsay said he visited in Bangor the day his brother was killed?"

"She didn't see him until that night, as he said. Which still leaves him enough time to kill Wallace and trot back up to Maine."

"If he was as angry at Harlan as his brother, thanks to the father cutting him out of the will, it'd make sense he wanted to frame Harlan. Despite what he said about 'cursed blood money.'"

Jinks jammed her cellphone back into its waistband holder. "Or that's precisely what he meant by blood money. Only he was the one doing the spilling."

"A lot of motives, a lot of opportunity, and not a lot of hard evidence. My favorite kind of case."

"We could pick up a case of beer from the store. That's the kind I feel like opening right now."

Adam pointed to her cellphone. "That text you got. Everything okay?"

"Jacob's being a pain. I should stop by and check on him."

"I'll drive you to the station to pick up your car."

Adam had no sooner dropped Jinks off than he saw a familiar figure leaning against her SUV, arms crossed over her chest. He drove over and rolled down his window. "Fancy meeting you here."

"Did you talk to the brother?" Beverly didn't waste any time getting down to business.

"Nice to see you, too," he replied, with a touch of sarcasm. "We did talk to Ramsay Ryall. Thanks for the tip, by the way."

"And?"

"He has a good reason for being friends with the victim's neighbor. Too good a reason." Adam stared at her. "You're popping up in all kinds of places lately. Coincidental places."

"Like at the pub last night?" Beverly's smile had a way of mocking without mocking, although he felt a flush crawling up his neck.

"I met an old private eye friend."

"So Zelda's a private eye, now?"

"No, she's a busybody. Creighton Querry's the friend. Seems like I saw you with Wallace Ryall's ex, Fern Gery."

Beverly rubbed the sleeve of her sweater. "Getting to know her better."

"Did she happen to say anything that could shed some light on Wallace's murder?"

"Why don't I hop in, and we can compare notes?" She walked around to the passenger side, where she opened the door and slid in.

He didn't turn off the engine, keeping the heater running, and wished he'd taken Jinks up on her offer of getting a case of beer. And a thermos of coffee. "I'm listening," he said.

"Fern thinks our killer was Vernon Atkinson, the neighbor. Or in second place, Ramsay Ryall."

"I'd be thrilled if she had a video or photos or a confession. We're long on gut feelings and short on court-proof evidence." Adam sighed. "Ms. Gery didn't say anything about being assaulted by Wallace Ryall, did she? Or knowing someone else who was?"

"You mean, sexual? Rape?"

"Something like that."

"She said she'd heard rumors about Wally. Nonconsensual rumors. But in Fern's case, she would have been more likely to buy him some Viagra, I think." Beverly thought for a moment.

"From your question, I'm guessing you're talking about Braddon Hopper's ex, Jane Campen?"

Adam turned to face her. "How did you hear about her?"

"I asked Fern why Wallace and Braddon didn't get along. She mentioned jealousy. And then said she heard them arguing about this Jane Campen, but she didn't get any details."

Adam looked at his watch. Fern Gery should be at the flower shop. He glanced at Beverly and asked, "Want to come along as I ask Ms. Gery point-blank?"

"If you think it will help."

"Mind if we drive by Harlan's shop first? Prospero's installing a new security system, but I like to keep an extra eye on the store when I can."

Adam doubted the chief would be thrilled with him allowing Beverly to come along on interviews, but she'd proved herself useful and level-headed. And he certainly didn't mind her company. Not that he'd tell her that.

Adam also didn't tell Beverly it killed him to not be able to talk to Harlan except in his role as a cop. He had to keep all his interactions strictly professional. Although he knew Harlan understood, it still rankled.

He didn't really need to surveil Harlan's antiques shop, since the man was never there without Prospero and had his ankle monitor in place. But it was the closest he could come to his old friend without raising any eyebrows.

One thing was sure, when this was all over, Adam was going to take Harlan ice fishing or bar-hopping. Or over to Cy's Point to get some of his favorite venison medallions. Whatever the hell he wanted. That is if Harlan still wanted to have anything to do with him.

24

After the quick drive by Harlan's shop where everything looked okay from the outside, they made it to Fern Gery's flower shop. A tattoo parlor lay around the corner, something Beverly hadn't noticed on their first visit.

She pointed it out. "I guess you have to choose between getting your sweetie a bouquet of flowers or getting her name tattooed on your whatever."

Adam replied, "Think I'd go with the flowers. That tattoo shop was hit up with prostitution charges a few years ago. They've tried to stay legit since, but we're watching them."

Fern greeted them warmly, but as she motioned them back to the same room as before, she asked if it would be okay if she continued working while talking. "The extra-long Christmas season may not be as big as Valentine's Day, but it's still busy. I've got a wedding tomorrow," she motioned to a table of corsage picks and boutonniere lapel vases waiting for their red roses and carnations.

The irony of discussing failed relationships and possible sexual assaults in the shadow of wedding decorations wasn't lost on Beverly. She looked at the flowers in the refrigerated cases and wished them luck.

Beverly had suggested on the way over that she take the lead in asking the questions due to the subject matter, and Adam reluctantly agreed. Although she should have let him take over since Fern seemed to be spending as much time studying Adam as she was her projects.

Beverly asked, "Fern, when we were at the bar, you said you overheard an argument between Wallace and Braddon Hopper about Hopper's then-girlfriend, Jane Campen. Did you catch any snippets of it?"

"No words. But reading their body language, I'd say Braddon was accusing him of something, and Wally was on the defensive."

Beverly chose her words carefully. "You said Wally didn't get too aggressive with *you*, is that right?"

"Aggressive?" Fern stopped in mid-twist fashioning a carnation with florist tape. "You're thinking Braddon believed Wally propositioned Jane Campen?"

"Make that 'forcibly' propositioned."

"Rape? That's preposterous. I never saw anything of the kind. And if he'd been like that, I would have known. This Campen woman must have an axe to grind. Sour grapes."

"Another woman made the same claim."

"You must be mistaken. Or she must be mistaken." Fern started working on the carnation again, but she used so much force, the tape broke. With a sigh, she put down the flower. "Look, Wally was no saint. But with his OCD, he wouldn't have risked rape."

"What do you mean?"

"Sexually transmitted diseases. He'd have to make each woman get a lab test first. I can't see a rapist asking his victim to do that and get back with him later."

Adam spoke up, "He was never violent toward you?"

"We argued. But he was about as violent as a puppy."

Adam continued to stare at her, and Fern folded her arms across her chest. "Wallace may have scared me once or twice, okay, but it was only when he got drunk."

Adam added, "Then the reason you called off the engagement—"

"As I said before, it was mostly the OCD. A little more eccentricity than I was willing to put up with. I know that makes me sound shallow."

Beverly asked, "Was he on meds for his OCD? Some of those have nasty side effects, like depression or aggression." Beverly smiled to herself at Adam's approving look at her question.

"He'd been on some years ago. But he stopped taking them." Fern finished the boutonniere and held it up. "Red carnations and baby's breath. I can't tell you how many of these I've done. Just once, I'd love to see someone think outside the box. Take a walk on the wild side. Eucalyptus and tallow berries. Maybe some bavardia and dusty miller."

Beverly pointed at a phalaenopsis orchid in the case. "Like that."

Fern turned to look. "A purple girl? I'm a fan myself. Wally hated purple. I have no idea why."

Adam asked, "Did you have any interactions with Braddon Hopper? Know him to be a liar? If he wanted to be Rapier Marshal so badly, he might have tried to sully Wallace's reputation."

Fern nodded. "I can see that. He was frosty toward Wally and me both."

"Did he make any threats toward you?"

"He told me I wasn't welcome at rehearsals. Not that I cared to go. Those people can be scary."

"Scary?"

"As in a few drams shy of a full goblet, if you get my drift. Like that Joss Warder. Sorry, His Excellency, Richard Symonnet."

"The park ranger?"

"Park ranger by day, fantasy geek by night. He and Wally liked to go drinking together."

Adam asked, "Did you ever see them drunk together?"

"I'm not much of a drinker. The occasional beer, but that's about it."

Adam glanced at Beverly. "We can see you're busy. Thanks for your time, Ms. Gery."

Fern winked at him. "Please, it's Fern. If you have any more questions, give me a call. Except between one and four o'clock tomorrow. The apocalypse could come calling, and I wouldn't answer, thanks to this wedding."

She added to Beverly, "I had fun chatting with you last evening. If you want to have another beer night, let me know."

Adam waited until they were inside the car again to ask, "Did you buy any of that? About Wallace being a gentleman and the accusers having an axe to grind?"

"You're asking me because of my shrewd insights and intellect? Or because I'm a woman?"

"Both." He grinned at her.

"Braddon certainly did have an axe to grind. Or perhaps we should say sword. Which means Jane Campen could have, as well. Did you track her down for questioning?"

"Jinks is on it."

"I think Fern is being honest when she says Wallace never abused her. She has none of the signs of a recent sexual assault victim."

"Just how many sexual assault victims have you been around?"

Beverly didn't answer and looked out the window.

"Beverly?"

She licked her lips and shrugged. "Enough."

His voice softened, and he gently put his hand on her chin to turn her face toward him. "Are we talking about other people or about you?"

"All women experience unwanted sexual advances."

"How unwanted and severe were these advances?"

"I haven't seen him in years. It's ancient history."

Adam leaned against his seat and stared straight ahead. "He'd better not come around here, or I might kill him. Or Jinks will castrate him."

He reached for her hand and gave it a quick squeeze.

"Thanks," she said.

"For what?"

"For being the kind of guy who would say something like that. For knowing how to make me feel better."

"Wait until you try my patented Guinness and jalapeño jack cheese omelet."

"That's unusual."

"Tastier than it sounds. Unless you're a vegan? I made a tofu spinach quiche for a vegan friend once."

He seemed flustered, and it occurred to her they'd never had one real meal together yet. Despite him asking her for dinner—how many times was it now? She probably knew much more about him than he did her.

Adam said, "I should drop you off at the station to pick up your SUV." He paused, then added, "I'd like to stop by my house first. I need to grab some files to take back to the office. It'll be quick."

Her heart beat faster at the thought of being anywhere near his house, but she forced herself to smile. "Whatever will help."

Help with Harlan's case, with Adam's schedule, with life, the universe, or whatever. More than anything else, she was glad to be by this man's side. She silenced her inner psychiatrist when it started to question what Beverly meant by that thought and sat back to enjoy the ride.

25

Adam pulled up in front of his house, looking at it critically for the first time in years. What would Beverly make of it? The same woman who was used to places like the Apple Valley Resort, with its marble this and crystal that? Zelda had picked out this house, falling for its Adirondack style with a slate roof, board-and-batten siding, and wraparound front porch.

He noted the peeling paint around the windows and how the siding had faded a notch or two. When had that happened? To be honest, he hadn't paid much attention to the house since the divorce.

He said, "This should only take a few minutes. You can keep the heater running."

Adam ducked inside, looking around for the files, but didn't see them right away. Where had he worked on those? Last night while watching the game or at the kitchen table? After checking the floor and the countertops, he came up blank. He headed toward some boxes near the wood stove, when a turn of the doorknob stopped him in his tracks.

The front door opened, and Beverly walked in, with a tentative smile. "I didn't want to run the engine too long. Carbon monoxide."

"Ah," he said. "Sorry about the delay. Can't seem to find those files."

Beverly looked around the room, then pointed to his bookshelf in the corner. "You mean those folders?"

He walked over and grabbed the folders off the top of two books that were appropriately titled *Criminal Investigations* and *The Case Files of Sherlock Holmes*. With a grunt of disgust, he tossed the folders onto the table next to the couch that also served as his bed most nights. "Gotta get more organized."

"I don't know," Beverly put her hands on her hips as she surveyed the room. "It's better than I expected."

"Oh? And what did you expect?"

"Clothing everywhere. Day-old pizza cartons. Bachelor kibble."

"Bachelor kibble?"

"You know, chips, nuts, pretzels—things that come out of bags."

"Have you been talking to Jinks?"

"She might have mentioned something like that."

He shook his head. "I had too many lectures from Zelda about picking up after myself, I guess."

Beverly snorted. "You are not a dog needing kibble."

"A lot of people still refer to cops as pigs, so there ya go."

She giggled. "That is so not the image that comes to mind about you, Adam."

"Really?" Adam raised an eyebrow.

"More like Fern's Bruno Giacometti."

"The Italian Stallion?"

"Better than that."

"Any better than that, I'd make millions running in the Derby."

She bumped into a table and knocked over a picture frame, rescuing it before it fell to the floor. She looked at the photo and asked, "Where is this?"

He moved toward her to remind himself which photo it was, and then he remembered. "It's a cabin overlooking Beaver Pond Brook, not far from the Nature Preserve."

"A vacation home?"

"I just liked it." At her questioning look, he added, "It's where I wanted us to live when we first got married."

She studied the photo. "I love this wooden bridge over the brook. And you can walk right out your front door and sit on the patio next to the water. It looks peaceful."

"You've got the sound of the water, but it's a gentle sound. Nature's lullaby."

"It's beautiful. Did someone else beat you to it?"

"Zelda didn't like it. Too far out of town and isolated, she said." He waited for her to agree with his ex, but she didn't say anything. She put the photo down, then spied the open case next to the table and exclaimed, "A guitar! I didn't know you played."

"I dabble."

"Play something for me." She sat on a chair and looked at him expectantly.

"I don't know. I should get you back."

"Not 'Classical Gas' length. Something shorter."

He picked up the guitar and brought it to the couch, where he checked the tuning. It was weeks—months?—since he'd touched the instrument, but when he started to play, it felt more like yesterday. Like reuniting with an old friend, and when he finished, he didn't want to stop.

Beverly clapped her hands. "That was beautiful. What is it?"

"It's a Spanish dance by Granados, 'Andaluza.'"

"Where did you learn how to play?"

"My father taught me. Now there was a guitarist. Puts me to shame."

Beverly pointed at the guitar. "Was that his?"

Adam got up to put the instrument gingerly in its case. "Yeah. Playing it makes me feel close to him somehow."

She hopped off her chair so fast, she lost her balance. He reached out to grab her arm before he fell backward and pulled her toward him. He was so concerned to see that she was okay, he didn't realize at first how close they were. And when he did realize, he also knew that he liked it. A lot.

But he didn't want to be like the man in her past who'd hurt her. There was a fine line between wanted and unwanted advances, and he was slipping and sliding all over that line.

Her lips were so soft-looking, so inviting. Alarm bells were screaming in his head. He should back off, drive her to the station.

To his surprise, she leaned toward him, not away. Her lips parted ever so slightly as her face grew nearer to his. He bent his head so close to hers he smelled her breath that held hints of wintergreen. The spell of that first kiss, so tantalizing, so electric, so. . .

A knock at the door broke the spell in one explosive vexation of sound. He sighed and looked into her wide blue eyes. She said, "I guess you should get that?"

He stomped over to the entry and opened the door. No mailman, only a lone truck disappearing down the street. One of those small white trucks, like online stores used to ship purchases. But he hadn't bought anything lately. A gift? A look at the brown-paper package showed a computer-printed label with his name and address. But no return address. And no postmark.

They say instincts are a cop's number one defense, and in that one moment, something about that package made him toss it into the front yard and slam the door. Moments later, an explosion of sound hit his ears, followed by a percussive blast wave that hit the front of the house and knocked him backward onto the floor.

He struggled to rise up to protect Beverly, but he didn't have to. Once again proving how smart she was, she'd already hunkered down next to him, with her arms over her head.

He waited for a few moments and then helped her off the floor. They both turned to the door, which was still intact but bowed inward. Remarkably, it opened, and they stepped outside to survey the damage. A mini-crater lined his front yard, and the passenger side of his car was blackened. He walked out to see if he could open the car door, and it did, but he knew he was looking at a pricey repair job.

He scowled at it. "This car is cursed. I just got it fixed after it went into the pond three months ago. It's totaled, anyway. I'll have to get the department to loan me a rental until I can buy a new car."

Beverly took his arm and turned him around toward the house. "Could have been worse," she said. And she was right—the front windows were partly shattered and would have to be replaced, as would the door. But otherwise, the house was intact, livable, and not on fire. All good things.

"This was a smallish pipe bomb, a warning of some kind. If they'd wanted to kill me, it would have been quite a bit bigger."

"There's always lemonade." She smiled at him.

"Lemonade?"

"Fix up the broken bits and use this opportunity to buy that cabin."

He could have kissed her right then and there. But instead, he reached into the car to use his police radio and alert the station. There went his nice, relaxing evening. He held out his hand toward the house, motioning for her to precede him inside. "Well, Miss Laborde. Never let it be said I show you a dull time."

Her eyes glinted with something he hoped was silent laughter. "Let's see. One near-drowning, one near-shooting, and now one near-bombing. Or not-so-near-bombing. You definitely know how to show a lady a good time."

"I'm beginning to think I'm underpaid."

Then, she really did laugh. And he joined right in.

26

Saturday, December 8

Beverly looked at the clock on the nightstand and groaned. Nine-thirty, way later than her usual five a.m. She'd considered asking the resort's staff to give her a wake-up call but decided against it.

Wrapped in the luxurious down comforter, she felt like a human chrysalis, safe and warm in her own cocoon. But the face that stared back at her in the mirror across the room didn't look like a butterfly. More like a moth that had gone nine rounds with a spider.

After the bombing at Adam's last evening, she'd answered questions from the arriving police on site, refused medical care, then answered dozens more questions down at the station.

Jinks, bless her heart, had brought in buckets of espresso and tomato-basil focaccia sandwiches from an all-night cafe a block down the street. Adam had popped in from time to time, but he was busy with his own third-degree with Chief Quinn, the Vermont State Police Bomb Squad, and ATF.

Beverly had wanted to see more of him, to see for herself he was all right. But when ten o'clock rolled around, and he was still in meetings, she realized how tired she was. Given the all-clear to leave, she'd said yes to Jinks, who wanted to trail

Beverly back to the resort to make sure she arrived okay. Too exhausted for even a soak in the enticing hot tub in her room, she gave up and went to bed.

She'd tossed and turned in the night, which could explain her new moth-woman look. Mostly, she was worried about Adam and Harlan and the depths someone seemed willing to go to hurt them.

Dragging herself out of bed was hard, but she managed to make it to the bathroom for a long, hot shower. She had a few bruises on her legs from diving to the floor of Adam's house. Knowing the way he had dived down, he probably had a lot more. But as she'd told him yesterday, it could have been far worse.

After making her way downstairs to the resort's tea room, she expected to overhear some of the staff talking about the explosion but not a word. It was as if it had never happened. But she hadn't dreamed it, had she? No, dreams didn't usually give you bruises.

She wasn't particularly hungry but ordered a double espresso. Caffeine in hand, she'd no sooner sat down at her favorite table overlooking the White Mountains in the distance, when someone plopped down on the chair across from her.

In her wildest nightmares, she'd never have expected *this* person to join her. Zelda Lehmann. Beverly considered whether she could beat a hasty retreat to her room and crawl back into bed but decided against it. She'd never run from a challenge.

Beverly knew a "size-up-the-competition" look when she saw it, and Zelda made no effort to hide it. So Beverly took the opportunity to do the same, more in the way a seasoned detective like Adam might do, instead of a tabby gearing up for a catfight.

Zelda was attractive, no doubt about it. It was easy to see why Adam and the mayor had both fallen for her. Although not a natural redhead, the color suited her grayish-green eyes and milk-white skin. The emerald and diamond earrings she wore looked several pay-grades above a detective's salary. As did the green-and-white floral lace and tulle dress straight from Saks.

"You're that woman who was involved in the Forsythe case, aren't you? Beverly Laforde?"

"Laborde. And yes."

"I'm meeting a friend here and happened to see you. What a fortunate accident of timing."

Like hell, it was. Zelda wasn't here to see a friend, not dressed like that. Beverly herself probably still looked like "hell" and had opted for a knee-length plain white sweater over simple black leggings. But she really didn't care. "Yes, fortunate." She took a sip of espresso and stared back at the other woman.

"My husband, the mayor, was so distraught by the Forsythe case. I mean, being innocent and having his name dragged through the mud. Just because he made the mistake of trusting a master criminal."

"He shouldn't have trusted him."

"You should know since that man is your uncle, right?"

"Estranged uncle, yes."

"I can't help thinking if you'd never come to Ironwood Junction, none of this unpleasant business would have happened. And poor Adam, it's been so stressful for him. I've never seen him look so despondent."

Beverly wanted to pull out her cellphone and call up a dictionary to shove in Zelda's face. "Despondent" was not an emotion she'd ever seen Adam exhibit. Disappointed, determined, driven, maybe, but never despondent.

"Adam is perfectly capable of handling all kinds of pressure. Even political." Beverly punctuated that last bit with a loud slurp of the espresso, trying not to laugh at the expression of anger and disgust on the other woman's face.

"My husband, and perhaps everyone in town, wonders if you're somehow involved with Forsythe's activities. Or perhaps you're a femme fatale who led your poor uncle astray. Like you're trying to lead Adam astray."

And the claws had come out. Beverly kept hers sheathed long enough to give Zelda a nice, friendly smile. "Adam's a big boy." And then, she couldn't help herself, adding, "In all the right places."

Zelda's face paled further, but then a crimson flush spread out across her nose and cheeks, coordinating nicely with her hair. "I heard about the pipe bomb. And that you were there when it happened. You may be in this for selfish reasons, but you should consider Adam's well-being for a change. He's been almost killed four times now since you arrived in town. You're not just bad luck, you're a disaster magnet."

Since her words echoed Beverly's own words to Adam, she couldn't disagree with that part, could she? Her angsty soul-searching must have shown on her face when Zelda stood up with a triumphant look of her own.

"Take my advice, Miss Laforde. Stay away from Adam, and he'll be a lot healthier for it."

Beverly stared at her. "This from the woman who broke his heart."

Zelda's arrogant expression deflated, and for a moment, her eyes looked like they might be forming tears. Beverly felt a twinge of sympathy for the woman right then, torn between her ambitions and her emotions. Ambitions so strong, they blinded her to the wealth she already had—the love and respect of a good man.

Zelda trounced out of the tea room, leaving Beverly alone with her espresso. A "walking disaster magnet?" That was a new one. She'd been called a thief, a con woman, a female Robin Hood, a righteous crusader, and an avenging angel.

But disaster magnet? Maybe she should heed Zelda's advice and stay away from Adam. Maybe there was a cosmic reason she'd never settled down or formed lasting bonds. Then why was she so ready to kiss him last night? And something more?

She picked up the sugar container, adding a spoonful to the other two in her drink. For some reason, it now tasted bitter. As she stared down at her drink, she became aware of someone sliding into the seat across from her. Thinking Zelda had returned, Beverly looked up with a frown.

The woman giving her a careful study smiled at her. "I know that look. A human hornet ready to sting. And I think I know why. That woman who was sitting here, Zelda Lehmann, the mayor's wife?"

Beverly immediately relaxed. Gloria Gelling was not only the very best waitress Beverly had ever met, but she was one of the best listeners. "Zelda and I aren't what you'd call bosom buddies."

"Good thing, too. I have a feeling those bosoms of hers aren't real." Gloria grinned, and Beverly couldn't help but smile back.

"Zelda is also the ex-wife of Detective Adam Dutton."

"Yes, I've heard of her." She leaned on the table and said in a conspiratorial tone, "If you want, I think I could take this Zelda. She looks too dainty to put up much of a fight."

"She has a sword for a tongue, though."

Gloria shook her head. "Can't see what Adam saw in her. He's such a great guy. I really do owe him so much."

"For arresting your ex."

"Exactly."

Gloria looked at her watch and called out to her assistant that she was going on break for fifteen minutes. She waved for Beverly to follow her to an upstairs break room with a view out to the snow-capped Presidentials. They sat on comfy chairs next to a fireplace.

Beverly cupped her hands around her mug. "Thought I saw with you some books taking notes the other day."

"Didn't I tell you? I'm starting my business degree in January."

"You're quitting the resort?"

"I'll continue to work while going part-time. Then, who knows? Harvard MBA? They have a good drama department, too."

"Then, you'll have to start coaching me in disguises and costumes."

"Deal." Gloria looked toward the direction in which Zelda disappeared. "So…you and Adam are…?"

Beverly blurted out, "Friends. Good friends."

"Must be nice to have such a sexy friend." She took one look at Beverly's face and laughed. "Oh, honey, you may be 'just' friends, but somehow I don't think you want it to stay that way."

"Right now, I'm only helping Adam on a case. Consulting."

"Consulting?"

"Whether he likes it or not. It's about a dear friend of mine, Harlan Wilford."

"Oh, you mean that murder case? It's so ridiculous. Everyone knows Harlan couldn't hurt anyone."

"Absolutely not."

Gloria leaned back in her chair. "The victim's brother, Ramsay Ryall, works here. He's a great guy. But quite honestly, I wouldn't put it past him to have killed his own brother."

"Why?"

"I knew Ramsay's wife, Mai. She was Vietnamese but had lived here since childhood. Not the usual shy, shrinking violet stereotype of Asian woman, you know? But she confided in me once that her husband's brother, Wally, gave her the creeps. Always commenting on her body. And trying to kiss her when his brother wasn't around. Poor thing. Between that and her father-in-law never accepting her, she was miserable. And then there's that whole inheritance thing."

"You mean, cutting both sons out of the will?"

"The father did that? I hadn't heard. Well, yes, then, but I'm referring to the way Wally tried to poison his father's heart against Ramsay. Mai didn't like her father-in-law but loathed Wally. The things Wally said about Mai, too. Calling her racist names while trying to molest her on the side."

"So you'd put your money on Ramsay as our murderer?"

"I do hate to say that. Ramsay's been nothing but kind to me and all the other staff."

"What about Mai's own family? One of them could have found out about Wally's dark side. Then took matters into their own hands."

"Mai was an orphan, far as I know."

"Don't get too dispirited yet. I'm not. There are other suspects besides Ramsay. And I trust Adam."

Gloria got up and walked over to a coffee machine, poured herself a cup, and raised it to clink against Beverly's. "A toast to Detective Adam Dutton."

"And may he never have to beheld-a Zelda again."

27

Adam looked at his handiwork through bleary eyes. Was it lack of sleep clouding his judgment, or did he just want the task to be over with? But it didn't matter. It was good enough. The boards over the windows would suffice until the new panes arrived. And at least he could open and close the front door.

The chief had offered to let Adam stay with him and his wife last night, and even Jinks had said she and Felicia had an extra room, but he'd decided to stay in his own place. He was never one to run from a fight.

The damage was more to his pride than anything else. He didn't like having people make a fuss over him, and he didn't want to appear vulnerable. In cop terms, that was like saying you were a coward, and being a coward was a sure-fire way to lose respect. Might as well quit after that.

He'd wanted to call up Beverly to see how she was doing but was afraid he might wake her. So he waited until ten-thirty to send her a text that was straight out of high school. *RUOK?*

She'd replied back with, "Just had coffee with Zelda. Off to see Agnes next."

Coffee with Zelda? It that wasn't her way of making a joke, then he knew he was in for an earful later. But which one would it come from? Beverly or Zelda? Or both?

After showering off the grime and sawdust, he headed in to confer with Jinks. She was already waiting for him in his office when he arrived, with her feet up on his desk. "Good morning, gorgeous. Aren't we looking gruff and grizzled on this lovely Saturday? I know how you love working weekends."

He growled at her, realizing he sounded like a bear. "Any lab tests on that bomb yet?"

"Preliminary results indicate it was your garden-variety pipe bomb. Probably got the plans from a website and went down to the hardware store for the bomb guts. The explosive was black powder. Enough to shake, rattle, and roll. And potentially seriously injure whoever was holding it."

"The bomb squad track down the purchaser?"

"Not yet. Could have had the components lying around. Or bought them out of state. They're still checking the shrapnel for prints."

"Looks like somebody doesn't want me clearing Harlan's name. And putting theirs in the pot instead."

"If that's the right pot."

"Forsythe and his stew of crooks and thieves?"

"Could be. We still haven't tracked down Redbeard. He ran from you at the hospital, which indicates he knew you. Feared you, perhaps? Held a grudge?"

"We'll find him soon enough. In the meantime, now that you mention grudges, I think it's time we talked again with the victim's neighbor, our randy professor."

"Good idea." Jinks pointed at a piece of paper on Adam's desk where he'd scrawled out a note. "Couldn't help seeing that little puzzle. Moody Blues NH lieutenant? A classic rock-and-roll flashback, or are you taking up crosswords?"

"Called one of Sergeant Moody's former colleagues up in New Hampshire."

"Ah. Keeping an eye on the enemy?"

"You gotta be able to trust your fellow cops when the chips are down. And I don't trust Moody."

"What did you find?"

"Moody's old colleague hemmed and hawed. Didn't want to come right out and say anything bad. But I got the impression they were glad to get rid of him."

"Swell." Jinks hopped off her chair and reached over Adam's desk to open his top left drawer. She pulled out a couple of Tootsie Rolls and threw one at him. "I'll wager you had as little breakfast as I did."

"Late night with Jacob?"

"Yes and no. He's doing better. But I also stopped by the Hardin Technical College campus this morning at the Student Activities Center to talk to a few students. Off the record. Turns out, Dr. Atkinson is a serial womanizer. The woman Beverly saw him with the other day matches the description of his T.A." Jinks gave Adam a wicked smile. "Guess T.A. really stands for tits and—"

"Yeah, I get it. Sounds like he's pretty blatant about it."

"Might be why his wife looked so down in the dumps when we saw her."

"Also sounds like he and Wallace Ryall had quite a bit in common if those assault complaints against him are true."

"Atkinson made up all those stories about Ryall's vandalism? And they're rapist-best-buds?"

"I checked the police files, and Atkinson did file a couple of complaints. Not to say he didn't throw eggs at his own house and blame Ryall."

Jinks said, "Wait right here." She disappeared down the hall, then reappeared moments later with some stale sandwiches left over from last night.

He pointed at them. "You're not going to eat those."

"No mayo, no salmonella. Better than oatmeal. Or Tootsie Rolls." Jinks knew Adam's aversion to "gruel" or anything that remotely resembled gray food. He grabbed one, and they wolfed them down with warm sodas before heading off to see Professor Open-Fly.

When they arrived, Vernon Atkinson didn't seem either surprised or distressed by their presence. He explained his wife was visiting her new niece again. "We thought about having a baby ourselves at one time. But they do tie you down, don't they?"

Adam said, "Especially when you're too busy having sex with other women. Including your students."

Atkinson smiled, exposing his unyellowed teeth. Did he think whitening made him more of a babe magnet? He looked amused as he replied, "I've had lots of relationships with other women, Detective Dutton."

"Was Wallace Ryall blackmailing you about those women?"

"He tried. I told him what I'm going to tell you. That it wouldn't do any good."

"And why is that?"

"My wife and I have what is commonly called an 'open marriage.' She knows about those other women."

"And your fellow professors and the college administrators?"

"I have tenure. Those students are all of majority age, none are in my own classes, and our relationships are consensual. No story there. Truth be told, I think my colleagues are secretly jealous."

"Did Wallace Ryall ever try to join you in these 'consensual' encounters?"

"A threesome, you mean?"

"I mean, did he express an interest in dating any of these women? Consensual or otherwise?"

Atkinson sat on his hands. And then he crossed his legs, and Adam had the wicked thought he probably didn't do it all that often.

The other man said, "I do hope you're not going to bring the 'R' word into the conversation. As I said, the women I'm with want to be with me. As for Wallace Ryall, I have no idea what his status with women was. Other than the one girlfriend he had. She was quite a looker that one. Now that she's on the market again, perhaps I should—"

Jinks butted in, "She's dating this big, burly Italian dude. I wouldn't go there if I were you. Unless you already have. Were you and Fern Gery getting it on?"

"I do love that term. But no, alas."

Adam was proud of Jinks's restraint. Left to her own devices, she'd be perfectly happy to chop up this cretin into professor-burger and feed him to her dogs.

Adam asked, "Does the name Jane Campen mean anything to you?"

Atkinson shook his head.

"Did your friend Ramsay Ryall ever mention his brother Wallace coming on to Ramsay's wife?"

"No, not that I recall."

"Did he ever come on to your wife?"

"She kept as far from him as possible. That's interesting about Ramsay and his wife. If that happened, I could perfectly understand him wanting to kill his brother. Although a sword seems very over-the-top for his style."

"And what would his style be?"

"He's an expert woodsman. He could have arranged all sorts of 'accidents.'"

"Do you own any swords, Dr. Atkinson?"

"I don't. But if that question is a sign you're ready to charge me with something, I should call my lawyer."

"We have to check all the angles, sir. We know where the murder weapon came from."

"Yes, I read about that in the papers. Wills, bequests, and such. Don't these things usually come down to money?"

Adam stood up and motioned to Jinks. "Thank you for your time, Professor. We'll be in touch."

They'd barely got outside the door when Jinks pounded her fists against her sides. "God's gift to women, he is not. Despite what he says. If I weren't already a lesbian, he'd be enough to turn me into one."

"I'm uncomfortable with him dating naïve, impressionable eighteen-year-olds. But unless he does something illegal, and the college doesn't complain, there's nothing we can do."

Jinks growled. "His poor wife. Judging by her expression last time we were here, don't think she's as happy with this 'open marriage' arrangement as he is."

"Atkinson never said Wallace Ryall didn't hit on his wife. Only that she 'kept as far from him as possible.'"

"If he pulled a Jane Campen-style attack on her. . ."

"Then both she and Atkinson have reason to kill Wallace."

Jinks grimaced. "I'll check on that story of hers about visiting her sister and new niece when Wallace was killed. Sometimes I think I should keep a phone glued to my ear. Go to bed wearing one of those over-the-ear jobs. Would save a bunch of time."

"And be a charming fashion accessory. You could patent some phone cozies. Make a killing."

Jinks groaned at his choice of words. "Just for that, I'm not feeding you any more stale sandwiches."

Adam silently cheered at that. The one he'd eaten was currently causing his stomach to complain in no uncertain terms. He rode out another wave of rumbling and promised himself he'd make a proper meal soon. With lobster and roasted acorn squash. And maybe he'd finally get Beverly Laborde to join him. At the moment, he'd settle for a heaping serving of Pepto with an antacid chaser.

28

Still smarting from her encounter with Zelda, Beverly was only half paying attention to Agnes as they walked into a lamp and lighting shop. After the third store they'd popped into along the downtown's main street, they were all beginning to look the same. But Agnes was excited about picking out some last decorative touches for her wine shop, so Beverly had gone along for the ride. Or walk.

"Besides," Agnes had explained to her. "Shopping cures everything. Depression, tummy aches, bombings."

Agnes had agonized over whether to opt for the kitschy-country side or a more sophisticated yuppie sensibility when creating her new space. Since the small stage in the cafe section might end up hosting rockabilly one night and an open-poetry event the next, she decided to split the difference. Beverly wouldn't have dreamed floral needlepoint wall hangings and contemporary geometric mirrors could coexist happily, but Agnes made it work.

All that was left was to find the perfect Zen water fountain to sit next to the cash register. They'd come to the right place—it might as well be called "Water Fountains R Us." It was a gardening and patio shop, but in the middle of winter, that meant less emphasis on the gardening and more on the patio end.

Then Beverly caught sight of three figures, and she spun around to face away from them. Agnes looked at her in surprise. "What's wrong, dear?"

"Those teens in the back. I recognize two of them as the punks who tried to rob me three months ago. The same kids who may be responsible for your shop damage."

Agnes glanced toward the trio. "And the third one is Blaine Morland, the boy I told you about. I hate to see him hanging around those other two older teens. They're trouble with a galaxy-sized T."

Beverly chanced another quick peek. "One of the older boys shoplifted what looks like blasting caps." She patted Agnes's shoulder. "Wait here."

"What are you going to do, dear?"

Beverly headed straight for the front counter, where two men were involved in a tense conversation. She noted the title "Manager" on one man's nametag and directed her comments at him. "I saw those teen boys over there shoplifting some blasting caps."

The Manager, Mr. Brand, looked at the other man and then replied to Beverly, "We're aware of it. We have a security guard monitoring the situation until the police arrive." The sound of the chimes on the front door alerted them to a new arrival, and Brand nodded toward the sound. "And there they are."

A uniformed cop headed toward the young men as Beverly watched. The two older youths took one look at them and sprinted for the rear door, but a man wearing a security guard's outfit stood in their way. The near-escape-artist duo were quickly shuffled out the back by the guard and a police officer.

Beverly went to check on Agnes, but Agnes wasn't where she'd left her. Beverly looked around frantically and then spied the older woman in an animated discussion with the second cop who had his hand on the shoulder of Blaine Morland.

When Beverly drew closer, she could hear Agnes making a plea on Blaine's behalf. "I tell you, Officer Naigle, this young man was not stealing anything. It's obvious he's just in the wrong place at the wrong time. The only thing he's guilty of is hanging around with a bad bunch."

Officer Naigle uttered an exasperated sigh. "Look, Miss—"

"Flamm, Agnes Flamm."

"Miss Flamm, this young man's been in scrapes before. He's no angel."

"I knew his mother before she died, Officer. She loved her son very much and raised him properly. He would never do anything to hurt her memory, would you, Blaine?"

Blaine's shoulder-length shaggy hair and bangs half-hid his eyes, but Beverly caught a look of surprise in those eyes. The officer nudged the boy toward the door, saying, "Looks like you've got a fan, Morland. But I still have to take you to the station. Maybe it'll finally put the fear of God into you. Before you end up in juvie. Or Southern State Correctional Facility."

Agnes called out after the boy as Naigle took him away, "I'm a firm believer in second chances, Blaine. As long as you're still breathing, it's never too late."

Tears formed in the corners of her friend's eyes, and Beverly said, "What's wrong, Agnes? Why do you care about this one boy so much?"

Agnes picked up a table fountain shaped like a lion. "He reminds me of my youngest son."

"I didn't know you had another son."

"Did have. Willem died while on a trip overseas with some other kids. Did some drugs, fell into a lake, and drowned."

"So that's where the name of your store came from, Willem's Wine & Cheese." Beverly put her arm around Agnes's shoulders. "Oh, Agnes, I had no idea. And I'm so sorry."

Agnes put down the lion fountain and patted Beverly's hand. "It's been decades. Seems like a lifetime ago."

"If it helps, I think you may be right about Blaine." Beverly wasn't about to let Agnes know of Beverly's social-worker pretense she'd used to talk to Blaine's aunt.

Agnes wiped her eyes and headed for a shelf in the corner. With a triumphant, "Ta-da!" she held out an object for Beverly to see—a small stone fountain resembling a Grecian-inspired bust. And it was perfect.

While Beverly and Agnes waited for the clerk to wrap up the fountain in tissue paper and put it in a box, Agnes said, "You looked disappointed when those officers arrived. Were you expecting Adam Dutton? But I guess since he's a detective, he doesn't bother with petty crimes."

"He's working hard on the bombing. And Harlan's case. Although they may be connected."

"How's the case going? I know it's only been a week, but if Harlan is innocent—"

At Beverly's frown, she hastened to say, "Since Harlan *is* innocent, that means the real murderer is still walking the streets."

Beverly replied, "Have you ever watched a piece of pottery being hand-glazed?"

Agnes shook her head.

"Okay, have you ever pulled taffy?"

The older woman nodded.

"It's like that. Maddeningly slow. And sticky. I don't think I'd have the patience to be a detective."

"We are definitely an instant-gratification society."

"It's not that. It's knowing a huge injustice is hanging out there, like the Sword of Damocles. And sometimes, it stays like that. No resolution."

"There's always resolution, dear. If nothing else, death evens the playing field for us all. Not to be morbid, but—"

"Death pays all debts." Beverly smiled. "Grammie used to say that."

"She probably stole it from me." Agnes winked at her.

§ § §

Beverly dropped Agnes off with her new purchase at the wine shop and decided to take a drive. It only took about ten minutes to the edge of town and beyond, but as she maneuvered the twisting road to her target, it seemed as if she were in a pristine forest.

At about the time she thought she'd taken a wrong turn, she came upon a cabin overlooking Beaver Pond Brook. Well, Adam had said this place wasn't far from the Nature Preserve, so that would explain the forest feel.

She climbed out of the car and crept toward the front door. It looked exactly like Adam's photo, save for the missing patio furniture. But what a soothing place to be, sitting in the evening, listening to the water. It was good to see the wooden bridge over the brook from the photo was still there.

After getting a tip from Gloria, the waitress at the Apple Valley Resort, Beverly learned not only where this house was but that Gloria thought it was for sale. Sure enough, a Crawford Realty sign stood next to a stately red pine tree shaped like a tin soldier, with its tall, straight lines and double trunk.

She couldn't see much through the windows, but the empty interior looked roomy, with vaulted ceilings and a massive fireplace. An image of a soft area rug in front of the fireplace, a comfy recliner, and a glass of wine came to mind.

Beverly strolled out to the arched bridge and examined it. Looked like it could hold her weight. She walked on it gingerly at first and then headed to the middle where it was easy to see up and down both sides of the brook. It might be a cliché, but it even babbled. Listening to nature's version of a meditation mix-tape, the near-permanent knot in her shoulders from months of tension and stress begin to relax.

She could see why Adam loved this spot. Why hadn't Zelda? Oh, right. According to Adam, Zelda said it was too far out of town and isolated. But for Beverly, that was its number one attraction.

After spending fifteen minutes soaking up the sounds of the brook, the winds through the pines, and the calls of Bohemian Waxwing birds, she knew she should head back to town. But first, she jotted down the number of the realtor. Adam did suggest she find a permanent residence instead of the resort, right?

29

Adam dropped Jinks off at the station to follow up on her research into other women Wallace Ryall might have attacked. Next, he headed for a place where he wasn't sure he'd be welcome.

He stood outside the door, with his hand on the knob, debating with himself whether this was a good idea or not. When a customer behind him cleared her throat, he opened the door for her to enter and followed on in.

Prospero greeted the customer, then waved toward the back office when he saw Adam. Of course, Harlan was in. Where else could he be? The court had settled that with the restrictions on his travel, hadn't it? Adam popped his head inside the office and had a twinge of guilt when he noticed Harlan rubbing his ankle.

Adam walked in and pointed at it. "That monitor causing a rash? I can request a new one for you if that one's too tight."

"Naw, it's winter eczema. Get it all the time." Harlan reached into his desk and pulled out a tube of hydrocortisone cream. "See?"

Adam cleared his throat. "Ah. Well. I came to take a look at those swords again, the ones from Reuben Ryall's estate."

Harlan hopped up, and Adam said, "You don't have to bother showing me. That is if they're in the same place as before."

"I may have eczema, but I'm not a cripple. And Prospero and I did move some of the Ryall pieces around yesterday."

Adam followed him to a wall of display cases and pointed to a free-standing sword rack. "All the swords on that right there are Ryall's. I haven't sold any."

"Sword market not big right now?"

"I decided not to sell any Ryall pieces until. . .well, until after. You know."

"You're not legally bound to do that, Harlan."

"Felt like the right thing to do."

Since Adam knew Joe Brimm had dusted these weapons for prints, too, he didn't think anything of picking up the top sword. "This is a falchion, right?"

Harlan chuckled. "Didn't know you were an enthusiast."

"Prospero gave me a Swords 101 lecture." Adam turned the sword over and studied the handle. "Huh. This one doesn't have Ryall's monogram on it. Like the murder weapon."

"Don't think any of these others do, you see. Don't know why the man would engrave only the one."

"In the original display, the Tritonia was the fourth sword down, not the one on top."

"So it was. Better for slicing and dicing?"

Adam gave a sharp look at Harlan, who was grinning at him. Good to know his humor was still intact. "If I were looking to frame someone for a murder, I'd want the evidence to be pretty blatant. Say, a sword with a traceable monogram on it."

"Then said murderer would have to know such a piece existed, right? Since he didn't go for the one on top?"

"How long were these swords on display prior to the murder?"

"A day or so. Still got some boxes with estate pieces in 'em we're just now getting around to."

"There's a good likelihood our killer was inside Ryall's home at some point. Legally or otherwise." Adam replaced the falchion in its holder. "Those boxes you mentioned. Where are they now?"

"In the storeroom. You wanna see 'em?"

Adam nodded, and once again, he followed along behind Harlan, feeling like a puppy currying favor from his master. Harlan showed him about a half-dozen boxes, and Adam bent down to take a closer look. "Have you opened these yet?"

"Haven't had a chance." Harlan poked his head out into the store and yelled out, "Prospero, you opened any of these last Ryall boxes yet?"

Adam heard the assistant yell back, "Not yet. It's on my list, I swear."

"No probs, just checking."

Harlan rejoined Adam as he stooped down and pulled a glove from his pocket that he put on. "What's that for, Adam?"

"You say neither you nor Prospero has opened these boxes. But someone else has."

"Why do you say that?"

Adam ran a finger along the edges. "Someone removed the tape recently. Then re-taped to make it look more-or-less like it was originally."

"Why would somebody do that? Thieves aren't usually that neat."

"Looking for something. And didn't want to draw attention to it." Adam stood back up. "I'll have the guys come and dust these. Is there any way of knowing what's supposed to be in them?"

"Reuben Ryall's estate only came with a partial packing list. Sorry to say the answer to that question is likely no."

Adam removed the glove and stuffed it back in his pockets. He started to exit the storeroom, then stopped. "Duane Sher been in contact with you?"

"Checks in once a day. He's a bang-up attorney, Adam."

Adam smiled briefly. "That's good. Glad to hear he's doing right by you." Adam cleared his throat. "Guess I better run. Jinks'll drink all the coffee before I get back."

Harlan gave Adam a knowing look. "You didn't really come here to check on those swords, did you?"

"Turns out, it was a good idea." Adam shifted his feet. "You're looking well. Eating enough?"

"Prospero's a big mother hen. Who knew? And Beverly and Agnes Flamm have dropped by a few times each."

"Agnes?"

"She was 'checking on my antiques,' too. Like you. I'm fortunate to have so many people who care about my. . .antiques."

"Well, we're all worried about those. . .antiques."

"I've been around a long time. Done just fine. Reckon I'll go on doing just fine. So don't you worry."

A nice thought, but Adam wasn't as far along in the investigation as he'd hoped to be. And the theories rolling around him were all filled with crater-sized holes. Time to head for the bar, but not to drink. He had an appointment with a giant.

§ § §

Adam made his way through the bar that was as empty as a church on Monday. But being early afternoon, this particular bar didn't have an array of television screens like the fancier bars, with every flavor of sports broadcast from Vermont to Vladivostok.

The room in the rear of the place had barely enough room for one six-five, three-hundred-pound private eye and a narrow table that doubled as a desk. Adam squeezed himself into a corner and stayed standing. As if there'd be any place to sit down.

"Since you're back in the private eye biz, Cray, why are you keeping the bouncer gig, too?"

"The only thing I'm bouncing is the occasional check. I did a favor for the owner of this place. So, he let me keep this little office here."

Adam gauged the size of the room. Eight-by-eight, if you were generous. "Where do you put your clients, in a hammock strung from the ceiling?"

"Funny man. I meet them elsewhere. This shoebox is to have an address that isn't my house."

"Why aren't *we* meeting elsewhere?"

"Wanted to see you brought down to size. For a change."

"You still haven't forgiven me for that case where you almost ended up in an orange jumpsuit?"

Cray shrugged. "I let by-grudges be by-grudges." He grabbed his cellphone and snapped a photo of Adam. "You look quite miserable, all squished up in that corner. That's a keeper."

"When you're finished being cute, I'd love to hear where you stand on your investigation. Those missing rare-earths shipments."

"Why are you so suddenly interested?"

"Harlan's case. One of the suspects is a prof. He teaches this eco-design stuff now, but I found out this morning from some online research the guy used to teach chemistry. Since he's a regular sleazebag, I couldn't help but wonder if he's somehow involved in your pot of poison."

"Seems a bit of a stretch."

"Perhaps. Have you run across the name Vernon Atkinson or even Nyssa Atkinson?"

Cray pulled out his phone again and opened a notepad app. "How do you spell that guy's first name? Is it short for something?"

"Might as well be. The man has a rather high opinion of his attractiveness to the fairer sex. But it's V-E-R-N-O-N." Adam waited for Cray to finish typing in the names. "You said those rare earths are used in wind turbines. What else?"

"Dysprosium and neodymium are the main elements. Dysprosium is known as the 'Kryptonite' of heavy rare earth elements.' It's a bitch getting it out of the ground." Cray paused to ask, "How much you remember from your chem class?"

"Bits. Probably enough."

"Dysprosium has two paired electrons. Helps in working with radiation, batteries, lasers, digital storage. Added to neodymium-iron-boron magnets, it's used in hybrid and electric cars. And neodymium's got similar uses."

"Who hired you?"

"It's classified."

"Military?"

"Like I said, it's classified."

Adam studied his friend's face. "Atkinson doesn't appear to be the cloak and dagger type. Skirts and daggers, sure."

"Don't see how any of this would tie in with Harlan's case. But thanks for the tip on this professor guy. If I hear of anything—"

"I'll be the last to know."

Cray put a hand over his heart. "If it were just for you, maybe. But since it's Harlan we're talking about. I swear I'll give you a call."

"Thanks, Cray."

"Be sure and wipe your feet on the way out, will ya?" Cray grinned. "Otherwise, it'll take the cleaning lady five minutes to clean this place. She gets cranky if it takes over three."

Adam managed to unwedge himself from the corner and shoehorn himself out of there. The rare earths angle was likely a dead end, but a part of him wanted to nail something on Atkinson. Outside of a jealous marshal-wannabe, a vengeful brother, and some potential assaults, he was running on empty in the motive department.

When his cellphone rang, he didn't recognize the number but answered it. It was one very agitated Agnes Flamm. He held the phone away from his ear, wincing. He wanted to tell her he didn't have time for this, but then he remembered the property bond. He hung up with a promise to stop by the wine shop and found himself hoping one particular raven-haired beauty might be there, too.

But then his phone rang again. Sometimes, he wished he could turn the damn thing off. Half-expecting Agnes again, he was in for a surprise when he heard the familiar smooth monotone of Mr. X. "Detective Dutton, my condolences for the forced redecorating of your home. However, if you'd like the name of the decorator, I might be able to help."

"Oh, really? We don't have any witnesses. And the lab struck out on prints."

"This particular gentleman, and I use the term loosely, is someone you've nicknamed Redbeard."

Adam's ears perked up. "I'm listening."

"His real name is Darnell Warner. A rather slick operative who's frequently in the employ—off the books, mind you—of Ivon Kozak."

"Kozak? That's a new one."

"He and Reggie Forsythe are cut from the same cloth. And both NAL 'kingpins.' With Forsythe out of action, Kozak pretty much has a corner on the dirty dealings market in the Northeast antiques world."

"Do you have proof this Darnell Warner was behind the bomb at my house?"

"I'm afraid that's your department, Detective. I see the big picture. You get to tear it apart pixel by pixel."

"Gee, thanks." Adam wanted to follow up right away, but he'd promised Agnes. "If this pans out, I owe you one, Xenakis."

"Oh, it will. But I'll wait and cash in on my winnings some other time."

Adam was also going to thank him for looking out for Beverly, but the man had hung up. He was one of the strangest informants Adam ever had. But right now, he'd take a tip from a magic elf, if it would help.

30

Agnes placed the new Grecian-bust fountain on the wine shop's counter. She moved it forward six inches, back four inches, then forward again. The woman was still agitated over Blaine Morland at the garden shop, and Beverly didn't see any signs of her mood changing for the better.

With a groan, Agnes reached for her purse, grabbed a bottle of pills, and dry-swallowed one.

Beverly asked, "Headache?"

"Pep pills. Doc Wilson prescribed them for me."

"Pep as in caffeine or pep as in—"

"Anti-depressants. Something ending in 'ine,' I think."

"But you don't seem depressed."

"Guess those pills are doing their job."

"They have so many side effects. Are you sure you need them?"

Agnes rubbed the pill bottle and slipped it back into her purse. "They've become a crutch. I never got over David's death. He was my one true love. And then when our son died, too..."

Beverly patted her on the shoulder. "It's okay. If you need them, you need them." She looked around. "Do you have any bottled water to use in this fountain?"

Agnes directed her to the cafe area, where Beverly extracted a bottle and brought it to the counter. She followed the instructions, plugged in the fountain, and watched as the soothing sound of running water bubbled out the top, flowed over the statuary, and down into a square basin.

Agnes patted the bust's head. "He looks very classically Greek. I think I'll call him Dionysus."

"The Greek god of wine?"

"Can you think of a better name?"

Beverly eyed the male statuary with its wide-open stone eyes that seemed to be staring back at her. "Dionysus will make a fine mascot."

The chimes over the door Agnes had installed signaled a new arrival, and Beverly bit back a smile when she saw who it was. But then her jaw hung open when Agnes started in on Adam right away, haranguing him about Blaine Morland. "They hauled that boy out of there like he was a worthless piece of garbage. Police brutality, pure and simple. He hadn't done anything wrong."

Beverly didn't miss the quick look in her direction from Adam before he replied, "I checked on those three boys before I came here. They've been tied to other thefts in town."

"All three of them?"

"Well, the two older boys."

"There, you see? Not the youngest one, not Blaine. He shouldn't go to jail just for running with the wrong crowd. If each of us had to go to jail for having bad friends, we'd all be in jail."

"If Blaine Morland doesn't have any priors, and the store owner can't prove he saw him shoplifting, he'll be okay."

"I may not be a mind reader, but I don't feel that boy means any evil. He's directionless, a lost boy who lost his mother. And lost little boys tend to latch on to anyone or anything who'll give them the time of day."

Adam walked over to the fountain and appeared to be hypnotized by the water. "If he's innocent, then we'll see what we can do about changing that course of his. Those older two—I wouldn't be surprised to find they're tied to several unsolved burglaries and break-ins. I'm glad Prospero is installing a security system for you and Harlan. An antiques store up in Crawford was vandalized two weeks ago."

Beverly mused aloud, "Can't help but wonder if those older two boys were behind the break-in here at Agnes's shop."

She realized her mistake the moment the words came out of her mouth. Agnes glared at her for letting the details slip, and Adam glared at her, too, as he asked, "What break-in here at Agnes's shop?"

It was too late to turn back, so Beverly added, "Two days ago, Agnes found her shop in disarray. Some items were broken, others strewn about. It was a mess."

"Anything stolen?"

"Agnes couldn't find anything missing."

"Why didn't you tell me about this? We could have sent in a team to check for prints or other evidence."

Agnes said soothingly, "You're so busy with Harlan's case, this bit of nonsense hardly seemed worth troubling you about."

Adam stewed over that briefly, then surprised Beverly by asking, "Didn't Harlan send over some items for your shop?"

Agnes replied, "Why, yes, he did. He didn't have to do that, mind you. I wasn't expecting anything in return for putting up the property bond."

"Were any of those items among the ones broken or rifled through?"

"Now that you mention it, yes. Is that important?"

"Can you show me those items?"

Agnes waved her hand, motioning for him to follow her to the small inventory room as Beverly trailed along behind. Agnes pointed to a table where several small items lay waiting for repair.

Adam studied the broken halves of a Davenport terra cotta wine bottle cooler and the pieces of a cranberry-red Prussian-style glass decanter. "It's likely an effort in futility, but I'd like to send someone out to try to print these pieces."

Agnes hesitated, and Adam reassured her, "Look, if the boy is guilty, it will come out anyway. But the prints could as easily prove he wasn't behind this particular nasty business."

She relented, and when he asked for a list of the things Harlan had loaned her, she bounded toward the front. Adam looked at Beverly, "She seems happier all of a sudden."

Beverly grinned. "She got a new combo fax-copier-printer she's quite proud of."

"Ah. Glad to christen it for her." He picked up a black lacquer papier mâché coaster decorated with gold flowers and leaves. "Did you contribute any items to Agnes's shop?"

"What you're holding in your hand right there."

"Looks expensive."

"Good prices can be had if you know where to look."

"You did come by it the old-fashioned way, right?"

Beverly gritted her teeth. Did he think so little of her he'd believe she'd conned somebody out of those coasters? But then, did they really know each other that well at all? Sometimes all they did was avoid, evade, and dance circles around the other.

Adam must have picked up on her mood, or her expression said it all. "I didn't mean it like that."

"Oh? How *did* you mean it?"

"Ever since that whole Forsythe saga, the NAL, the disguises. I don't like the idea of you putting yourself in danger."

She tilted her head. "You mean like pipe bombs?"

"That's different. I do this for a living. It's expected I'll piss some people off."

Agnes rejoined them and handed a paper over to Adam. "There you go." She waited for him to glance at the list before adding, "I think I saw your ex-wife, Zelda, the other day. Going into the new fashion designer boutique in Hanover. She had on a red coat and red shoes, as I recall. With her red hair, it made her look like a walking strawberry."

Beverly almost choked, and Adam stared down at the floor. Beverly was afraid Agnes had gone too far with her underhanded matchmaking when she saw Adam trying to suppress a smile.

"Or a red bell pepper," Beverly added, helpfully.

Adam chimed in with "Or a candied apple."

As much as Beverly was enjoying their little game at Zelda's expense, her curiosity got the better of her. "Where are you off to next, Adam?"

"Thought I'd check with Braddon Hopper again. Jinks found out something interesting about that ex-girlfriend of his."

"Since Braddon already thinks I'm your 'consultant,' mind if I tag along?"

She expected him to say no when he surprised her again by agreeing. On the way to the car, he asked, "So. Coffee with Zelda?"

"Oh, that. I bumped into her in the tea room at the resort. We had a nice chat."

"A nice chat. Is that code for catfight?"

"You wish. Men go in for that sort of thing, don't they? Kind of a turn-on?"

"This man doesn't. Too much like my day job."

She could tell he was pissed at her refusal to elaborate further. But she wasn't about to tell him what Zelda had said—accused, was more like it.

She punched him lightly on the arm. "Come on. Let's go chat with Manfred Urdangarin, also known as Braddon Hopper. Is he an excellency, baron, lord, or sire? I can't keep all that straight."

"Don't worry. When in doubt, I'll use what I do on crooks, 'hey you.' Works pretty well."

"Ever tried that on Mayor Lehmann?"

He grimaced. "Don't tempt me."

Adam's cell rang, and he mouthed a "sorry" to Beverly as he took the call. From her end, she heard Adam say, "Is that a fact? You got it that soon?" He listened some more and added, "Sure sounds like him. I'm heading that way. I'll keep you posted."

After he hung up, Beverly stared at him expectantly. "Well?"

"Jinks."

"It must be about Harlan's case. So what did she say? What did she get so soon?"

"Jinks checked Wallace Ryall's DNA with samples she got from her a sex assault victim, a case she's working. She said she might have bribed Joe Brimm to get it fast."

"Was Wally the same guy who attacked Jinks's victim?"

"No, the DNA wasn't a match. Although Jane Campen, Braddon Hopper's ex, is still pretty sure Wally was the man who attacked her one night. But she'd blocked out something until she recently went into therapy."

"I'm all ears."

"After Jinks tracked her down, Jane recalled seeing another man with Wally the night she was attacked, wearing longer hair and a full beard and mustache. Sound like someone we know?"

Beverly's eyes widened. "Mister 'you may address me as Your Excellency, Richard Symonnet.'"

"Yep. Think I'm going to have to chat with our park ranger. And soon."

31

Adam pulled the car in front of the alpinesque A-frame conference center and spied a familiar figure swigging a bottle of root beer. He pointed out the man to Beverly. "Isn't that our park ranger, His Excellency, Baron Richard Symonnet?"

"Looks like the same ranger to me."

"Let me take the lead on this one. Don't want to spook him too soon." Adam hopped out of the car and approached him. "Ranger Joss Warder?" Adam wasn't about to call him "Your Excellency" to his face.

The ranger squinted at him in the late afternoon half-sun, half-haze. "Detective Dutton, wasn't it?"

"That's right. Last time we chatted, you said Braddon Hopper's father had a stroke, which is why Braddon had to shelve his fencing dreams and run the family business. Do you recall the circumstances surrounding that stroke of his?"

Warder set the root beer bottle down on top of a nearby post. "It was following a car accident. Lucky he survived. Although he may not feel he's all that lucky, since he's paralyzed on his left side and can't talk all that good."

"Hit and run, wasn't it?"

"The cowards could have stopped and helped. First few minutes are critical with strokes."

"So I've heard. There's another question I have…the first time I ran into you, you said you didn't know Wallace Ryall well, only as part of the Society for Creative Anachronism."

"That's true."

"I have a source who saw you and Ryall drinking together."

"Some of us got together sometimes after meetings. Doesn't mean we hung out otherwise."

Adam nodded. "I see. During any of these bar meetings, did Wally become drunk? Perhaps aggressive?"

Warder laughed. "Sure. We all did. Shit-faced mean drunks. Who doesn't?"

"Were you also drinking buddies with Braddon Hopper's ex-girlfriend, Jane Campen?"

"Jane? I hardly knew her."

"Did you ever try to get to know her better? Possibly after one of those 'shit-faced' bar crawls? With or without her consent?"

Warder's face turned deep red. "I don't think I like what you're implying, Detective Dutton. Any more of that nonsense, and you'll have to talk to my lawyer. Now, if you'll excuse me, I have important work to do."

As he stormed off in his truck, Adam said to Beverly, "Awfully jumpy for a man with nothing to hide."

Beverly fished into her purse, pulled out a tissue, and gingerly picked up the root beer bottle the ranger left behind. "Will this help?"

Adam grinned at her. "If he left behind some saliva, you bet. I'll get a rush warrant, and Jinks can use her magic bribery skills on Joe Brimm again and run the DNA stat." Maybe Beverly did have the makings of a bona fide detective.

With the bottle secure in Adam's car, he and Beverly headed into the center to track down Braddon Hopper. They ran into a young woman who introduced herself as the conference center's secretary, Sharon Bogren. "It's a pleasure to meet you, Detective Dutton, Miss Laborde. I do hope you solve

Wally's murder soon. It's cast quite a pall over the place. Although I understand the main suspect is out on bail?"

"He is. But he's on strict monitoring."

She bit her lip. "This might not be a popular opinion around here. But I don't think he did it. I've seen him around town. Such a kindly looking man. And always friendly."

Adam said, "He is that."

She smiled. "Or I'm antiques-blind. Always wanted to get into the antiques business."

Beverly said, "I know lots of people in the biz." She pulled out a scrap of paper from her purse, wrote down her cellphone number, and handed it over. "If you ever want some advice, give me a call."

"Thanks. I may do that. Braddon is here today in his office. Should I tell him you're coming?"

Adam replied, "That won't be necessary," and he and Beverly found Braddon in the same office at the same desk, with a cup of his "mud coffee." It was as if the intervening three days hadn't happened. Adam had a sudden feeling of being stuck in a time loop.

"Hello again, Braddon."

Hopper lived up to his name and hopped up to shake Adam's hand. "Detective Dutton. What can I do for you?"

"First off, an employee of Tossed Treasures antiques saw you there not too long ago looking at swords."

Braddon frowned. "I have an interest, sure. When I was in the Olympics, I saw actual swordplay in Asia. More interesting than the sabre fencing I'm used to."

"Fair enough. I also wanted to ask you about Jane Campen, your former girlfriend."

"Jane? Haven't seen her in months. Moved to California. Guess she's a fan of movies and wines." The forced smile on

Braddon's face told Adam he thought the attempt at humor was as lame as it sounded.

"The car that hit your father and didn't stop. Do you know who was behind the wheel?"

"I thought you wanted to ask me about Jane."

"Is it possible she was the one driving that night?"

Braddon's fists were clenched by his sides, and he didn't answer at first, staring out the window.

"Braddon?"

"She wasn't driving, but she knows who was."

"And she wouldn't tell you?"

"She didn't have to. I guessed."

"It was Wallace Ryall, wasn't it?"

Braddon's attention snapped back to Adam. "How did you—"

"We tracked down Jane. She feels pretty badly about it now, that she didn't go to the police with the info. And I guess it made her feel better to tell the truth." Well, Jinks had done most of the work, and Adam owed her some more lutefisk for it.

"Fat lot of good that does Dad now."

"With Wallace Ryall dead, I guess your father was avenged, in a way, isn't that right?"

"Damn straight. And I know what you're thinking. But I wasn't the one who killed him."

Through a connecting glass panel, Adam saw some SCA members practicing swordplay in the larger room beyond. He pointed at the group. "Thought we'd see you in full Rapier Marshall mode this time."

"The SCA board wants to wait a while before filling the position. Out of 'respect' for Wallace."

Beverly chimed in, "I'm sure that's the honorable thing to do. But I'm curious—you're an Olympic competitor, but where do other people learn how to fence and fight with swords? I mean, how did Wallace learn?"

"His brother taught him. He's a pretty good sabre-handler, himself."

Beverly raised her eyebrows at Adam, who nodded. He was surprised at how well they were getting at reading each other's body signals. He made a note to follow up on that sabre tidbit later.

But he needed to address something else first. "Braddon, you run your father's lighting shop now, so I imagine you're pretty knowledgeable about the various types of lights. You sell more than lamps, right?"

"We're not Home Depot. We sell everything from commercial troffers to dock lights to lighting poles and ballasts."

"And you'd sell metal halide lamps?"

"Sure. Mostly outdoor flood lamps."

"I understand metal halide lamps are also used in automotive applications, aquariums, even car headlights."

"Yeah, but those are called xenon headlamps due to the xenon gas in the bulb instead of argon used in other halide lamps. They're more intense than incandescents."

Adam was enjoying the puckered-skin confusion on Beverly's forehead, but to her credit, she kept her face blank as if she knew where he was going with this. She made a fine detective assistant.

"Do you ever do lighting repair? Or make your own lighting?"

"Sometimes, mostly the former, not the latter."

"Are you familiar with dysprosium?"

"One of those rare-earths minerals. Some high-end commercial lighting uses it. Makes for a high color temperature. But there's not enough of a market for those types of lights for us to carry them. And China's got a corner on the market for dysprosium mining and processing. They could pull the plug at any time. This country's playing catch-up. There's only one working mine in all of the U-S-of-A."

Braddon folded his arms over his chest and sat down on the edge of his desk. "This all feels like a far cry from murder."

"Tree roots in the ground spread out in strange patterns, but they all lead back to the trunk. Which leads me to my last question, have you heard of Dr. Vernon Atkinson?"

"Wallace's neighbor, sure. And since Wallace ragged on him all the time, even hated him, I guess, that made me want to meet the guy and thank him. But I never did."

"Thanks for your time, Braddon. Mind if we take a peek inside to watch the practicing?"

Braddon waved them in, and Adam and Beverly went into the main hall and parked themselves in a corner. Beverly started in with a flood of questions, but Adam held up his hand. "I'm not sure where I'm going with this. I wasn't kidding about those roots, even though the tree can seem pretty far away."

They watched the two pairs of combatants, both suited up in armor helmets and shield and wielding "swords" made of rattan. There was some thrusting-and-parrying, but mostly starting and stopping. Near as Adam could tell, if one participant on the receiving end of a blow from the sword felt it was a "death" blow, that round was over. Judging from the amount of contact and lack of effective defense techniques, Braddon's work as potential Rapier Marshal wasn't going to be easy.

That brought his thoughts to Wallace, pinned to a tree with a very accurate sword thrust. If a Rapier Marshal was supposed to be an expert at the craft, why wasn't he able to defend himself better?

Beverly poked him in the arm. "They're not that good, are they? You think Wallace Ryall was as inept as these guys? How did our killer swordsman get the better of him?"

Adam stared at her, blinking slowly. "You haven't added reading minds to your long list of unusual talents, have you?"

She stared into his eyes and put her fingers on her temples. "I think I'm getting something. Yes, it's clearer now. You are bored, you are hungry, and you have a craving for a fudge mocha latte at Uncommon Grounds."

He shook his head in mock astonishment. "I see I'm going to have to be more careful around you, missy."

She laughed, and he hoped she'd forgiven him for his comment earlier in Agnes's shop. A tiny sliver of doubt crept into his conscious mind—how committed was she to her new con-artist-free lifestyle? But he pushed that thought away. If she really was reading his mind, he didn't want to hurt her again. Trust had to work both ways, didn't it?

32

Saturday, December 9

After a restless night's sleep and some Apple Valley Resort signature cranberry maple scones that were disappointingly stale, Beverly felt the need to get out and do something. Anything. She enjoyed getting out on the open road, driving endlessly, going nowhere. But this morning, she had a destination in mind and pointed the SUV down the road.

Her thoughts turned to her outing with Adam yesterday afternoon, which she'd secretly enjoyed. Not just going to talk with Braddon Hopper, but stopping at Uncommon Grounds afterward. She knew Adam wanted her to go to dinner with him, and going out for coffee or a quick bite was a poor second-best. But dinner felt so. . .committed. A Real Date. Before she knew it, she'd have makeup and clothing in two different houses and be choosing between a German chocolate or red velvet groom's cake.

She pushed those images away when the familiar mini-castle came into view. Although less agitated than her last visit here, she still felt restless, unsettled. She wanted to be a more thoughtful guest this time and had stopped along the way to pick up a vase of bamboo and birds-of-paradise from Fern Gery's florist shop.

Mr. X thanked her and placed the vase in a prominent spot on the marble-top étagère. "The usual or perhaps some Portugal port?"

"Hmm?" She saw him looking at her questioningly and realized he'd asked her a question. "Oh. Sorry. The port sounds lovely, but I'm driving."

"Depends upon how long you're planning on staying. A woman your size after one glass and two hours should be fine."

"You sound like a walking breathalyzer."

"Did you know they sell those now? Portable ones."

"Wonder how Adam feels about those?"

"I'm surprised not to find him with you today."

"He's busy. Harlan's case."

Mr. X disappeared long enough to bring her a glass of the port. "That sounds promising."

"I wish." She rushed to add, "It's not Adam. I'm frustrated. Police work is like skating on molasses. Harlan's case, the vandalism at Agnes's shop. Guess I'm used to making things happen on my schedule."

"It's only been eight days since the murder, six days since Harlan was arrested, and only three days since Agnes's shop was broken into. The average time for a typical murder investigation is ten months, last I checked."

Beverly smiled and shook her head. Mr. X obviously had a lot more first-hand knowledge about crime and the legal system than she knew. She was dying to hear about his background and could have done a little investigation, herself. But she respected him too much for that. When he was ready to tell her, he would.

"Adam told me about a separate antiques store theft two weeks ago. Could it be related to Agnes's case?"

"I learned of that event through my network. That same network tipped me off as to who the prime suspect might be. I still like to keep apprised of the business."

"Do you have a name?" Beverly hoped it wasn't Blaine Morland, for Agnes's sake.

"Dmitri Chekhol."

"Russian?"

"Originally. Raised in New York, moved here recently. He's a lone operator, an ordinary thug. Not part of the small, but active, Eastern European organized-crime faction in New England."

Beverly sat up straight. "Do you know where he lives? Works?"

"Yes. I know about Mr. Chekhol. Most of it distasteful."

"I want to check him out. To see if he's been anywhere near Agnes's shop."

"I'm not sure I like that idea, Beverly. It didn't turn out so well last time."

Beverly patted her purse. "I won't forget my gun this time."

"I still don't like it. But if you are bound and determined to go, then I must go with you."

Beverly beamed at him. "This is wonderful. Agnes puts on a brave face, but I think she's terrified the vandals might come back."

The ever-thoughtful Mr. X gave her a thermos of some yak hot chocolate, and they were on their way. Their target was a small house near Crawford, "house" being a generous term. The warped siding and rotting boards were topped off with a roof with half its shingles missing. Beverly had heard of "lean-tos" before, but this seemed more of a "lean-away."

Upon spying a car in the driveway with its motor running, Mr. X had her drive past the house so he could get a good look at the place and then circle around the block. When they came around again, the car was pulling out of the driveway, and they followed.

"Are you sure this is the right man?"

"Balding, with a scruffy patch on the crown to match his scruffy stubble. Hooded eyes, a small beak nose, and a large black spider tattoo on his neck."

They followed him to a smallish warehouse-barn combo, and Beverly parked a short way down the road, partially hidden by a stack of brush. She said, "I'll bet that's where he stores the hot merchandise. I need to get closer." Mr. X didn't have time to protest before Beverly was out of the car and scurrying toward the same door where Chekhol disappeared.

She quietly turned the knob and opened the door a crack. It led into a closed-off vestibule, and she silently cheered. She'd be able to get in and take a peek, then get out.

Getting in was easy, and she immediately saw boxes and shelves with antiques. Stolen? Most likely. Getting out wasn't as simple, because right as she turned to duck toward the door, a man's voice growled from behind. "You shouldn't be snooping around in other people's business."

She batted her eyes innocently at him. "I'm sorry. Guess I got lost. Or my friend gave me the wrong address. This sure isn't Reuben's Tire Shop." Not her best line, but she hoped it would fool him.

It didn't. "Don't know of any Reuben's Tire Shops around here. You look waaaaay out of place. You a cop?"

He started toward her, and she quickly fumbled around in her purse, but her fingers were shaking, and the gun fell out. She swooped down to pick it up, but right as she straightened up, she heard a loud "thwack." Looking toward the sound, she saw Mr. X with his hand out in a flat-palmed chop—and Chekhol lay flat on the floor.

"Karate?" she asked.

"The shuto, or knife-hand, strike. It can be deadly. When you want it to be."

Chekhol groaned, and Mr. X planted his foot on the man's forehead. "Now, Mr. Chekhol. What we want is simple. We want to know if you recently broke into a wine shop in Ironwood Junction. And I strongly encourage you to be honest. Two hundred pounds pressing down on a man's skull is not very pleasant."

"Look," Chekhol managed to choke out. "I didn't rob no wine shop. And I ain't been near Ironwood Junction in months."

"But you did rob the Saffell Antiques Market?"

Chekhol hesitated, and Mr. X pressed down harder. "Okay, okay. I robbed it. So what? A man's gotta make a living."

"I'll assume for now you are being honest. So here's what I want you to do. You will return all the stolen items, anonymously if you choose. I have very little interest in adding to the prison system's bloated membership."

"Yeah, okay. Okay, already."

Mr. X removed his foot and nodded at Beverly, his way of indicating they should exit. On the way back to the car, Beverly kept an eye on the door, half-expecting to see Chekhol running after them, but he didn't.

"How did you get in there?" she asked.

"A second door."

"Weren't you afraid he had weapons?"

"I could see he didn't." Xenakis pulled two guns out of his pocket and tossed them into the back seat. "And I made sure he wouldn't be able to use the ones I found."

Beverly looked over at him as they climbed into the car. "You really believe he'll take those antiques back?"

"I will make sure he does." The tone of his voice let Beverly know she shouldn't press it any further.

He tapped her purse. "Although having a gun in there is better than nothing, your struggle with it was distressing. Have you considered a holster? I understand they make some rather attractive ones for women. So invisible, you can't tell someone's packing."

"Gun cozies? That should be fun to shop for." She grinned at him, but he didn't return her smile.

"Beverly, your willingness—and even eagerness—to dash into danger troubles me. Perhaps you are missing something in your life that makes such endeavors a replacement? Being reckless almost got you killed once."

"Guess I'm an adrenaline junkie." But that wasn't exactly true, was it? She loved nothing better than to browse through stores looking for bargains or curl up with a good book and a glass of wine. To a true adrenaline junkie, that would be worse than death.

Missing something in her life? Well, she wasn't about to run out and get a cat. Even if she liked cats. Or get a husband, even if. . .

No, she wasn't missing anything. She loved her life, loved her freedom, loved the type of thrills she got from a successful con. Maybe Adam was right in questioning whether she'd ever truly be able to go "straight." Then she thought of the cabin by Beaver Brook Pond. Could she still travel around and use the cabin as a home base?

She glanced over at Mr. X. "Do they make gun holsters shaped like a penis?"

Finally, something that made him laugh.

33

Adam liked this time of morning, right after the first blush of sunrise, when everything felt new and clean. As if the dark cloak of night had swept away yesterday's mistakes and started the world over again. Although that wasn't true in the human world, was it? Man's criminal ways continued without pause— or Adam would have long been out of a job.

He knew Beverly wasn't happy with the slow pace of the investigation into Wallace Ryall's murder. Adam wasn't exactly dancing a jig over the lack of a big break in the case and had stayed up late going over his notes. The truth was in there, somewhere. Or pieces of it.

Lulled to sleep by the fisherman's channel on TV, he awoke with a desire for a salmon-and-egg bagel, which was a gourmet feast after last night's takeout cardboard-burger. He didn't try asking Beverly to go to dinner with him. What was the point?

Maybe the time for that had passed, maybe it wasn't in the cards, maybe he really was married to his work, as Zelda had said. He comforted himself with the thought Beverly was safe, probably sleeping in or taking advantage of the resort's spa.

His cellphone rang, and he briefly entertained the notion of letting it go to voicemail. In the world of a cop, phone calls were as likely to be bad as good. But he picked it up and was surprised by the caller, although whether the call was good or bad remained to be seen. He agreed to meet her for brunch and told himself at least he'd get a good meal out of it.

On the stroke of noon, or so his atomic chronograph watch said, he walked into the Hanover's Embers Bistro. He didn't even check with the hostess, although he recognized her, and she smiled back at him, pointing into the dining room. Zelda was already there, seated in their "usual" booth, the one they used to ask for.

He'd lost count of how many times they'd eaten here when they were married. The food was above-average, the service outstanding, and the Drunken Chocolate Truffle Cake was something that should be enshrined in the *Guinness Book of World Records* under "most decadent."

Zelda reached out for his hand as he sat down and squeezed it. "I'm glad you came. I ordered us the usual."

"Does the mayor know you're here?"

"He's out of town this weekend. A sudden last-minute thing."

"Zelda—"

"It's all right. I'm just here to check up on Harlan. He's my friend, too."

Adam raised a skeptical eyebrow but went along for now. "I saw him the other day, at his shop. He looks good. Holding up well."

"I don't understand how anyone could possibly believe he's guilty. You don't, do you?"

"The evidence is circumstantial, but it was enough to charge him."

"But you don't believe it. Tell me you don't."

He looked into her eyes and realized it was as hard to lie to her as always. "I don't. But that doesn't mean I get to play favorites."

"I'm glad you got to see him. Titus doesn't want me to. Says it would look bad."

"For him or for you?"

She reached up to play with her gold double-hooped earrings that jangled when she touched them. "Both. He's also quite upset that woman is still in town. The one involved with the Forsythe scandal. He's afraid she wants to settle down here."

"And that's a bad thing, how?"

"Oh, you know. Appearances. Of the town, its moral fiber."

"He didn't think it was that immoral to associate with the same man who kidnapped me."

"He associates with a wide variety of people. He doesn't do a background check on everyone he meets."

"Maybe he should."

"That woman. . .Beverly, isn't it?"

Adam nodded, knowing full well she knew Beverly's name. After all, she "had coffee" with her the other day. And Adam had the sudden feeling he knew precisely why Zelda wanted to meet him today, which was verified by her next question.

"She's a lovely woman, and you seem to be getting closer to her. But surely you understand she's not right for you?"

"Like you weren't right for me? Or more the reverse—I wasn't right for you."

"Adam, I didn't come here to quarrel. I'm not in the mood for it." She grabbed her napkin as the butternut cider bisque arrived and took a tentative taste of the soup. "As good as always."

He had to agree with her there. He also had to agree he wasn't in the mood for a fight with her. So he kept it apolitical. "Yep. Pretty good."

After a couple more spoonfuls of the soup, she said, "My mother isn't doing well. It's the rheumatoid arthritis acting up again."

"Sorry to hear that. The methotrexate not working anymore?"

"Not as much. The doctors are thinking they'll try biologics. They're genetically engineered proteins."

"Hope it works."

Zelda drew circles in her soup with the spoon. "She tells me all the time what a mistake I made by divorcing you."

"Kalinda said that? Thought she hated me."

"That's what she wanted people to think. Mom had such a rotten childhood, being abandoned at a gas station. She finds it hard to trust anyone, but she did trust you."

"I guess I'm flattered."

They continued eating their soup in silence, Adam struggling for what to say. He was married to the woman sitting across from him for ten years, and yet he couldn't think of anything to talk about. Make that anything "safe" to talk about.

She only ate half her soup then pushed it away. "I overheard something. Something Titus said, and it made me troubled."

He waited expectantly and put his spoon down to focus on her.

"It was his end of a phone conversation, so I'm not sure who he was talking to. But he said he 'hoped this would teach Detective Dutton a lesson and keep him in line.' I can't believe he was behind framing Harlan. But I don't know what he might be talking about."

Adam wracked his brain, trying to think of anything other than Harlan's case that would fill that bill. He knew the mayor wouldn't truly rest until Adam was fired. Or worse.

"I heard him say something about a property bond, Adam. Did you secure Harlan's bail with our house?"

"With *my* house, no. It was Agnes Flamm, a former antiques store owner who's setting up a new wine shop. I guess antiques people stick together in times of need." He wasn't about to add that Agnes was Beverly's friend. "Was there anything else your husband said that's worrying you?"

"Not recently. He mostly talks shop or rants and raves about Vermont's cap on political action committees. The other day I heard him going on and on about some thefts. Minerals, rocks, dirt, something like that."

"Rare earths?"

"You know how I am with science. I flunked chemistry. Twice."

Creighton Querry's case suddenly got more interesting. If Mayor Lehmann was involved somehow, that opened up multiple cans of political and legal worms.

He was still mulling that over when he noticed Zelda's blouse sleeve had pushed up further when she rested her elbow on the table. He grabbed her arm and pulled it closer to him. Her eyes widened as he fingered the needle marks, and she pulled her arm out of his grasp.

"When did you start shooting smack?"

She picked at her earring so violently, it threatened to fall out. "Don't get angry, Adam. I got bored. It's only a phase. I can quit any time."

"Did Lehmann get you into this?"

She didn't reply, but her look toward the windows and away from him spoke volumes. He said, "I should turn him in. I should turn the both of you in."

"But you won't."

Adam rubbed his eyes, trying to quell the desire to speed over to the mayor's house, tie him to a tree and run one of

Harlan's swords through him. Instead, he reached for her hand, gently this time. "I won't turn you in if you'll go to a doctor about this. Get him to prescribe some Suboxone."

"Adam, I—"

"Promise me."

She rubbed along his thumb with her own. "You do still care. I knew you did." Then she looked at him with a watery smile. "I promise."

He relaxed and held onto her hand. Maybe Zelda's mother had a hint of all this. She'd always seemed like the perceptive type. And he knew she was probably right—if Zelda had stayed married to Adam, this likely would never have happened. But Zelda hadn't stayed married to Adam. And now she was hitched to the closest thing to either a non-jailed or non-comatose enemy Adam had.

He wanted to hold her, tell her everything was going to be all right. But they were already in dangerous territory if one of Lehmann's spies reported back to him about this "brunch" of theirs. Adam could take what Lehmann dished out, but the part of him that still did care about Zelda didn't want Lehmann taking out his anger on her.

So he said simply, "Want some cake?"

34

Cray Querry was mostly silent on the ride from Ironwood Junction to Concord, New Hampshire, as Adam filled him in on the case to date. Then Cray turned the tables by filling Adam in on his rare earths case while Adam listened.

As they arrived at a modest-looking house with Georgian architectural roots, Cray said, "So, Beverly Laborde was at your house when that bomb went off?"

Adam gave him a sideways glare. "Don't go there, Cray. It was business-related, okay?"

"Business, right." Cray hauled himself out of the car. "Let's go do some business, shall we? The real kind that is."

They knocked on the door which opened to reveal an elderly man, eighty-ish, with a surprising lack of white hair to go with his facial map of wrinkles. Bill Rotheimer guided them to an old-fashioned den with vintage Queen Anne chairs and antique glass lamps. Adam had a momentary twinge at the sight of the antiques, thinking of Harlan.

Adam thanked Rotheimer for letting them drop by after taking a page from Beverly and introducing Cray as his "assistant." Then he asked, "I hope you don't mind if we ask about your late brother Payton's lawsuit with Wallace Ryall."

The other man's face darkened. "That evil bastard. A frivolous lawsuit, but Ryall pushed it through the courts. Payton fought hard and won eventually, but not before he'd lost a lot more than money."

"I understand his health failed him afterward."

"Health, yes. He became so obsessed, he lost his job with the bank. His wife left him because he couldn't let it go. And she turned the kids against him, too."

"Kids?" Adam couldn't imagine sixty-year-olds being so easily swayed.

Rotheimer explained, "My brother married a much younger woman, Mori, about fortyish. They had a couple of small kids when all this happened."

Adam struck the kids off his list of possible suspects in Wallace's murder, and he'd already learned the wife was in Europe when the murder happened. "Must have been hard on you, too."

"I hated Wallace Ryall. That's why you're here, isn't it? I heard about the murder. You want to know if I did it."

Adam stared at the man. That was direct and to the point. "We need to cover all bases. And hear your thoughts about the victim and any persons who might have wanted him dead."

"The news reports didn't say how he died, but like most of my friends, I've got ail-itosis."

"Ail-itosis?"

"My heart's on the fritz, my kidneys are barely hanging in there, and I've got one new hip and two new knees, all titanium."

Adam had noted the man's shuffling gait when he led them inside. It wasn't impossible he'd be able to run a sword through Ryall but highly unlikely. Not that he couldn't have hired someone else to do it for him.

He started to ask about those friends of his, when Rotheimer added, "And I've got an alibi. That's what you need, right?"

"It certainly helps to know where people are when something violent occurs."

Rotheimer pulled out a piece of paper from a pocket and handed it over. "That's my doctor. I was in the hospital for tests the day Ryall died."

Adam took the paper and smiled. "Thanks, and I hope the results of those tests were in your favor."

"At my age, they're never in your favor. But the doc says I'm good for another year if I live right. Whatever that means. Hardly a day goes by that some study says something you've done all your life is bad. Until the next day, another study says, no, it's good."

"Mr. Rotheimer, your brother's lawsuit involved a business deal, is that correct?"

"That Wallace fellow duped my brother into investing in some pie-in-the-sky project of his. He was a pretty talented woodworker, near as I understand it. Custom skis, or snowboards, or boogie boards, or something. It had to do with that."

"Did any of your brother's friends have any dealings with Wallace Ryall?"

"You mean, did they kill him? Nah, they've all got ail-itosis, too. It was brutal what that lawsuit did to my brother, but people move on, that's how it goes. When you don't know how much time you have left, you tend to want to spend it on family. 'Cause you never if you'll see them again."

That brought an image of Harlan to Adam's mind, and his distress must have shown on his face because Rotheimer added, "Sorry not to be much help, Detective Dutton."

Adam smiled reassuringly. "Every bit of information helps. To rule something in, you have to rule other things out."

After he and Cray had bid the older man farewell, they headed for the car as Cray said, "That man didn't have anything to do with your murder, you know that?"

"He could have hired—"

"No, he couldn't. Or wouldn't. I got instincts, you got instincts, we both know it."

Adam sighed. "Hope springs eternal."

As they drove off, Cray asked, "We going to see my contact next?"

"That's the plan. And thanks for the tip."

"When you told me about your Sergeant Moody, it rang a microscopic bell. Okay, not so microscopic. Former colleague of his is a friend of a friend. Didn't have very many good things to say. Make that no good things to say."

"Which is why this may be the highlight of my week."

Cray laughed. "Just follow my directions, and pick up the tempo, slowpoke. You drive like a little old lady. Actually, I've known little old ladies who drove faster."

Cray had set up the meeting, and when Adam reached their destination, he did a double-take. The term "dive" was a polite way of describing the falling-down wooden structure held up by hope and a prayer and rusty nails. Half a dozen Doberman Pinschers were penned in a caged-in area in the back.

Adam looked at Cray. "You sure this is the place?"

"Yep, come on."

They entered and spied a man about Cray's height sporting a blond buzz cut and a black eyepatch who was working on a '60s-vintage Chevy. He turned to them with a scowl, but at the sight of Cray, he started smiling. "You owe me twenty bucks, Cray."

Cray grabbed his wallet and handed over a twenty. "You cheat at poker, Joey."

Joey McCullock grabbed the bill. "I'm just good. But you won't admit it." He gave Adam a close scrutiny. "Detective Dutton, I assume?"

Adam nodded. "Cray says you know Sergeant Mike Moody?"

Joey snorted. "Knew, as in we were colleagues."

"In the Concord police department."

"That's right. Until he pushed me out."

Adam kept his expression blank but wasn't sure about Cray's tip after that. A man with an axe to grind wasn't the best character witness. "How's that?"

"He's very competitive. Wants to be first in everything. Has aspirations to climb the blue ladder, chief or higher someday. Anyway, he wanted our chief to think he was hot shit, so he planted evidence at a crime scene."

"Drugs?"

"Heroin. The perp was trash, I'll hand you that, but planting evidence is not in my code. When it was found out, Moody blamed me. He's got the connections, I don't."

"Connections as in…"

"He's cousins with your Mayor Lehmann, for one. Was dating a Concord councilman's daughter at the time, too. Me, I'm a poor farmer's kid."

"Ah. You didn't appeal?"

"What good would it do? Although you'd think that with his record, questions would have been asked long before he got this far."

"Record?" Adam looked at Cray, who shrugged.

"Moody was in the army for a while. Discharged dishonorably for fighting and other code violations. Worked in an explosives unit."

"And no one else questioned this planted evidence scheme?"

"A lot of the guys were suspicious. They knew it wasn't like me. Most of 'em were sure it was Moody, but what could they do? They didn't see it happen. Everybody was thrilled when he left, though, that's a fact."

Adam raised an eyebrow at that. He wanted to ask more questions, but Joey said, "Look, I got a work gig in forty-five minutes. Part-time security guard at a warehouse to pay the bills."

Adam took the hint and thanked Joey for his time. When he and Cray were back in the car, he mused, "Was the pipe bomb courtesy of the red-bearded NAL thug Mr. X told me about? Or Sergeant Moody's handiwork?"

Cray snorted. "I'd give 'em fifty-fifty right now."

"That puts me in a dilemma. I should alert the FBI and ATF working the bomb case, but they might think it's sour grapes on my part about Moody. No evidence and all."

"Hold off for a bit. Until you absolutely have to." Cray scratched his chin. "This Mr. X fellow who thinks the Redbeard burglar is the bomber…you said he also thinks Redbeard has ties to the NAL and Reginald Forsythe's goons? I thought Forsythe was in a coma after shooting himself."

"Doesn't mean he can't have an accomplice from his one of his criminal pursuits who's on a vengeance kick, does it?"

"Maybe it'll help to know I'd heard of Ivon Kozak before, the guy Mr. X mentioned as being Redbeard's boss."

"How?"

"You're going to love this. Mike Moody mentioned him to Joey McCulloch once."

Adam stared at him. "Moody? In what context? Why didn't you tell me sooner so I could ask Joey about it?"

Adam started to turn the car around when Cray stopped him. "Wouldn't do any good."

"What do you mean?"

"Because I can tell you verbatim what Moody said. And because Joey doesn't want to talk about Ivan Kozak. He'd clam up. Or toss you out on your ass."

"Cray—"

"Ivan Kozak's a nasty piece of work who has his tentacles into everything. Joey's up for a job with the Nashua PD, and he doesn't want to queer the deal."

Adam uttered an exasperated sigh. "What did Moody say, then?"

"After Moody framed Joey for the planted evidence, Moody told Joey he should walk away. That he was friends with a guy who could make Joey regret it, if he didn't."

"Ivan Kozak."

"The same. Joey wasn't afraid for himself so much as he was his family. So, he walked. Resigned before he could get fired."

"And the Nashua PD aren't aware of the reason for his resignation?"

"It's a small state. Word gets around. Let just say Moody's the one who better watch his back if he tries to return. Or do anything funny."

"I wish Joey the best of luck, then."

"I'll tell him that. He thinks highly of you."

"Me? Why?"

"Your infamy precedes you, Dutton. You're a regular Detective Do-gooder. In the best sense."

"Thanks, I think." Adam sniffed the air. "By the way, I keep getting a whiff of something that smells like fresh compost. Or wet sneakers. You changed colognes recently?"

"My sister's a door-to-door cosmetics rep. I bought some cologne to make her happy. And believe me, you wanna keep Cherry happy. It's called 'Manly Muse.' Like it?"

Adam rolled down the window and used his hands to push the air out. "Try some motor oil or baking soda or something."

Cray laughed. "Now I know you hate it, I'll put on double next time."

"I've got a bunch of clothespins at home. Thanks for the warning."

Dubious cologne aside, Adam was grateful to Cray for looking out for him, especially regarding Sergeant Mike Moody. But what Adam had thought was a simple case of zealous ambition was turning out to be something else altogether. If Moody and Redbeard both had ties to Ivan Kozak and Kozak had ties to Reginald Forsythe—who had painted a bullseye on Adam's forehead—then Cray was right. It was fifty-fifty as to which of the two might behind the bombing at Adam's house. And how did Harlan's case and Ryall's murder fit into all of this?

What was intended as a geographical detour with Cray for a brief Q&A had turned out to be a detour into some pretty dark waters. Adam just had to find the right bridge to get across it all.

35

After dropping Mr. X off at his castle, Beverly headed over to the Apple Peel, a combination cider presser-brewery, gift shop, and cafe. She needed something to bring her down off her adrenaline high. Plus, the place had a small stage with live music like Agnes wanted to add to her wine shop. Beverly didn't think it would hurt to do some scoping out the competition, and besides, Fern Gery had suggested they meet there.

They browsed through the gift side, mostly basket samplers of honey and jam and, of course, cider. Beverly bought some maple fudge for Adam since it was his favorite, and the two women found a table in the luncheonette area. Beverly wasn't hungry at all, but she ordered some of their "world-famous" cider donuts and some coffee.

The entertainment turned out to be too loud and out-of-tune for their tastes, so they hurriedly finished the donuts and headed toward the Maple Kingdom Artisans Gallery. Beverly ignored the "kingdom" part since it brought to mind images of the SCA jousts she'd witnessed yesterday.

This place was much more to her liking. Watercolors, stoneware, wood and metal sculptures, fiber arts, glass. Fern seemed every bit at home as she did. How long had it been since Beverly had done anything friend-ish with a woman other than Agnes?

Fern picked up an iridescent, multi-colored glass bottle. "That would look nice on an end table." She looked at the price tag and put it back. "Too rich for my blood."

Beverly had seen that price tag, and it wasn't as high as she'd expected. In fact, it was very reasonable. Work as a clerk at a florist's shop wasn't enough salary to buy yachts and Picassos, but surely this bottle was within reach? She toyed with the idea of buying it for her but didn't know how she'd react. Mr. X warned her to be less impulsive, so perhaps she should take that to heart.

She asked, "Where do you live? Are there any less expensive home decor stores there?"

"A few miles west of Ironwood Junction. But I don't need much. More things I have to dust."

Beverly sighed. "Guess if I'm going to staying around here, I should look for more permanent housing than the resort."

"You could rent a house for what a few nights at that place costs."

"Can you suggest something?"

"I'm no real estate expert. I'm surprised Adam Dutton hasn't given you some suggestions."

"He's terribly busy."

"And terribly hot. Seriously, I always thought cops were, well. . ." She formed a figure like a beer barrel with her hands. "And bald."

"Definitely neither. But I wasn't kidding about the busy part."

"Is it Wally's murder?"

"Mostly."

"Bruno says I should let it go. But I can't help but wonder if I hadn't broken up with him, he might still be alive."

"The what-if game will drive you crazy."

Fern picked up a stoneware pitcher and peered inside. "If Adam is that busy, he must be getting close to solving the case."

"He's following several leads."

"My money's on Braddon Hopper. He hated Wally. It was like he became obsessed with him. You should have seen the way he looked at Wally. You could see the wheels turning in his head about how he'd get rid of him."

"Did Wally ever say anything to you about a hit-and-run accident?"

"I don't recall everything we talked about. But nothing like that jumps out at me." Fern looked at the price of the pitcher and shook her head before setting it back down.

"Did you ever meet Braddon's girlfriend, Jane Campen?"

"I saw them together. Braddon made sure to steer her away from Wally and me."

"To keep him from becoming interested in her?"

"Jane? She wasn't Wally's type. Too mousy. And a little overweight. And that voice—nasal, like a honking goose."

Fern pointed to a bowl crafted from spalted maple. "This is the color of Adam Dutton's eyes. That's one of the first things I noticed about him."

So had Beverly. Lovely, warm, mocha-brown. "Why, I think you're right," she said as if noticing for the first time. Beverly liked Fern, but this interest in Adam kicked the borders of those feelings around a bit.

She said, "Have you and Bruno set a date?" Meowrrr. She wished she could have retracted it as soon as she said it. She hated catty women.

"After one broken engagement, I'm in no hurry for that. Bruno's nice. But I'm not sure he's The One."

"But no OCD?"

Fern laughed. "Thank god, no. The most 'O-C' he gets is ordering the same toppings on his pizza. Anchovies and olives. He's Italian, after all."

Beverly grimaced. "I guess that's better than living with someone worrying about germs all the time."

"Wally couldn't help it. It's the way he was. No main suspects yet? I have to admit I'm disappointed."

Despite her own frustrations about the pace of the investigation, Beverly felt compelled to defend Adam. "I'm betting on Adam and Detective Jinks."

"Aren't you consulting for the police, too?"

"I worked another angle this morning." Well, Beverly *had* set out her unofficial shingle, hadn't she? Couldn't back down now. "Someone broke into Agnes Framm's wine shop, and I tracked down the thief who'd robbed a similar store recently. But it's not the same guy."

"How does that relate to Wally's case?"

"It probably doesn't."

She focused Fern's attention on a yin-and-yang brass and silver bracelet. "This one is more affordable."

Fern tried it on. "Fits, too." She held her arm up in the air. "And no sliding. That drives me fucking insane." She said it with such force, it took Beverly by surprise. So Fern had a spicy side. Good to know.

That aspect was further deepened when a woman headed into the shop and stopped short when she saw Fern, who mumbled under her breath, "Just what we need." The woman abruptly turned on her heel and headed outside.

Beverly gaped after her and laughed. "Was it something I said? Who was that woman?"

"Nyssa Atkinson. She's married to Wally's former neighbor."

"Ah. Wally and her husband had a feud. Did she blame you?"

"Maybe, maybe not. But I don't trust Nyssa. When Wally and I were dating, I thought Nyssa came on to him. Guess it's not surprising since her husband's a big swinger. Perhaps she is, too."

"A swinger? Hadn't heard that."

"Wally was envious of the guy. But if Nyssa didn't go along with all of that, I should feel sorry for her. At the time, I was pretty upset."

"Did Wally succumb to Nyssa's advances?"

"Oddly enough, he wasn't interested. Or he picked up on some weird vibes from her. You know, takes one to know one. I'm not sure."

"Would she have been upset he rebuffed her advances?"

"She may seem meek and mild, but she has an iron streak when she needs it."

So did Fern, apparently. But then, so did Beverly.

As Fern was paying for her new purchase, Beverly's cellphone rang, and she answered, despite not recognizing the number. "Yes?"

"Miss Laborde? This is Sharon Bogren. We met at the Salt Rock Lodge and Conference Center yesterday."

"You're the secretary there. The one who was interested in antiques."

"Sorry to bother you, but I got some awful news. And I want you to tell Detective Dutton that I don't believe it for a minute."

"Don't believe what, Sharon?"

"It's Braddon Hopper, he's at Dartmouth-Hitchcock Hospital. They're saying it's a suicide attempt. But I know it can't be true. Please tell Detective Dutton I said so."

Beverly listened to Sharon's entreaty, then hung up and made her excuses to Fern that she had to leave. As she raced to the hospital, she wondered if she should call Adam but figured if Sharon knew, Adam knew.

A million thoughts flew through her head as she ran through various possibilities. Whatever the reason for him being in the hospital, Beverly's gut feeling was it had something to do with Harlan's case. And maybe, just maybe, this was the big break they'd hoped for.

36

Adam sat by the hospital bed, listening to the ventilator's whooshing as it forced air into the lungs of the man lying in a green hospital gown. It was eerily similar to what he'd seen at the hospital where Reggie Forsyth lay in his coma, but it hadn't bothered him then. Was it because he took a perverse pleasure in seeing The Monster that way?

But Braddon's prone form, the sounds, the sights, the smells of the pungent antiseptic—it all brought to mind the time it was Adam who was lying here. After a madman kidnapped and tortured him. He took a few deep breaths like his therapist has instructed.

He shook off the darkness as a woman burst into the room and stopped short of the bed. Beverly looked over at Adam. "I got a call from Sharon Bogren."

"The conference center secretary?"

"She says you're calling it suicide. And asked me specifically to tell you that you're wrong."

"Wrong?"

"She and Braddon started dating a few weeks ago. She said he was happier than she'd seen him in, well, since Jane Campen left. And he got the news the SCA board had decided to give the Rapier Marshall slot. That's why she doesn't believe he was suicidal in the least."

Adam held up his cellphone, so she could see the text message, then he read it to her. "Couldn't live with the guilt. I killed Wallace. I am a rabbit coward. Sorry."

"He texted you a confession? And suicide note? That's convenient."

Adam pocketed the phone. "The preliminary blood analysis is monkshood poisoning. The only reason we knew to test for it is the bottle of monkshood tincture in his desk."

"Monkshood? Isn't that the type of poison used in the Middle Ages? Makes it sound like something an SCA person would use."

"Like you said, convenient."

Beverly moved closer to the bed. "How's he doing?"

"They pumped his stomach, gave him activated charcoal, and have him in an induced coma. The doc said it's touch and go, but there are positive signs he'll pull through."

"So, he just tipped up the bottle and drank it?"

"There was a cup of coffee nearby, so it may have been added to it."

"Braddon's 'mud' coffee?"

"Didn't he say it was espresso, the more bitter, the better? With extra shots? Funny thing, that. Monkshood has a bitter, unpleasant taste. Braddon's mud coffee'd be a perfect way to disguise the flavor."

"You think Sharon Bogren is right?"

"Not necessarily. Still, very—"

"Convenient," she finished for him.

"The lab'll run prints on the cup, the bottle, Braddon's cellphone. Not that I'm expecting anything. If this was a murder attempt and not suicide, it was carefully planned. Gloves would be on the checklist."

Beverly gripped the bed rails. "I have to confess I've felt sorry for Braddon. A man with big dreams and big roadblocks."

Adam rubbed his chin. "Too bad it's winter."

She stared at him. "Why?"

"Dr. Vernon Atkinson is an avid gardener. Everything's died off now. Couldn't tell if he grew monkshood or not."

"It could be dried or refrigerated, right?"

"Yep. And Atkinson has a chemistry background."

Adam stood up as he noted a new arrival. The man slowly pushed a walker into the room, dragging his right foot with each step. Adam scanned the man's face and saw that the mouth, eye, and muscles on his right side drooped.

Adam asked, "Mr. Hopper?"

The man looked over at him and nodded. Then Mr. Hopper pushed the walker beside the bed and reached out with his good arm to stroke his son's forehead.

Adam said, "The doctor thinks Braddon's going to be okay. They put him in an induced coma. But that's to give his body time to recover."

When he spoke, the older man's voice was soft and hoarse, and the slurring made it even harder to hear him. "I can't lose him. He's all I've g-g-g-got. He's a good boy. He's such a good b-b-b-boy."

Adam asked, "Mr. Hopper, had Braddon been unusually upset lately? Possibly depressed?"

"There's a lot of . . . p-p-p-pressure. But not worse. Maybe b-b-b-better."

Adam motioned toward a big, oversized recliner in the corner. "Why don't you sit down. You can see him from there."

Adam and Beverly helped him ease into the chair just as a woman around the father's same age entered the room. She moved the walker out of the way and hovered over the older man, speaking soothingly to him. Adam introduced himself and Beverly, and she explained she was the man's sister and Braddon's aunt.

"They're saying this was a suicide attempt, aren't they? Well, they're flat-out wrong. Not Braddon."

"Then, do you know of anyone who'd want to hurt your nephew?"

"Not a fly. Could it be an accident?"

"Unlikely, I'm afraid. Our department is checking everything we can."

"Thank you, Detective. Whichever pond scum lowlife did this deserves a taste of their own poison."

When a doctor and nurse arrived, Adam put a hand on Beverly's shoulder to guide her out of the room. He'd be getting regular updates, anyway. He started to lead the way toward the lobby when Beverly yanked him into a small supply closet and pulled the door closed except for a crack.

He stared at her. "What the—"

She put a finger on his lips and peeked out the crack, then whispered, "Mayor Lehmann's here. Didn't think you'd want to be caught in a pissing contest right now."

"Good thinking." Since he couldn't see through the opening, he had to rely on her observations. Which gave him a brief moment for a few observations of his own. Like how close they were. How soft her body felt against his. How he smelled something sweet on her breath again, this time like summer-fresh raspberries. He also heard the loud thumping of his heart in his chest and wondered if she could, too.

He felt a twinge of disappointment when she whispered, "The coast is clear," then opened the door all the way. If the nurse at the desk down the hall saw them duck into the closet, she wasn't looking in their direction. Or was pretending not to.

He wished he could pretend that all he was thinking about was Braddon or Harlan or cases or justice. He reluctantly followed Beverly toward the lobby and the bright light of day streaming through the tall paned windows.

Once outside the building, Beverly asked, "Jinks have the day off?"

"It's Sunday. She and Felicia were taking their kids skating."

"That means you're in need of a partner. Where do we go next? Wally's neighbor with the potentially deadly garden?"

"We?" he asked.

"My presence might set them more at ease, particularly Nyssa. I should tell you that Fern Gery and I were at the Apple Peel when Nyssa walked inside, saw Fern, and walked out. Fern thinks Nyssa tried to come on to Wally. And may have blamed Fern for some of the bad blood between him and her husband."

"She might transfer that dislike to you. If she remembers you from the shop."

"I could do something about that. If you'll let me."

"Beverly…"

"She didn't see me for long. Only a wig. I promise."

Adam sighed. "If it's just the one time, and I'm there with you. That blond wig you used when you came charging to my rescue three months ago was pretty fetching." He hastened to add, "If you like that sort of thing."

She grinned at him. "Blonds have more fun, right? Lead on, partner."

37

It took more arguing on her part, but Beverly eventually won Adam over. So, now-blonde Beverly and Adam were standing in Professor Vernon Atkinson's living room, which was currently a mess. The furniture heaped in the middle and covered in plastic tarps looked like a haunted-house prop, and more tarps covered the floors. Atkinson welcomed them in with a speck of paint on his nose and a roller brush in hand.

"Nyssa's hated that yellow color for years, haven't you, dear?" His wife, wielding a paintbrush in the corners, nodded silently.

Beverly looked at the walls with the new coat of paint. "That's a lovely shade of maroon."

"Cranberry," Atkinson said, pointing to the can. "We should all be wearing face masks and air filters, considering what they put in this."

Beverly walked over toward Nyssa to study the color more closely. "You have more patience than I do. I'd happily hire someone to do it."

Atkinson said, "But we love home improvement projects, don't we, dear?"

Nyssa pasted on a smile. She did give a quick side glance over at Beverly before returning to her brushwork.

Adam pulled out his small notebook as he asked Atkinson, "Do you know a man named Braddon Hopper?"

Atkinson stood back from the wall to examine his progress. "If he was a former student, I might remember his face. So many students come and go."

Adam pulled out a photo and handed it over. The other man peered at it, then shook his head. Adam asked, "You didn't see this man over at Wallace Ryall's place?"

"Despite our tiffs, Detective, I didn't stay glued to the window with a video camera watching everything that man did twenty-four-seven. Or people coming and going."

"You said before you didn't see any women there except for his ex, Fern Gery."

"He didn't have wild parties if that's what you mean. Although he and Fern got into it now and then."

"Arguing?"

"Typical engaged-couple nonsense."

Nyssa had a pained expression on her face but kept painting. Just what did her husband consider a "typical" argument? The toilet-roll, toothpaste-tube kind, or something more violent? Beverly would love to know the answer to that one.

Atkinson added, "I believe Wallace got Fern on the rebound after her ex-husband ran off with some floozy. So there was a reason, eh? This woman was hard to get along with, hence the arguments."

Adam asked, "You're an avid gardener, isn't that right?"

"Avid, but not fanatical. I'm not like those people who go to rose shows or build greenhouses for their precious, pampered orchids."

"What do you grow, mostly?"

"Organic herbs and vegetables. Things my wife can use in her cooking. We dry many of them. Beats all those store-bought brands with their MSG, or synthetic anti-caking agents, or concentrated toxic pesticides."

"Speaking of toxic, you haven't noticed any unusual weeds growing in your yard? Things like white snakeroot, belladonna, wolfsbane?"

"Funny thing about poisonous plants, they're often very lovely. Belladonna bushes are often grown for their beautiful drooping, bell-shaped blue or red flowers. And wolfsbane has these lovely purple clusters."

"But you haven't grown any?"

"Not intentionally. I use organic herbicides to keep most weeds like that at bay. To avoid any cross-contamination from seeds of such plants with my herbs."

"Are you aware of any specific gardeners who might be cultivating them?"

"No, and they'd better not have any pets if they do. It only takes a tiny bit to kill an animal. I certainly wouldn't want Muttley getting into them."

Atkinson put down his roller brush and frowned. "Are you hinting that the poison used on my dog was something like wolfsbane?" He mumbled to himself. "Never saw it in Ryall's yard."

Beverly wanted to try to get Nyssa alone since it was clear her husband was the controlling type, at least with other people around. Should she ask for some water as an excuse to follow Nyssa into the kitchen and get her alone? No, Atkinson would likely barge ahead and go get it himself.

Adam snapped the notebook shut and put it back in his pocket. "That's all for now, Professor. Don't want to interrupt your painting any further."

Beverly smiled at Nyssa on her way out and gave a quick look back as she and Adam let themselves out. "Dr. Atkinson appears pretty cheerful, but his wife is one sad, depressed woman. I guess it takes one to know one."

Adam raised an eyebrow. "You don't seem like someone who gets depressed. More the active, take-charge type."

"In my former life."

He didn't press her on it, and she was grateful. He looked at his shoes, one of which was now sporting a smear of cranberry paint, which prompted Beverly to say, "I guess we'll have to accessorize your wardrobe to match. We can start with a cranberry tie, add in some cranberry cufflinks. Plus, a cranberry pocket-handkerchief."

"I loathe cranberry."

"The fruit or the color?"

"Both." He held up his foot and wiggled it as if he could make the paint go away.

"You don't think Atkinson grew the wolfsbane and planted that bottle in Braddon's desk?"

"If he did grow it, he's already got rid of the evidence. Makes me wonder if his dog got poisoned accidentally by his master's own stash."

"Poor little guy. Regardless of who did it, it was a horrible thing to do." She sighed. "Grammie was allergic to dogs. Still, every Christmas I used to dream there'd be a Golden Retriever puppy under the tree."

"Guess it's hard to have a pet if you move around often." He paused for a moment. "Looked for places here, yet?"

"Haven't had time. What with Harlan's case and Agnes's shop." Once again, her excuses rang hollow to her, and she knew they would to Adam, too. She blurted out, "Maybe you could recommend a real estate agent?"

A slow smile spread across his face. "I could do that." He started whistling "Little cabin in the woods," and she joined in. She wasn't going to tell him about her visit to "his" cabin, not yet. She was still too skittish to feel ready to settle down, but she could play the pretend game, couldn't she?

Adam got a call on his cell, and from his end of the conversation, Beverly knew it was Jinks, excited about something. When he hung up, he relayed to Beverly, "The fingerprints and DNA from the root beer bottle you rescued from the park ranger did the trick. They match Jinks's sexual assault case. The woman picked him out of a lineup, and now our park ranger is in jail."

"That's wonderful, for Jinks and her victim. Doest his help Harlan, too?"

"Time will tell. I need to hurry back to the office to help Jinks interrogate 'His Excellency.' Hopefully, I'll learn more then."

38

After Adam dropped Beverly off at Agnes's shop, Beverly was pleased to see no trace whatsoever of the damage from the vandals. The older woman joined Beverly in admiring the place. "Sorry Detective Dutton couldn't be here. I wanted to thank him."

"For what?"

Just then, a box on two legs walked in from the rear of the store, or so it appeared. Two arms gently laid the box next to the cash register, revealing the bearer to be none other than Blaine Morland. "I've got a few more of these to catalog, Miss Flamm. That should be the lot, I think."

"Thank you, Blaine. It would have taken me two days to do all that." She pointed to her face. "Aging eyes."

The boy headed back to his task in the other room while Agnes beamed at Beverly. "That's what I want to thank Adam for. He got Blaine released into his custody, although it's more of a supervisory thing. Blaine lives with his aunt, but she has to work. It's so hard on her."

Yes, Beverly knew that quite well from her social-worker ruse. "Why not his father?"

"His father works two jobs. Doesn't have extra time to spend with his son. Truth be told, I'm not sure he cared one way or the other about the whole arrest business. He's a bit heavy with the bottle."

"So, this is community service in lieu of jail time?"

"No jail time's forthcoming. Lack of evidence, you see. For Blaine, that is. The other two were caught with stolen items on their person and at their homes. But don't think this is slave labor, either. I'm paying him."

Beverly lowered her voice. "How's he doing so far?"

"He was a tad surly at first. To be expected. But he's really quite handy. I think I won him over with my famous chocolate-pecan pie."

Beverly looked at Agnes in mock indignation. "You have a famous chocolate-pecan pie? And why was I never told this?"

Agnes laughed. "You can have some any time. I'm thinking of adding it to the cafe menu when it gets going."

"Are you still thinking you might open the store this week?"

"Saturday. If all goes according to plan. Took that idea you had about advertising in the *Junction Jive* with a coupon and ran with it. Twenty-five percent off any item."

Agnes's phone rang, and while she answered it, Beverly wandered back to the room where Blaine was working. She introduced herself, then took in his tousled hair, which was in desperate need of a comb. But his jeans were clean, sneakers neat, and he had on a gray mock turtleneck that matched his eyes.

She complimented him on the sweater, then added, "I appreciate you helping Agnes out. It's tough starting a new business, but she's excited about making it work. It's like having a second chance for her." Beverly doubted he would get the double entendre, but hoped it might sink in later.

He looked up from the notes he was making from the items of the box on the table. It was one of the same boxes Adam said were part of Harlan's donation.

He said, "My aunt bought it for me. The sweater."

"She has good taste." Beverly pointed to an item from the box. "Know what that is?"

"Looks like a wooden shoe. With palm trees and huts carved in it."

"It's a wine bottle holder. See the hole in the middle?" She pointed to another item. "That one is a vintage French silver-plated wine champagne bottle combination holder and pourer."

"People really use all this stuff?"

It hit Beverly hard, thinking about Blaine's absentee father, whose idea of drinking was tipping back a bottle and guzzling it down whole. The boy had likely never seen a fancy table spread. Most of the items in this shop would be foreign to him, making him a rockfish out of water.

She replied, "Sometimes. People use them mostly for special occasions."

He pulled out another item. "And this one?"

"A silver wine funnel. The curved spout directs wine down the side of a decanter to prevent it from dropping straight to the base. It also helps to remove impurities and sediments from the wine."

"Are they worth a lot of money?"

Her heart skipped a beat, thinking he was trying to gauge how much money he'd get for them if they "went missing." But when she said, "That might fetch a few hundred dollars," he wrote it down in the notes section on his list with the reply, "I hope she sells that one, then."

Warming up to his task, he started peppering her with questions about each item as he rescued it from the box, carefully jotting down the details in the ledger. "How did you learn all of this, Miss Laborde?"

"My grandmother ran an antiques store. I learned most everything I know from her."

"Is she going to be here on Saturday for the big opening?"

Beverly swallowed hard. "She died a few years ago. But I have a feeling she'll be here in spirit."

"My aunt likes things like this. Maybe I'll get her to come."

Beverly felt increasingly simpatico with the young man, seeing the parallels between them. The sense of being cast away, the feeling of isolation, having to fend for yourself, choosing risky behavior. Stubborn, independent, yet yearning for something stable.

She hoped Agnes and Adam were doing the right thing by trusting this boy, giving him that second chance. So many throwaway people—Blaine, Braddon's ex-girlfriend Jane, Vernon Atkinson's treatment of his wife and all his conquests, Fern's ex-husband running off with "some floozy."

All the little battles and little wars in all the households around the world—too often, they boiled over into violence. Like Reggie Forsyth killing his father. Or a sword pinning a man's body to a tree.

39

Monday, December 10

Adam woke up with a headache, something that didn't get any better after getting a call from Creighton Querry. Not that Adam minded getting up at the crack of dawn, but four-thirty was a touch early, even by his standards. The early hour was necessary if they wanted to meet with someone who said he was too busy to talk except from six to six-thirty.

So here Adam was, standing on a chilly concrete floor staring up at a bright yellow gantry with large hollow metal tubes hanging below. His "handler" pointed out parts in various stages of assembly, from giant fiberglass blades to nacelles to heat exchangers. Men and women in hard hats scurried from one station to another.

Catching sight of Cray, Adam waved him over, and their guide escorted them to the main offices, specifically the office for co-owner, Kirk Joffe. The man motioned for them to sit, adding, "Sorry for the early hours, but we're swamped right now. Working 'round the clock. My calendar is divided into fifteen-minute slots."

Adam said, "This is an impressive plant you have here. Wind turbine components must be in high demand."

"They are. We were the first company to manufacture these parts in the Northeast. Unfortunately, we're no longer the only company. Competition is cut-throat."

Adam pulled out his notebook to make sure he got the terms right. "You use dysprosium and neodymium in your plant, is that right?"

"They're crucial. And the Chinese control almost the entire market. When a shipment goes missing, it's huge. We need those rare earths to stay afloat. Without them, we'd go bankrupt. The bigger companies have more leverage, so they're first in line for anything else. This supplier was our last hope."

Cray butted in, "Why did you choose this particular supplier?"

"They had a more reasonable price. And willing to deal with small potatoes like us."

Adam asked, "Mr. Joffe, I'd also like to ask you about how your business got started. Your wife is your partner, I believe. But she's not your first wife, is that correct?"

Joffe leaned back in his chair. "If this is headed where I think it is, I want you to know I'm not proud of the way I handled the breakup of my marriage, running off with Jenny like that. But I'm much happier now. It was the best thing for me. Fern was controlling, micromanaging, jealous, suspicious— well, that part came true. But maybe what I did was a self-fulfilling prophecy."

"By Fern, you mean Fern Gery?" Adam owed Cray for finding out that bit of news.

"Yeah."

"How acrimonious was the divorce?"

"My wife, Jenny, well she was my girlfriend at the time, was afraid for her life. *I* was afraid for my life. Fern left dead rats in my car, my wife got a package with a bloody cow's heart, and more. She was clever, though. Nothing that could ever trace the harassment to her. On the surface, she was all gracious and polite in the court proceedings. But as you watched her, you see the wheels turning in her head as she schemed."

If she was everything Joffe said, then Fern was indeed a good actress, for Adam hadn't suspected anything of the kind in talking with her. Nor had Beverly—someone used to disguises and playing roles to fool other people. "Mr. Joffe, do you think she could have had anything to do with the missing rare-earths shipment?"

"I hadn't heard anything from her for a couple of years and thought her vendetta had faded away. She doesn't have much money. Not enough to buy off the supplier or pay someone else to steal the shipment. And she's smart, but not that smart. I can't see her being able to pull something like this off."

A floor supervisor skidded into the office and shouted something about a computer malfunction before ducking back out. Joffe sighed and rose to his feet. "Sorry I can't chat with you more, Detective Dutton, Mr. Querry."

"We understand, sir. If we have more questions, we'll give you a call."

"If it's all the same to you, I'd rather the next phone call be good news about finding that shipment."

The same handler led Adam and Cray through the labyrinth and back outside, where Cray scanned the front of the building and the sign that read, "Windfall Manufacturing." He said, "Wind-FAIL is more like it. Or will be soon."

Adam's guide had told him the plant employed close to fifty people, not huge by most manufacturer standards. But jobs weren't all that plentiful in this part of Vermont. Those people and their families would suffer mightily if the plant went bankrupt.

He said, "On the phone, you said you had a very good reason for believing Fern Gery may have some knowledge of this rare-earths theft. But even her ex doesn't think she's capable of it."

"I didn't say she did it, now did I?"

"No need to be cranky, bar-boy. So what's her connection?"

"I ran down a petty thug who specializes in low-level crimes. In and out of jail, doing whatever dicey gig he can find in between. He stays under the radar, leaving the big plays to other people willing to take the risk. But his checkered history means he's developed an address book filled with lowlifes. Said he 'thought' he mighta heard about a guy with a loose tongue."

"And this 'loose tongue' likes to lap up rare dirt, I take it?"

"So he said. Or my contact said. Second-hand tips, you know."

"You got a name for Mr. Loose Lips?"

"Bruno Giacometti. He's—"

"Fern Gery's new boyfriend." Adam recalled how Fern had smiling referred to him as her "Italian Stallion." He was their new dark horse.

"You met him, Adam?"

"No, but I think I need to. You got an address?"

"Lives in a trailer park not too far from here. The one behind the old burned-out mill. On Larson Lane."

"You up for a nice chat with this guy?"

Cray grinned. "Sure. We can stop and pick up some cupcakes with pink icing and some tea."

Adam rolled his eyes, and Cray said, "Should get some for us, then. I need energy for a rumble. And I have a feeling this tête-à-tête may end badly. By which I mean well."

"How would your mysterious client feel about all of this?"

"He's paying me for results. Any way I have to get 'em."

"I should get back-up."

"Nah, it'll make him more suspicious. We can take him."

Adam agreed, somewhat against his better judgment. But Jinks was in the middle of her usual hectic morning rush of getting the kids to school and herself to work. And it was just a "friendly" little chat, minus cupcakes, to find out what this Giacometti character knew or didn't about Clay's case. Or even Harlan's.

Since Clay knew the way, Adam let him take the lead in his car, with Adam following behind. He half-hoped they had success, half-hoped they didn't. If Fern Gery were tied into this, it would be a blow to Beverly. Almost everyone she'd ever formed an attachment to had died or disappointed her. He wanted to protect her from that kind of pain, not add to it.

40

Beverly woke up early, after having dreams of confronting a ghost in a field of red flowers. She tumbled out of bed toward the shower, wondering what had prompted that bit of nocturnal theater. Ghosts from her past haunting her subconscious? Reliving the very real nightmare of her villainous uncle shooting himself?

Then she realized the ghost was a sad-faced woman with olive skin who looked a lot like Nyssa Atkinson. The red flowers must be taken from the new paint in their living room.

She'd obsessed about Nyssa after her visit to the Atkinson home with Adam. That woman was hiding something but wasn't about to speak up with her husband around. Or any man, especially a police detective.

It was Monday, so the Professor would be in classes, wouldn't he? With her post-shower hair in a towel, Beverly munched on a room-service breakfast sandwich and checked out the college website on her laptop. Atkinson had a class at ten. Perfect.

Beverly hadn't paid attention to the garden behind the Atkinson's house on her first visit. Dormant, brown stubs of plants and layers of straw mulch filled the planters. Not much to look at now. Was there purple monkshood next to the strawberries and basil when the yard was in full summer bloom?

She briefly debated about sneaking around looking for a shed or peering into any basement windows looking for dried purple flowers. That would have to wait for Adam. All official and logged into evidence.

Beverly hopped in her rental car and headed for the address, wearing the blond wig again. Nyssa Atkinson was surprised to see her but didn't turn her away. She graciously invited Beverly in, offering her some homemade herbal tea. "That's a mix of violet flowers, chamomile flowers, dandelion petals, and calendula petals."

Beverly took a sip. Surprisingly good, if a touch odd. She looked around. The wall painting was finished, everything back in its place. It was every bit as red as the flowers in her dream. Blood red.

On the way over, she'd tried to decide what question to open with, and the Atkinson's former neighbor seemed a safe bet. "It must have been frightening to have such an unpredictable man next door. Wondering what he might do next."

A cute, fluffy dog wandered into the room, and Nyssa called out to him. "This is Muttley, a Golden Retriever, Corgi mix."

"That's the dog who was poisoned?"

"Fortunately, he hadn't eaten much of whatever it was. He'll eat anything, won't you, boy?" She reached down to stroke his head. "I don't know what I'd do without him. He's both family and my best friend."

"Since you and your husband both suspect Wallace of poisoning Muttley, I'm surprised your husband wanted anything to do with Wallace's brother, Ramsay. Seems like he'd rather make friends with a snake."

"I have no idea why. They're so unalike. But my husband's ways are pretty mysterious." Nyssa took a sip of tea, lost in thought.

Beverly wasn't sure how to broach the subject, but sometimes direct was the best. "I understand you have an open marriage. That must be. . .interesting. Very Bohemian."

The other woman put her tea cup down on a table next to her chair and squeezed her hands together in her lap. "Interesting? More like devastating."

"It wasn't your idea?"

"My husband can get very loud and forceful and doesn't take no for an answer. He kept badgering me about this 'experiment,' saying it would save our marriage. I finally gave in."

"Did your husband or Wally ever assault you?"

"Vernon is too aloof with me for that. Wally scared me once when he was drunk, and my husband wasn't home."

"How so?"

"Threw himself on me, but I managed to get away. And he'd also say sexually suggestive things from time to time. I never told my husband for fear of what he would do. I mean, he was already upset with Wally."

Beverly thought back to what Fern had told her—that the reason Nyssa turned around on seeing Fern at the Apple Peel was because Nyssa was the one who'd come on to Wally. So who was telling the truth? "If you're unhappy in your marriage, could you try some counseling?"

"Vernon would never go. I could go on my own, but what good would that do?"

"Well, maybe get a job, then, something outside the home?"

"I haven't worked since the year before we got married. Ten years without a job or experience or references. Who would want me?"

Perhaps sensing his owner's distress, Muttley jumped up on her lap and licked Nyssa's chin. "At least I have good ole Muttley."

"Do you think Wallace Ryall poisoned Muttley?"

"I don't know what to think anymore. But since you asked, it bothers me very much Vernon is friends with Ramsay Ryall."

"It's bound to be awkward for you."

"It's not just that. I overheard a conversation between Ramsay and Vernon. About Ramsay's father's collection and how he used to lord it over his son. That the father had something valuable Ramsay would never get his hands on."

"Something valuable? Like what?"

"I didn't get that part. But when I first heard about Wallace's murder, guess I jumped to the conclusion Ramsay killed Wallace after he'd inherited this valuable whatever and stole it from him."

She muttered, "Maybe with help."

Beverly's ears perked up. "With help?"

Nyssa hugged Muttley to her. "Why else would my husband suddenly be friends with the man?"

"You really think your husband helped Ramsay commit murder?"

"In my undergrad days, I majored in psychology. You'd think after all that, I would have noticed I was dating a man with Narcissistic Personality Disorder."

Beverly had taken some psych classes herself. Vernon Atkinson certainly fit the narcissism profile. Excessively vain, check. Lacking in empathy, check. Obsessed with prestige, check. "If your husband and Wallace did steal this item, whatever it is, perhaps they've sold it. Has your husband been spending more lately?"

"If anything, he's spent less. We hardly ever go out anymore. Not even to restaurants. But I guess in an 'open marriage,' he takes whoever out whenever. I'm one of many."

Beverly finished her tea, noticing it had a somewhat bitter aftertaste. "You know, Nyssa, I've been staying at the Apple Valley Resort. There's a job opening waiting tables in the tea room. Not very lucrative, but it would be something. I could put in a good word for you."

Nyssa's expression grew thoughtful, and then she sat up a straighter, making Muttley reach up to lick her face again. "That's such a lovely place. And it would be a change from these dull four walls. But we only have the one car, and I'm afraid my husband would say no."

"I would say no to what, dear?" Vernon walked in from the kitchen. Beverly looked at her watch. She and Nyssa had talked for an hour, and Vernon's class must be over.

Nyssa patted Muttley and put him on the floor. "Oh, trying out that new Italian restaurant in Woodstock."

He sniffed. "You know how I hate pasta. It'd be a waste of money."

Beverly stood up, thinking she didn't want to be here in the middle of these two, then noticed Vernon was giving her a thorough once over. "You were here with Detective Dutton, weren't you? You're a lovely creature. I haven't seen you around before. If you're new to town, I could give you the grand tour."

"That won't be necessary. I'm not new to town, and I hate tours. Too overbearing and dull." Beverly winked at Nyssa and hurried to her car, away from the clouds of unhappiness inside and into the gray clouds of the winter day.

"Arrogant prick," she said to herself.

Eager to tell Adam about this "valuable item" Nyssa had mentioned, she dialed Adam on her phone. But all she got was his voice mail, which made her worried. Was he in an interview and couldn't be interrupted? Or perhaps he and Jinks were on the road, and he was driving?

She continued to fret, imagining all the various possibilities, some not so pleasant. Where the hell was he and what was he up to? This must be what Zelda had experienced as a cop's wife, right? Every day he went to work, he might come home...or not. Although Beverly didn't want to admit it to herself, she had a sudden moment of sympathy for Zelda Lehmann.

41

Adam and Cray stood outside their cars, looking down the road at the mobile home. In better shape than similar homes they'd driven past but not a candidate for Palace of the Year. The siding was more grayish than the original white, and the maroon shutters hadn't seen a new coating of paint in years. Adam had the fleeting thought the occupant should ask Vernon Atkinson for some of that leftover cranberry paint.

"You like cranberry?" He asked Cray.

"The fruit?"

"And the color."

"Can take or leave either. You thinkin' of getting into interior decorating, Dutton?" Cray unzipped his jacket revealing his gun holster.

"Just asking." The blinds on the unit were shut, and Adam didn't see any fingers lifting up the slats as they approached. He led the way up the three stairs to the tiny front deck and rapped on the door.

The man who answered the door looked like he could be Italian. Olive complexion, black hair swept back with a healthy dose of hair gel, pencil mustache, and a "soul patch" goatee. He also wore a leather necklace with small silver metal beads—suspiciously like the silver circle Adam had found in the woods at the crime scene.

Adam asked, "Bruno Giacometti?"

The man licked his lips. "Yeah. Who's asking?"

"My name is Dutton. Detective Adam Dutton. I want to ask you about a shipment of minerals that—"

He didn't have a chance to finish his sentence before Giacometti slammed the door in their faces. Cray said, "Well, now, that's downright rude. Too bad we're past the days of battering rams."

Just then, they heard the sound of a door being slammed in the rear of the trailer. Cray took out after Giacometti, with Adam following through the woods. Their quarry didn't look like a star athlete, but he set a fast pace. Cray was falling behind, and Adam made a note to tease him about his cheeseburger diet later.

Adam was gaining on the guy. He kept an eye on flashes of the guy's blue shirt as they hurdled over fallen tree stumps and zigzagged around tall pines and shorter barberry shrubs. When he recognized a tree they'd passed, with two knothole-eyes and a mouth-like opening that made it look like a screaming face, Adam suspected Giacometti was doubling back toward the mobile home.

Sure enough, Giacometti headed straight to his truck in the driveway. But when he fumbled in his pocket for his keys, Adam saw his chance. He lunged at the other man's legs and tripped him to the ground.

Cray got there seconds later, picked up the prone man as if he were a mere sack of potatoes, and put him in a headlock. He waited for Adam to cuff Giacometti and stuff him into Adam's car.

"Now see, Dutton, here's what I don't get. This fellow here could have saved himself a trip down to your lovely little police station by answering a few questions. Or maybe he's training for a marathon."

Giacometti scowled at both of them.

Adam headed back to the station with Cray's car following behind. As they stopped at a red light, Adam turned around to face his "guest" and said, "You're looking at some potentially serious charges. Grand larceny, evading, resisting arrest, murder."

"Murder? The guy ain't dead. He's in the hospital."

"I was referring to Wallace Ryall. Who is very much dead."

Giacometti clammed up after that, and they rode the rest of the way in silence.

§ § §

After leaving their catch to stew in a cell, Adam and Cray met with the chief to fill him in, with Cray promising to write up as much as he knew and felt he was able to tell. He wouldn't budge on his "mystery client," however. Adam could tell Chief Quinn considered throwing him into a holding cell along with Giacometti. But Adam had a good idea who the client was and raised an eyebrow at the chief as a signal, so Quinn relented.

Adam had hoped the time it took for the meeting, plus getting Cray's details, plus filling in Jinks, would make Giacometti ready to sing. Instead, the "Italian Stallion" took the opportunity to call an attorney. Or try to call an attorney.

The sergeant watching him through a glass partition said the first two calls didn't end very well, with the accused pleading and cajoling to no avail. According to the sergeant, Giacometti's mumblings afterward revealed he'd contacted lawyers who knew him well enough to tell him to take a hike.

Meanwhile, Adam discovered Giacometti had a rap sheet—fraud, theft, drug possession. Plus, his name was fake, and he wasn't Italian at all. He was really Bruno Smith.

Adam had Smith/Giacometti brought to the interview room where the first words out of the guy's mouth were "I want a lawyer. I know my rights."

Adam nodded. "You'll get one." He waited without saying anything else for several minutes, continuing to stare at the other man, which made the guy start to fidget.

"You can't pin anything on me. Not larceny or murder. You ain't got nothing."

"We'll see what your partner has to say about that."

"Partner?" Giacometti stopped fidgeting.

"She's been quite helpful."

"You're nuts. She wouldn't—" He bit his lip, then slipped down in his seat.

The door opened, and Jinks breezed in, a paper in hand. She handed it to Adam, then stood in a corner, putting on her very best "don't mess with me" look.

Adam read it and looked up at Giacometti. "Seems we got a partial fingerprint on the poisoned coffee cup that put Braddon Hopper in the hospital. Surprise, surprise, it's yours."

"You're making it all up. You cops always make it up. Get your jollies sending innocent people to prison."

"Be a shame if you go to prison, but your partner goes scot-free."

Their prisoner muttered. "I ain't no rabbit coward."

Adam gave him a sharp look. "Funny you should say that. Not a common phrase. Yet, it was on the alleged 'suicide' note sent to me on my cellphone."

He snorted. "So what? That the best you got?"

Jinks spoke up. "I looked that phrase up yesterday. *Un coniglio* is popular Italian slang for coward. And *coniglio* means 'rabbit.'"

Adam smiled, "Giacometti—that's Italian, right? Even if it's fake Italian?" The other man gave him a middle-fingered 'salute.'

"Come now, Mr. Giacometti. We're one big melting-pot happy family here, right Jinks?"

She grinned, and Adam asked her, "Jinks, remind me again. What's the difference in typical sentences between larceny, attempted murder, and murder? I keep forgetting."

"Grand larceny and attempted murder might get you eight to ten. Murder, well, that's life right there."

Seeing Giacometti's stoic expression and arms wrapped across his chest, Adam shrugged. "Guess we're done here, then. Be seeing you in court, pal."

Adam and Jinks got up to leave and had almost closed the door when Giacometti called out after them. When they ducked their heads in, he said, "That state's evidence thing. That'll reduce a sentence, right?"

Adam looked at Jinks, they walked back inside, and this time, their canary started to sing.

42

Beverly really should put an end to her habit of following Adam. She really should. Worried when she couldn't get him to reply to her texts or calls, she drove by the station in time to see him and two other men heading inside.

One of the two was a large man, the same fellow she'd seen Adam with at the Ironwood Pub & Brewery, while the other fellow was in handcuffs. A prisoner? The real murderer of Wallace Ryall?

Although her heart rejoiced at the thought, she didn't recognize the guy. Dark hair, European-looking, like he hopped out of a travel poster for Greece or maybe Rome. Rome? As in Italian Stallion?

Beverly parked her car in front of the police station and slipped into the lobby. She knew the receptionist by sight and strolled over to her, with a smile. "Good morning, Arline. Looks like Detective Dutton's been busy, and it's not yet noon."

Arline smiled. "That's Adam for you."

"Well, I'm glad he found his man. Have they processed Bruno Giacometti yet?"

Arline pulled up her computer screen and flipped through the records. "Preliminary only."

"The turtle tracks of justice. Slower than watching paint dry."

"Sometimes, watching paint is more fun." Arline picked up a notepad. "Should I let Adam know you're here?"

Beverly smiled. "Seeing as he's busy right now, I don't think I should bother him. I had some information for him, but it can wait."

"Suit yourself. He'll likely be tied up with questioning for some time."

With her suspicions regarding the identity of Adam's prisoner confirmed by Arline, Beverly returned to her car. She opened a suitcase in the trunk and stared at the wigs and makeup she still kept stashed there. Should she try the blond wig? With the brown contacts and cheek prosthetics?

With a shake of her head, she closed both suitcase and trunk. She'd promised Adam. Besides, Beverly didn't need a disguise with Fern, who was as much a victim as Jane Campen or Nyssa Atkinson—women used by men like sacrificial pawns in a game of sexual chess.

When Beverly called the florist shop, she learned Fern had left early, and Beverly got directions from the colleague to Fern's house. Only it didn't turn out to be a house so much as a small trailer on the outskirts of Ironwood Junction.

It appeared Fern's fortunes had taken a turn for the worse since her divorce. Or even since her breakup with Wallace Ryall. But if Bruno Giacometti was the type of man she'd turned to, he wasn't going to help her situation any.

Fern seemed surprised to see Beverly, but not as embarrassed as Beverly had feared. When Beverly told her about Giacometti's arrest, Fern rubbed her forehead and sighed. "I was afraid this was going to happen. I should never have trusted him."

"I'm sorry, Fern. I know you hoped he'd be a better catch than Wallace."

"My taste in men is only slightly better than my taste in housing," Fern waved her hand around the bare interior. "I suppose I should go and talk to him."

She looked hopefully at Beverly. "Could we take your car? Mine had a wobble when I got home last night. Think I might need a new tire, and I don't have the energy to change it."

Beverly agreed, and they started out on the road to town. But they'd only gone a half-mile when Fern looked in the side mirror and said, "Uh oh."

Beverly looked in her rear-view and spied a black pickup truck following them. She couldn't make out the man's face clearly, but one thing was impossible to miss—his red beard.

Beverly said, "What the hell is he doing here? He's the man who bombed Adam's house."

"We can get rid of him." Fern pointed to a fork in the road ahead and told Beverly to take a right turn. Beverly didn't know this area at all, so she let Fern direct her around several unmarked twists and dirt roads, packed hard from the recent snow. Fern directed her to a small clearing and had her pull behind an outcropping of rocks and park.

Fern slid out of the car and disappeared around the rocks. When she didn't return after a couple of minutes, Beverly grabbed her cellphone, called up the contacts, and punched a familiar number. Then, she slipped her cellphone into her pants pocket and rescued her purse with the gun hidden inside, which she slung diagonally over her shoulder.

Not seeing either Fern or Redbeard, Beverly started to head back to the car when a pair of strong arms grabbed her from behind. With her arms pinned to her sides, she couldn't reach into her purse. No purse, no gun.

She cried out, "What did you do with Fern?"

Then a feminine voice replied, "I'm right here, Beverly. I'm terribly sorry about this little charade. But circumstances have made it necessary to have a bargaining chip."

"Bargaining chip? I don't understand."

Fern walked in front of Beverly to face her. "That idiot Bruno. Got himself caught. I knew we shouldn't have brought him in." She nodded at the man holding Beverly. "Beverly, meet Darnell Warner. My original partner-in-crime. Or should I say grime? Minerals can get rather dirty."

The wheels in Beverly's head were spinning so fast, it made her head hurt. But she needed to stay focused, to record everything she could for when she got out of this. And she knew that somehow, some way, she would get out of this.

"Minerals? You must mean those rare earths Adam talked about. You're the rare-earths thief? But why?"

Fern replied, "My darling ex-husband, Kirk Joffe, ran off with his little bitch while we were still married. He had a dream of starting his own windmill manufacturing business. So he took everything in our savings and all our property and left me penniless. But he's about as good a businessman as he is a husband. His company is on the verge of bankruptcy. He needs those shipments of rare earth minerals to produce his wind turbines."

"You stole the shipment to push his company over the edge?"

"And it's working. Of course, we'll sell the minerals ourselves and make a tidy profit. A win-win."

"Where do I fit in to all of this? The bargaining chip?"

"Detective Dutton is very good, isn't he? Even if Bruno-the-weak doesn't say anything, Dutton will be able to trace the line back to me. And our sexy detective seems to have formed an attachment to you. We need to buy time to get over the Canadian border."

Beverly stared at her. "That's your plan? You do a lot of off-the-cuff crime. I'll bet you're behind the robbery at Agnes Flamm's shop."

"Didn't you wonder why I hooked up with mousy little Wallace?"

"You said he was loving and supportive, a kind man, misunderstood."

"He was none of that. But he did have a rich father. And I needed money to buy the rare earths before my ex got his hands on them."

"Buy? But—"

"When Wallace's father gave his estate to Harlan Wilford, that meant I wouldn't be getting a dime by marrying Wallace."

"So, you tried to steal some of the items back?" The only items touched in Agnes's shop were the ones from Harlan's consignment boxes. Once again, Beverly's suspicions were validated.

"Only one item. A 1927-D Saint Gaudens Double Eagle coin. It'd fetch over a million and a half at auction."

"But you didn't find it."

"It wasn't listed in the old man's will. So, I figured he'd hidden it somewhere. I had to go with Plan B, stealing the rare earths. Much riskier, but I couldn't wait any longer. If Kirk got that shipment, my plan to bankrupt him would be in pieces."

"Why kill Wallace? Why not just break up with him?"

"He found out about the plan. Wanted a cut. So I gave him a cut. A permanent one."

Beverly had a sudden image of Fern thrusting the sword into Wallace. "You're the one who—"

"Right over there," Fern pointed to a tree. That's when Beverly noticed bits of yellow crime scene tape left over from the investigation. Beads of sweat broke out along her neck. Fern might not need her bargaining chip alive.

Beverly uttered a small cry and sagged against Redbeard. His grip loosened ever so lightly, and that was all she needed. She took the heel of her boot and rammed it into the man's instep. When he hopped backward cursing, she ducked out from under his arms and took off running through the woods.

With an eye on the angle of the sun, she had a pretty good idea which way to take toward the main road, but she had to make it before her pursuers did. Even then, she knew it would be an impossible stroke of luck for someone to be passing through at exactly the right time.

Her boots made good foot-stompers but weren't quite as effective as running shoes. Should she take them off? No, ice-block feet would be worse.

Feeling like a panicked deer, she jumped over branches and fallen tree limbs and sloshed through ice mud puddle after ice mud puddle. She paused for a moment to catch her breath, then pushed on again, thinking she could hear the thrashing of Redbeard and Fern catching up to her.

She crashed through the woods for what seemed like hours. But when she risked a quick peek at her cellphone, it had only been twenty-five minutes. Beverly pressed on, trying to buy some time.

She was in pretty decent shape, but she hadn't exactly trained as a forest hurdler. Before long, she had to stop and catch her breath again. Another fork in the path—right or left?

She opted for left and started toward it when a burly figure loomed in front of her. Redbeard.

She looked wildly around for a rock when she remembered she still had her purse slung across her shoulder. Keeping her eyes locked with his, hoping he wouldn't notice what she was doing, she jammed her hand inside her purse until her fingers curled around the gun.

He took two steps toward her, but stopped, his eyes wide, when he saw the gun pointed at him. Now what? Winded, tired, and cold, what was she going to do with her "prisoner?"

A baritone voice boomed out, "We've got to stop meeting like this," but Redbeard's lips hadn't moved.

A woman's voice added, "You got that right," and soon Adam and Jinks came into view.

They had Redbeard quickly restrained, but Beverly said, "Fern. She's in on this, too."

Jinks grinned. "And she's also in handcuffs. One of the uniforms is taking her to the station to join Lover Boy."

Beverly followed Adam and Jinks and their prisoner to their car, realizing she'd doubled back during her run to end up at the starting point. And there was her own SUV, waiting for her like a faithful steed.

Adam smiled at her. "Brilliant idea to call me on your cellphone and keep it running the whole time."

Beverly pulled the phone out of her pocket and turned it off. She was equally amazed it had worked. Maybe the phone company would hire her to be in their ads. She could hear the jingle now, "When you're kidnapped, you want the very best cellphone coverage."

Adam said, "What made you think this was a setup, Beverly?"

"Years of playing cons, I guess. And maybe it was the fact when Fern was directing me through the woods to avoid our 'tail,' she never once looked back. As if she didn't care whether the route was working. Or knew it didn't matter."

Adam said, "Cray told me he thought you'd make a good private eye. I'd better not tell him just how good you are, or he'll be luring my unofficial partner away."

"Lure? I am not a fish."

Adam laughed. "Fishing, you say? I have a feeling Harlan is going to be able to do it again real soon, thanks to you."

"You're not going to let him go ice fishing alone again, are you?"

"Not on your life."

She put her hands on her hips. "What kind of bait do you use with ice fishing, anyway?"

"Damsels in distress." He grinned at her, then when her mouth opened in indignation, he added, "Damselflies. Fake ones."

43

Agnes expertly poured everyone a glass of wine, beginning with Adam, Beverly, and Jinks, and working her way around to Prospero and Harlan. They were all crammed into Harlan's office since the antiques store could get drafty at times, and the office sported a wall heater. When she'd finished filling the glasses, she raised her glass in a toast. "Here's to one of the nicest antiquers in the business. Long may he reign. And stay out of jail."

Adam did a double-take when Agnes winked at Harlan, and he winked back. He glanced at Beverly, who had a surprised smile on her face. Were their two older friends flirting? Nah, couldn't be.

Prospero lifted his glass to add, "Hear, hear," then asked, "So Fern Gery cooked up this whole scheme to get revenge on her ex? And framed Harlan?"

Adam nodded. "Framed him to throw suspicion away from her. And to allow her to go through Harlan's things while he was in jail, looking for that coin."

Prospero frowned. "But what about Braddon Hopper?"

"When Fern and her cronies saw that the evidence against Harlan wasn't going to stick, they had to come up with a new suspect."

Adam had checked in on Braddon last evening after the sessions at the jail with Fern, Redbeard, and Bruno, and was pleased to find the man sitting up in bed watching TV and feeling much better. Beverly had gone with Adam and struck up a long conversation with Sharon Bogren, the secretary at the conference center who hadn't believe Braddon tried to commit suicide.

Adam was pleased to see Beverly connecting with the young woman. He knew she was still reeling from having trusted Fern at first, hoping they could get to be friends, something rare in Beverly's life.

Harlan slurped some of his wine, but he didn't need any spirits to lift *his* spirits, because he was floating in a cloud of relief. "All this to get back at one cheating husband. Guess hell hath no fury, etc., etc."

Adam saw Beverly getting ready for a retort, but Agnes beat her to it. She bopped Harlan lightly on the arm. "Present company excluded." They all smiled, but Adam would never forget the way Beverly went after Reginald Forsythe after what he did to her grandmother. Hell and fury, indeed.

Prospero downed the rest of his glass, and Agnes filled it up again. Adam had the impression Prospero wasn't a regular drinker and was enjoying his encounter with the grape a shade too much.

But it reminded Adam of something Bruno Giacometti had told him. That Fern bumped into Wallace Ryall quite by accident at some function where he was soused. In his inebriated state, he told her about the valuable coin and his father's estate, and thus the whole, sordid, rotten-egg-of-a-plan began to be hatched.

Beverly perched on the edge of Harlan's desk. "Have to admit I'm disappointed Mayor Lehmann wasn't involved. I'd love to see him behind bars."

"I haven't ruled out any involvement on his part. Yet. But we may never find a way to tie him to it. And Fern wasn't exactly forthcoming. She was as tight-lipped as Bruno Giacometti was free and loose. And neither admitted to the bombing at my house."

Beverly asked, "What about Redbeard? Has he said anything yet?"

"Funny thing about Redbeard. One quick phone call, and he had a high-priced attorney at his service and was out on bail. Xenakis warned me about him."

Beverly paused with her glass in mid-air. "He did?"

"It appears Redbeard is pals with one Ivon Kozak. Another of Forsythe's colleagues."

Adam didn't like seeing the apprehension return to Beverly's face when she'd been looking happier than he'd seen her in quite some time. He probably shouldn't have brought up Kozak. And he certainly didn't want to bring up the fact that the bombing was still unsolved, and two of the leading suspects, Redbeard and Kozak, weren't yet behind bars.

Nor did he want to tell her about the threatening note he'd received after the bombing. Or the fact that the doctors at the hospital where Forsythe was lying in a coma said they thought they'd seen some brain activity on the monitor lately. That could wait for another day.

Jinks saw the look he gave her, warning her not to mention any of this, and she nodded and said, "Was this coin thing all a scam the father cooked up? To tease the two sons he hated so much? I mean, there are days I want to give my little Jacob a one-way ticket to Siberia. But seems like he could come up with something less goofy than a magic coin."

Harlan shook his head. "Not magic, but very valuable, you see. One sold at auction a few years ago for two million."

Adam rubbed his chin. "How big would you say that coin is, Harlan?"

"Silver-dollar size. Pretty heavy, 'cause it's gold. There are only about twelve of 'em left in the entire world."

Agnes sighed. "Fern and Bruno looked through all the pieces from Ryall's estate here and all the items at my shop and came up empty. Or it was all a hoax."

Adam got a tingly feeling in his stomach as he stared at Harlan's desk. "Maybe not *all* the pieces from Ryall's estate." He pointed to the ugly Syroco Clown Lux clock he'd noticed days earlier. "You said that's from Ryall's estate, too, didn't you?"

Harlan sat up straight and put his wine glass down. "So, I did. You don't think. . ."

Adam picked up the clock and held it up in the air, then shook it around. Nothing rattled. But, shouldn't the clockworks inside rattle, at least?

He reached over and grabbed a small screwdriver from a workbench behind the desk to pry open the clock face on the clown's stomach. He looked apologetically at Harlan when a slip of the tool caused some scratches, but then, at long last, he had success. He gently wiggled the clock face open and peered into the clown's belly.

Agnes had moved to stand over his shoulder, practically breathing down his neck. "Well?" she demanded.

He looked at her and shrugged. But then he poked his fingers inside the clown with a grin and deftly removed a plastic pouch containing a round golden coin. Handing it to Harlan, he said, "Please tell me it's not Monopoly money."

Harlan reached into his desk, fumbling around for something, but Prospero had second-guessed him and handed over a magnifying glass. Harlan scrutinized the coin. "It'll have to be appraised. But it sure looks like a 1927-D Saint Gaudens Double Eagle coin from here."

Agnes clapped her hands. "You're rich!"

"Well, now, I guess since Ryall left everything to me, that would include this here coin, right, Adam?"

"Reckon it would, Harlan."

The older man looked at the coin half dazed. Then he said, "Part of this belongs to you, Agnes. After what I put you through with the lien and all."

"Oh, I couldn't," she said. "I mean, could I?"

Agnes, Harlan, Prospero, and Jinks crowded around the coin to admire it, while Adam motioned to Beverly to join him outside the office. She looked around the store. "I guess all's well that ends well?"

"Mostly," he replied. "Lots of loose ends to tie up. Then there are the court dates and attorneys and plea bargains and, well, this could drag on for quite a while. I'm sorry to make you have to testify at some point."

"It'll be my pleasure." She smiled at him, but then her smiled dimmed as she grew more serious. "There is some other unfinished business, too."

"Oh?" Did she mean Reggie Forsythe? Or maybe Zelda? Or Mayor Lehmann or Ivon Kozak. But instead, she stood on tiptoe, so her mouth was level with his ear. "Right before that bomb went off, remember?"

"Oh?" His voice sounded high and squeaky to his ears. She kissed him lightly on the cheek. "I think I'd like to take you up on that offer of dinner. If it's still on the table."

She looked uncertain, and he realized his mouth was hanging open. He shut it with an audible snap. "Dinner—dinner, yes, I think that would be good. Great, no, great. I mean, it could be Italian or Mexican or Greek or whatever you'd like. Or I'd make something. Or—"

She smiled at him. "Did you know you babble when you're uncomfortable?"

He'd have to be careful around this one. She never forgot anything, not even an off-hand remark he'd made a week ago. "Touché, Miss Laborde. And who says I'm uncomfortable?"

She hooked her arm around his and dragged him back toward the office like he was hooked, and she was reeling him in. As far as he was concerned, Beverly Laborde could fish for Adam Duttons any day. And if she ever did, this was one fish who might bite on that line and never let go.